BOOK 3 OF COURAGE ON THE OREGON TRAIL SERIES

FRONTIER SISTERS

A.T. BUTLER

FRONTIER SISTERS

An Oregon Trail Western Adventure

A.T. BUTLER

"I'll not be paying more than twenty cents for that," Louisa Hudson declared in her stentorian tone. "I know what's fair, and you'll not be cheating me, Charlie Bryant. A pound of chocolate for thirty cents? Good gracious me!"

Every other person in the Bryant General Store had turned to look at her. Louisa was a short woman, curvy and stolid; many of the curious onlookers had to crane their necks to see who was talking over the tall shelves and stacks of boxes that filled the store. There were whispers and giggles as the other customers turned to pay attention to the drama going on at the counter. Many of her neighbors, however, easily recognized the sound of Louisa Hudson. This wasn't the first time she had voiced her disapproval so forcefully and so publicly.

Without allowing the storekeeper to reply, she turned on her heel and hustled out of the store empty-handed.

Out on the wide main street of Norfolk, Virginia,

Louisa wrapped her shawl more tightly around her. The autumn chill had recently descended on their coastal town, and she wanted nothing more than to be in her cozy little workspace, fire roaring in the stove, hemming the Sloan girl's new evening gown rather than be outside running errands. She looked both directions down the street, trying to decide if she wanted to risk Joshua Clark's general store instead. The Hudsons had always supported Bryant General Store, going back two generations when their grandfather had been given a deal on adding acreage to his estate by the Bryant family whose land bordered their own. But now, if Charlie Bryant was going to try to cheat her... charging thirty cents for a pound of chocolate? What was that man thinking?

In the end, after standing in the cold for more than five minutes, Louisa decided she had far too many other things to worry about than fighting with a man about a mere few cents. She could make more than that with her sewing in the time it took her to talk him down again. Instead, Louisa would take the high road and go back to Bryant's. She needed that chocolate. There was nothing else that would do. It was Annie's twenty-fifth birthday, after all. She couldn't be stingy on such a big day for her baby sister.

Maybe she'd only get half a pound, though. They could all share it just as well as they would more.

Louisa turned and reentered the store with no sense of shame or embarrassment as soon as she made her decision. She felt the eyes of her neighbors on her as she strode defiantly back to the counter, back to where Charlie Bryant still stood, though now helping old Mrs. Rowland measure out some rice. He glanced at her and smiled. She would let him have his amusement; the more important thing was that she got all that she needed for Annie's birthday without wasting any more of her own time. Men like Charlie Bryant could afford to dawdle, but Louisa Hudson could not.

As she waited, Elizabeth Helling approached her timidly. She cleared her throat. "Miss Hudson?"

"Yes?"

"I hope you are well, ma'am. With the cooler weather, I know for myself, I like to—"

"Is there something I can help you with, Miss Helling? It's only that I have much to do today."

"Oh, yes, of course," she replied, flustered. "I was hoping... that is, I was wondering if you perhaps have an available appointment this week?"

"You'd like to come see me for what purpose? An alteration? A fitting? What *specifically* can I help you with?"

Elizabeth blinked at her, as though confused and overwhelmed by Louisa's directness. Her mouth hung open.

"Well?" Louisa prodded.

"A dress." Elizabeth cleared her throat. "A mourning dress, if... You see, my grandfather has fallen ill, and we're not certain he will be much longer for this world, but I also don't have the skills to make—"

"Wonderful." Louisa beamed at her, now all smiles that the preliminaries were taken care of. "I would be happy to help you with that. Can you come by tomorrow?"

"I'll be teaching until—"

"Of course, yes. Will four o'clock work for you?"

Elizabeth nodded numbly, as though stunned. "Four. Yes. Thank you, Miss Hudson."

"My pleasure."

With that, she turned to give Charlie her attention, now that he had finished with Mrs. Rowland. Elizabeth stepped back and seemed cowed by the forthrightness of Louisa Hudson. The town's seamstress knew her reputation—she would be the first to acknowledge that she could be brusque and intimidating. But she also was the first to point out that she got things done no matter her tone. There was a reason so many women came to her for their fittings, despite her reputation for not beating around the bush.

"So you changed your mind, did ya?" the shopkeeper asked with a wink.

"Not hardly," Louisa replied. "I still think your prices are outrageous."

"But...?"

"But it is my sister's birthday, and we both know that I will ensure she has the most pleasant celebration that is in me to provide. You're taking advantage of a sister's goodwill, Mr. Bryant."

"Oh, well, I'm sure you'll forgive me in time. So, then what'll it be?" Teasing Louisa was only fun to a point.

"A half of a pound of the chocolate bar you showed me earlier, and..." She consulted her list, mentally making the adjustments that were needed for her guests. "And a pound of butter, a bushel of apples, a tin of baking powder, and a pound each of white and brown sugar. I'll come back tomorrow for the pins and ribbon I need."

"Been to see Healy yet? Mrs. Hodgman told me he's

running low on pork chops already today," Charlie said as he turned to fill Louisa's order.

"Is he? Well, then I thank you for the tip. I have so many other things on my list it might have been too late by the time I got over there."

"Did you want to take all this with you, or should I have Fred run it over later?"

"If you could send it with Fred, I'd be much obliged." She beamed at him.

"Anything for your family, you know, Miss Hudson."

Once Louisa had gotten what she wanted, she was all sunshine again. It wasn't that she begrudged Charlie Bryant his thirty cents or thought she was above paying a fair price. Once she had recognized the reality of her options, everything was fine. With the errand boy, Fred, taking the order back home for her, Louisa was free to finish the rest of the shopping for Annie's big birthday celebration.

And the first thing she would do would be to head to the butcher as Charlie had recommended.

The Hudson family had lived in Norfolk as long as she had been alive. When their parents had died, so many of their friends and neighbors had stepped in to provide the family with the support and community they needed to get through that first difficult year.

That was almost fifteen years ago. The shock and burden of suddenly being the guardian of three children had given Louisa the impetus she needed to start her little business making, altering, and repairing clothing. There were enough sailors, naval officers, and bachelors in the surrounding communities that she always had clients, but in the last five or so years, she had been able to expand her offerings to help women create full ensembles for themselves. Her reputation as a skilled craftswoman was growing, and women like Miss Helling were willing to pay handsomely for the privilege and convenience of a Louisa Hudson fitting.

Once outside the Bryant General Store again, Louisa pulled her shawl around her and headed east toward Joe Healy's butcher shop. Every person she passed on her way nodded their greeting or lifted their hat. Though it may have taken longer than she would have liked, Louisa was now the pillar of the community that she had always wanted to be.

The bell over the door dinged when she stepped out of the cold into the butcher shop. It wasn't much warmer inside; Mr. Healy kept the back door open in cooler weather to keep his offerings fresh as long as possible. At a glance, however, Louisa could see that Charlie had been correct in his tip—the pork chops were almost gone. Louisa silently scolded herself for not remembering; it was Thursday after all. Thursday mornings were when Joe Healy butchered a pig, and the best selection was almost always gone by mid-day.

"Morning, Miss Hudson," Mr. Healy called to her. "Can I tempt you with a juicy ribeye or roast?"

"No, thank you. Today I need half a dozen pork chops. It's Annie's birthday, you know."

"Is it now? Well, then let's see what I can contribute to that."

After some discussion, clarification, and negotiation, Mr. Healy was packing up the meat for Louisa, along with one of his largest ham bones that Josie could use later in the week to make soup. No other customers had entered while she was there, so she had some moments of quiet to think as she waited.

Her sister Annie was twenty-five now. Twenty-five and lonely, to Louisa's thinking. Though she'd had a beau years ago, after he had died, no other man had stepped into his place. Instead, Louisa's youngest sister had remained at home, slowly growing her list of piano students, helping with chores, and more or less settling into a life of a spinster.

But Louisa couldn't believe that was what Annie had really wanted. How could she? When she had been younger, the baby of the family, Annie, had been everyone's favorite. She had been a bright, kind child, always willing to go along with what her friends or sisters asked of her. Now Annie was on her own and growing more isolated by the day. Louisa imagined an entire life like this would ruin the sweet disposition she had always loved her sister for.

Annie deserved something better than this. And Louisa's job as the oldest sister was to make sure she got it.

Well, it was her birthday, after all. If Annie was ever going to accept help or a gift from Louisa, it should be today. She just had to go home and figure out what that would be.

CHAPTER TWO

There was the distant sound of someone stamping the wet off her shoes and then the creak of the front door opening. When she heard that, Annie Hudson quickly stuffed her letter under the cushion of the chair where she had been sitting. The very last thing she needed was for her older sister Louisa to get wind of what was in that correspondence.

"Annie!" her oldest sister called. "We only have a few hours before Margaret arrives. Have you finished everything I asked you to do?"

Annie smiled to herself. She never would have played hostess for her birthday dinner if it were up to her—but it wasn't up to her. In this, as in everything since their parents died when Annie was eleven, Louisa had been in charge. She had been twenty-one at the time, which was plenty old enough to know her own mind and decide for other people as well. She had turned down a betrothal from the son of a navy commander in order to stay home and take care of her younger siblings.

And so, in spite of the fact that she was a grown woman with opinions and wishes of her own, Annie found herself on her twenty-fifth birthday peeling potatoes and following her older sister's list of chores. Her sister had been gone for several hours, but Annie hadn't quite had time to finish the tasks assigned to her. She was close but had only this last opportunity to take a short break in the quiet before Louisa came in demanding action. Annie thought she'd sit, read her letter and then be ready for Louisa coming home and insisting she knew the best way for her to be spending her birthday.

It was all just one more reason Annie wanted to keep the letter to herself.

When Louisa entered the sitting room, laden with several bags and packages, Annie stood self-consciously.

"No, I'm sorry. Not quite ready."

Louisa frowned at her but moved to the sideboard to set down all that she had brought home.

"Well, you know what needs to be done," she said. "Josie will be home any minute to start cooking. I'll help when I can, but…"

She trailed off, already distracted by verifying all the packages that she had brought home. Annie was grateful. She waited until she was certain her sister's back was turned before she tried to sneak her letter back into the pocket of her apron. The oldest Hudson sister busied herself unpacking the deep woven oak basket that had been looped over her arm, pulling out brown paper-wrapped packages of various sizes while Annie held her breath, waiting for her moment.

When it seemed as though Louisa was most preoccupied with the packages, Annie slid her fingers under the cushion, touching the softness of the thin paper as she tried to pull it out without Louisa noticing. She cleared her throat to try to hide the sound of the letter crinkling, but all it did was draw her sister's attention.

"Annie, are you sick?" Louisa asked as she turned around.

Both sisters froze—Annie in guilt, Louisa in curiosity—and looked at the small, seemingly innocuous envelope the younger woman held.

"What's that?" Louisa asked.

Annie could feel her face go red, could hear the exaggerated innocence in her sister's voice. There was no question; Louisa would harangue and nag until she had ferreted out precisely every word that was in the letter she held. Annie sagged in disappointment, already feeling defeated.

"A letter," she said softly.

"Is it for me?"

Annie hid her irritation. "A letter to me."

"Who from?"

"From... um..." Annie cleared her throat. This was not how she had intended on revealing this detail. Annie'd had the letter for a week and had imagined every possible version of this conversation—except this. "From a man who wants to marry me."

There was a long silent beat as Louisa stared in disbelief. Annie could not have shocked her older sister any more if she had professed herself to be an ostrich.

Louisa laughed disingenuously as she set down the basket she had been unpacking. "I'm sorry, Annie, I must have misheard you. I thought you said that the letter was from a man who wanted to marry you. However, I'm absolutely positive you assured me you would never be getting married since John Sherman died."

Annie sighed. And there it was—exactly everything that she had feared from revealing her secrets to Louisa.

"I know," she said with a sigh. "I know what I said, and I meant it at the time, but... Well, Louisa, you know. It's been six years. That's so long to be alone. I still miss John every day, but... This isn't how I wanted to tell you."

How could she make Louisa understand? She didn't know how to quite express the full extent of loneliness and frustration that she felt that had driven her to finally give up her vow that she would die a spinster. It was a vow Louisa herself had made, much longer than six years ago, so how could she understand how Annie longed for love, longed for companionship. She already knew precisely how her older sister would react to the news.

"And who is this man who has the gall to write you a marriage proposal?" Louisa asked, aghast. "Why haven't I met him?"

There was no hope for it. Annie was caught now, and refusing to answer her sister's questions would simply prolong the inevitable.

"Well, a few months ago, there was a notice in the paper."

Louisa's jaw dropped. Annie would have almost enjoyed so scandalizing her sister if the situation wasn't so fraught. Conflict of any kind made her retreat, and with Louisa even more so.

"His name is Isaac Wheeler. He's from Richmond,

originally, but now he lives in Oregon Territory. His wife died on the trip out west, and he's looking for..." Annie paused to gather her thoughts. She felt like she knew enough about Isaac to make this decision for herself, but that didn't mean Louisa needed all the same information. "Isaac is looking to start a family and put a notice in the paper out here to find a suitable companion."

"And you answered him." It was a statement, not a question. Louisa's expression told Annie she could hardly believe her own certainty. "This stranger?"

Annie nodded.

"And, *why* is that again?"

The sarcasm was biting. "I... I wanted to see what else was out there," Annie responded in a small voice. "To see what it might be like somewhere else."

"But, Oregon, Annie! To marry a man you've never even laid eyes on. Why on earth would you do that?" Louisa demanded.

"I haven't said yet that I would marry him."

"You could have a dozen young men here every Friday night angling for your attention. Why do you need to go all the way out to Oregon?" Louisa sailed right on into her lecture, seeming to not hear Annie's protests at all.

"I didn't think you'd mind."

"Mind? Of course I mind. After everything I've given up to raise you girls..." Louisa trailed off, frustrated. "This is simply unbelievable. You're still young, still lovely. There must be something more that you're not telling me."

Annie shook her head, her blonde curls bouncing cheerfully in opposition to her heart. "I didn't mean anything by it, Lou. I'm just... I'm lonely." Her voice cracked with the last word. "Every part of Norfolk reminds me of John. If he had lived and we had married, I would have happily made my home here alongside all of you, not looking for anything else. But... he didn't."

"Well, that's just silly," Louisa declared. "You have an entire life here. The church choir, your music students, and your family. What else could you need?"

Annie stayed quiet. Trying to change Louisa's opinion would be a losing battle. What she meant, of course, was there was nothing else Louisa needed, so how dare Annie have the gall to suggest it wasn't enough.

"You have never had a strong opinion about anything in your life," Louisa said dismissively. "Don't tell me you're up and starting now."

Annie shook her head again, shoving down the pain that was now bubbling up. She felt desperate, suddenly, like it was essential her sister heard her, understood her, but she couldn't find the words. She needed more time, more consideration. Annie had not been prepared to discuss this with Louisa just yet.

"I'm hurting, Lou," Annie said miserably, at a loss of how else to explain it. "I can't... I don't want to be here anymore, seeing the same people, going to the same church, the same routine. Every day without John here feels like that first day all over again. Writing to this other man in Oregon at least let me feel like I was somewhere else for a few moments."

The two sisters looked at each other across the sitting room. Louisa seemed to soften at the expression on Annie's face.

"Well, of course, it must be hard," she began. "He was your whole life. Of course you're having a hard time without him."

She crossed the wooden floor and took Annie's hands in hers.

"I should have seen this coming," she said. "This is my fault. I should have done something for you, protected you better in some way."

"What?" Annie said, confused.

"It's my job to make sure you have everything you need, and I haven't been doing that. I thought you were happy. That what our parents had given us was enough for you, but I see that I was wrong."

Annie thought she heard a note of irritation in Louisa's voice, but she wasn't about to argue back. Just the effort of saying how she felt for the first time had been as much as she could manage. Annie prayed that this would all blow over before her birthday dinner that evening.

Louisa looked at Annie plainly for another moment before pulling her into a hug. The older woman was a good half a head shorter than Annie. When she wrapped her arms around her, Annie took a comforting breath, smelling the lemon in her sister's hair. In spite of all of it, Louisa had always been a conscientious caretaker for her sisters. She was trying.

She pulled away and returned to the sideboard without another word. Annie watched on, wondering, hoping that the discussion was over. She didn't think she'd get the same secret pleasure out of writing to the man in Oregon, now that Louisa knew, but at least maybe her sister would understand her a little better.

Louisa carried the butcher shop packages she had brought home and put them away in the icebox. The two women stayed in tense silence for a full minute. When Louisa turned to where Annie had been standing in the middle of the room, her expression seemed calm, resolute.

"I'm going with you," she said.

"Where?"

"To Oregon."

Annie laughed, awkwardly, uncomfortably. Surely her sister was making a joke. "Very funny."

"I'm in earnest, Annie. I think that you should go to Oregon, and build a new life there. And I am going with you. How else can I be sure you get there all right?"

"But..." Annie did not know where to begin with her protests. The idea of Louisa giving up her whole life here in Norfolk was so ludicrous that she could not formulate a coherent thought about it, let alone the fact that she had decided Annie was going at all.

"And we'll bring Josie and Margaret along too," Louisa continued. She returned to her unpacking of the basket as though the conversation was over. "Well, we'll invite them. I'm sure they'll want to come."

Watching her oldest sister, Annie could not think how to respond. Examining her feelings, she was surprised to find that she didn't object. Something about this felt right. She would still understand if Louisa changed her mind, or if either of the other two Hudson girls chose to stay in Virginia, but the idea of their entire family starting a new life in Oregon filled Annie with a peace she had not felt since John died. She could give herself a fresh start and make a good man happy at the same time.

"I don't know what to say. Thank you," Annie said softly.

"You're welcome," Louisa said grandly. Now that the moment of decision was passed, she was her old imperious self again. "I will handle Josie and Margaret. You just get to those chores I asked you to take care of. Are the potatoes peeled? What about the front stoop? Has that been scrubbed thoroughly?"

"I'll take care of that right now."

Though it was in no way how she had expected this conversation to go, Annie felt relieved. There was no doubt that Louisa would make her reconsider this whole plan before they got to Oregon, but there was also no doubt that Annie had never felt more loved by her sister in her entire life.

CHAPTER THREE

Louisa Hudson had never been one to second-guess herself. When she decided a thing, it *was* decided. And she had decided that all of the Hudson girls would be letting go of everything in Virginia and emigrating to the Oregon Territory the following spring. They had only a few months before they had to leave, and there was so much to do.

But first things first: Louisa had to inform Josie and Margaret that they were going.

Louisa was the oldest of the Hudson girls—for that's what they were still called, even though all were grown women. Louisa, Josie, and Annie had always been the Hudson girls to their neighbors. When their brother Tom married Margaret, she was occasionally included in that appellation. Now, however, Margaret was more often called the Widow Hudson around Norfolk. But even though she was a staid matron with a thirteen-year-old son, Margaret was far too enthusiastic and cheerful for anyone to remember she was a widow.

And so now there were four Hudson girls.

And all four Hudson girls, as well as young Lawrence, would be together that very night to celebrate Annie's birthday.

After Louisa had made her decision about Oregon, they only had a couple of short hours before supper needed to be ready. Josie, the middle sister, returned home from her own errand, and Louisa prodded and pushed her sisters to finish the final cleaning and cooking for the night's supper. Margaret and her son arrived only ten minutes late—though Louisa had, of course, accounted for that—and after all the hugs and greetings had been made, they were ushered into the dining room. Louisa had things she wanted to say, and the sooner she told them all, the better.

The very moment the whole family was seated at supper, Louisa called for their attention. Josie had only just served the basket of warm rolls when her older sister looked at her pointedly to take a seat. She stood at the head of the table and lifted her glass in a toast.

"Today is a day we celebrate our beloved youngest sister, Miss Annie Hudson," she began. Annie blushed and ducked her head. She was usually so good at avoiding attention, but her sister wouldn't allow it on her birthday. "Annie has been a gift to our family, always an ear to listen or a hand to help. She deserves to be happy, not just on her birthday but every day."

Louisa looked around the table at her sisters: Josie smiled encouragingly, Annie kept her eyes on her plate, Margaret was scolding her son with a glare before he knocked his water glass off the table. This was the family that she had built her whole life around, and Louisa couldn't imagine not seeing them again. She let her gaze fall on her youngest sister, the reason they were all together that evening.

"And Annie and I have made a decision that we think will make her happy, and I'd like you all to support that choice."

Now all were looking at Annie, who blanched and stammered, "Oh, me? But, I thought…" She cleared her throat.

"Tell them," Louisa prodded. She wanted to push her sister, force her to take ownership of this idea of hers. "This is your plan."

"You're the one who—" She stopped at the look on Louisa's face. "All right," Annie murmured. "Louisa said… Well, I have… That is, I will be moving to Oregon."

"Oregon Territory?" Margaret clarified. "The Oregon that is three thousand miles away?"

Annie nodded.

"But… why?" Josie asked, astonished.

Annie glanced at her oldest sister, but Louisa resolutely kept her mouth shut. She nodded at her to continue.

"I'm getting married," Annie stated, chin up, shoulders back, but with little emotion.

The room fell into a stunned silence.

"That's right," Louisa said finally, determined to get the worst over with. "Annie will be accepting a proposal of marriage from a quality young man in Oregon who is originally from our very own state of Virginia. She and I will be leaving in the next few months to move west, and I think you all should join us."

Margaret's mouth fell open in shock as she looked from one sister to another.

"Oregon?" Lawrence exclaimed. His outburst surprised Louisa; he was usually so quiet and well-behaved at family dinners. She often forgot that he was there at all unless he figured directly into her plans. "I want to go to Oregon. Did you know there are so many fish in Oregon streams you can just reach a hand in and grab one?"

"How do you know that?" his mother asked with a frown.

"Jimmy Miller told me. Said his cousin left this spring and should be getting there this fall. He got a letter a few months ago sent from just before he left Independence and—"

"There you have it," Louisa said with a smug smile, smoothly cutting off the boy's excited chatter. "Our next generation is already aching to go seek his fortune on the other side of the continent. From the mouth of babes, let his words be our guide."

Lawrence beamed, though his face fell noticeably when he saw his mother's expression.

"Margaret?" Louisa said, turning to her. "You wouldn't keep your son from such a dream of his, would you?"

She snorted indulgently. "Dream. Since this is the first I'm hearing about it, I won't put too much stock into such dreams. But I won't deny, the idea does have some merit."

Louisa nodded, satisfied. If Margaret was already allowing the idea to be considered, she was as good as decided. The balance of votes in the family was turning in her favor.

"Josie?" she asked, turning to her next sister. "I assume you are up for such an adventure?"

Josie took her time in answering, which surprised Louisa. Generally, the woman was quick to agree with whatever her older sister had planned. Instead, she picked up the large bowl closest to her.

"I'll start the peas, shall I?" she said, heaping some onto her plate before passing the dish to Margaret on her right.

In spite of her surprise, the oldest Hudson sister sensed that this might be a moment to keep her own mouth shut. Josie was agreeable up to a point, but past that, you couldn't make her budge if she didn't want to.

Louisa was still standing as the serving bowl made its way around the table. The clinking of dishes as Lawrence helped himself to a serving of mashed potatoes and passed the dish again was the only sound as the Hudson family waited quietly for Josie to give her opinion of her older sister's scheme. She took a bite of her vegetable, still not saying anything, but now looked right at Louisa. Josie swallowed, delicately wiped her mouth with her napkin, and turned her eyes to Annie.

"Are you really doing this?" she said. Though she was trying to remain calm, the stress and concern were evident in the strain of her voice.

"Yes, she—" Louisa began.

"Please," Josie said, turning back to her oldest sister. "We all know how you feel about it, Louisa. But this is Annie's life. I want to hear her say it."

Louisa grumbled under her breath but sat back in her chair as though magnanimously allowing the other woman to speak. She had already decided, so what did it matter what Annie said? Annie wanted to go to Oregon, and this was the best way to make it happen. She knew just what her younger sister would say, in fact; she knew what Josie was listening for. Louisa knew that she just had to stand her ground, not give in, and all her sisters would come around to her way of thinking eventually. They always did.

"Well, I guess..." Annie sighed and looked at Louisa, who remained silent as requested. Looking down at her hands, Annie sighed again and began. "It is what I want. A fresh start in Oregon where no one knew John is just what I need, I think. I can't... That is," she looked up at Josie, "I don't want to have to stay here where everything reminds me of him. I know it's a risk, and I know..." She cleared her throat. "I know the trail is dangerous, but to me, that seems far less scary than living the rest of my life here in Norfolk where everything says John Sherman to me."

Josie nodded. "So you asked Louisa to go with you?"

"No, she didn't," Louisa interrupted, sitting up straight again and taking control of the conversation. "No, she wasn't even planning on going in the first place, but I insisted."

"Well, that's not completely true," Annie protested quietly. "I just hadn't decided for certain yet. I would have figured out a way. There are always people going west, Louisa. There would have been a way for me too."

"You don't know that," Louisa scolded. "If it weren't for me, you would be staying in Virginia, miserable and stuck for the rest of your natural-born days."

"That's why you want to go?" Josie asked, eying her older sister carefully. "Because you are trying to protect her from being unhappy? Louisa, you can't take care of every little thing. It's very likely you won't be able to protect her from the dangers of the trail to Oregon."

"I hear the skepticism in your voice, Josie Hudson. Don't you sass me. I'm not so arrogant as to think I can thwart the will of the Almighty, but I'd much rather be there and *know* I did everything I could than sit at home and wait for news."

"Well, yes, but neither of you need to go at all."

Louisa shot a look at Annie, assessing for the first time how she was taking the conversation. "Annie isn't happy here. And I want that for her. So this is what we're doing."

Josie nodded thoughtfully, then grinned. "I would expect nothing less."

"So... what, then?" Louisa demanded. "Does that mean you want to go to Oregon too?"

She shrugged, still grinning. "I suppose so. With you two gone, there won't be much left here for me, will there? And who will cook for you if you leave me behind? You can barely get a cake to rise."

Louisa was more relieved than she expected to be. Though she assumed she would be victorious eventually, she had to admit that she didn't want to leave Josie behind any more than she wanted to let Annie go to Oregon without her.

"Wonderful." She took a roll while it was still warm and passed the rest of the basket to Josie. "Everything is coming together."

"What about us, Mother?" Lawrence asked.

All eyes turned to Margaret, the last of the Hudson girls to decide to uproot her entire life.

"Well…"

"I want to go," Lawrence cut in. "There will be boys my age, and I can hunt buffalo, and you heard what I said about the fish in Oregon, right?"

Louisa caught the hopeful expression on her nephew's face. "Think of the opportunity for Lawrence. Think of the experience in work and the life he can build for himself in Oregon from a young age."

Margaret looked to her son. "Is this really what you want? You've never mentioned anything like this before."

"I didn't know I could!" he insisted. "Mother, we have to go. Please say we'll go. What will be left for us here if they all go to Oregon without us? I want to go."

"All right, there's no need to pout about it," Margaret said with a chuckle. "I daresay your aunt is right, and a brand new territory will be just the place for you to grow into your manhood. It could be exactly the opportunity you need."

"Does that mean you're coming to Oregon with us?" Louisa asked, more anxious about the answer than she wanted to admit to herself.

With a deep sigh and a smile at Annie, Margaret said, "It does. We're going to Oregon. Happy birthday, Annie. This time next year, we'll all be celebrating on the other side of the continent."

Lawrence let out the most jubilant whoop of celebration, which made his mother and aunts laugh.

"Good," Louisa said. "Now that that's settled, Annie, would you be so kind as to start the pork chops?"

CHAPTER FOUR

Annie really should have known that Louisa would talk the rest of the family into moving all the way across the continent. She always meant well, and she always was generous, but Louisa also always got her way.

There were times—like when Louisa sewed a new dress in the most atrocious shade of green or when she finished all the apple pie—when Annie was rather irritated by her oldest sister. Louisa was pushy and particular and seemed incapable of compromise. She never quite seemed to remember other people's preferences, or even that they were entitled to an opinion at all.

There were also times when Annie loved Louisa, like when she refused to sell the excess butter they made and instead gifted it to a poor family from church. Or the very fact that she gave up everything to raise her younger siblings.

But, there were times when Annie tried to forget they were related at all. Living under Louisa's thumb her whole life had made her ready to agree to anything simply to keep the peace.

Everything was extreme with Louisa.

Now, when all four of the Hudson sisters were getting ready to cross the continent in just a couple wagons, Annie could not help but be grateful for her. Louisa was the kind of woman who got things done, and as such, Annie found she could step back and allow her sister to plan their three-thousand-mile trek.

The morning after her birthday, Annie sent a letter to Isaac Wheeler, accepting his proposal and outlining her tentative plans to come west. Though her hands shook as she passed the letter over to the postmaster, once it was truly and irrevocably done Annie felt at peace. Something deep inside her told her this was the best choice for her, and she felt another wave of gratitude for Louisa and all her sisters.

After that first conversation over supper, when they made the decision, it was never revisited. It was simply accepted as fact. Annie half expected one or another of the sisters to change their mind about uprooting their entire life for her, but it was never brought up again. All three of the other women seemed to be just as invested in getting there as Annie did.

As soon as she had agreed to accompany her sisters on the trek to Oregon, Josie took complete control of learning and researching everything they would need. There was no situation that she wouldn't be prepared for. She bought a guidebook and read the thing cover-to-cover in under a week, then immediately started again at the beginning. By the holiday season, she was able to quote long passages from memory. Annie found herself ignoring the conversation about Oregon as much as she could, to avoid having to be reminded that they needed to be sure to buy enough dried apples for the journey.

Through much discussion and disagreement—and Louisa making the final decision—the sisters finally managed to come up with a plan they all could be happy with. Much of the plan was driven by Louisa. But then that was no surprise—most of the Hudsons' lives were driven by Louisa. Annie would much rather keep the peace than try to voice any dissent. She would just sit back and fill whatever role Louisa had decided for her. It would all get done either way.

Louisa would need to shutter her seamstress business, and Annie would need to let her piano students know she was leaving. Josie would study the guidebooks and make sure their home continued running smoothly through all the upheaval. It was a joint effort, but slowly and surely, everything began falling into place. The houses and extra furniture and animals would be sold, and everything would be ready to head to Missouri by the beginning of the new year, 1850.

While both of the Hudson homes would need to be sold, Margaret's went almost immediately. She and Lawrence moved in with the sisters for the remaining months that they would be in Virginia. Annie shared with Josie, while Margaret took Annie's room, and they set up a cot just off the kitchen for Lawrence. The small house seemed crowded, but Josie kept reminding them all that living out of a wagon for six months would feel even more crowded.

Lawrence had been pulled out of school at the end of the previous year to support his mother after his father's death. Even before that, his attendance had been sporadic while Tom was sick. More than once, Annie caught the boy sneaking chances to read instead of the chores he should be working on. It was always some ghost story or another, but at least the boy was trying. Nevertheless, he begged her not to tell his mother. She would take such books away from him. Annie was sworn to secrecy.

As the months and planning went on, Louisa delegated everything she could, in part because she had a list of customers that needed their gowns sewn and coats mended before she left the state altogether. Annie had never before seen her working so much, sewing by candlelight during the long winter nights. Louisa had spent almost fifteen years building up her business as the most trusted and reputable seamstress in the region. It seemed a miracle she was willing to walk away from all of that for Annie.

The hardest thing for Annie to part with was her piano. It had been their mother's, and Annie had spent the last several years teaching a half dozen children who had wanted to learn how to play. It wasn't much, but the income from those lessons let Annie contribute to the household and gave her a reason for getting out of bed every day after John had died. She had much invested in her musicality, and the long stretch of months on the trail without it made her wonder if Oregon was such a thing to be reckoned with. But that piano sold quickly, and before Christmas, it was warm and snug in its new home with the Barnaby family. The two youngest Barnabys had been Annie's students; she comforted herself knowing that their mother's piano had gone to a good home.

The Hudsons were giving up their homes, Louisa's business, Annie's students, and much of their belongings. As much as they could spare would be sold so the five Hudsons could travel west to Independence, Missouri, over the late winter months. It all needed to fit in the smallest space, so they would then also have room for all the food they would purchase there.

But not everything was easy or quick to find a new home.

In fact, some things would be brought with them to Oregon, like entire trunks full of quilts.

Some things were brought along that Annie had no idea would be traveling with her, like three chickens and their nests.

The argument over whether or not to take Louisa's hen Camilla was particularly entertaining. Lawrence and Margaret were in favor of traveling with the animals, while Josie tried to insist that bringing livestock that couldn't walk itself would be far more trouble than it was worth.

"Plenty of families will be driving herds of cattle across the continent, will they not? We're bringing goats, aren't we?" Louisa asked.

"Well, yes," Josie reluctantly admitted. "But that's different."

"How?"

"I..." Josie threw up her hands in frustration. "I haven't heard of anyone else taking chickens on the Oregon Trail."

"But surely someone must have. How else do they have eggs on the west coast?"

"All right. Fine. Fine, we can take the chickens, and I won't protest, but you will be in charge of keeping their roost clean in the wagon," Josie insisted. "And I get to decide how the eggs are used."

"I don't see why I should clean any of that," Louisa protested. "You are to be in charge of the meals. I will be so tired from driving the team all day that I can't possibly be expected to take on an additional chore like that."

"Well, I'm perfectly happy to make all of our meals without eggs at all, so I can't be expected to do it either."

"Fine," Louisa said, unconcerned. "Annie will do it. It is because of her, after all, that we're all going on this journey and having to give up the comforts of our settled home here."

Annie merely listened and watched through all of this, trying not to get pulled into any of the disagreements. She'd written to Isaac to accept his proposal. She'd found a new home for her piano. She followed the instructions and did the duties that Louisa had assigned to her. But she tried not to rock the boat.

Whatever freedom she had felt when she had received Isaac's proposal had slowly been whittled down piece by piece as Louisa had taken over plans for the journey west. Annie was grateful for her help. She wouldn't have done this without them. She was lucky to have such care and support from her family, that she didn't have to make this enormous life change by herself.

But just the possibility of going to Oregon had been

hers and hers alone for what now seemed to be a minuscule moment in time. As soon as it was out in the open, in Louisa's clutches, it was no longer Annie's adventure. It felt like it was no longer even her life. All through it all, she tried to just stay out of the way. When Louisa had an opinion, the easiest thing was to just let her have it. With every step of their preparation to go to Oregon, Annie seemed to just be along for the ride.

Before they left Norfolk to begin the trek to their jumping-off point in Missouri, Annie received one more letter from Isaac. It began with enthusiasm and gratitude, as well as polite wishes for her safety. Annie smiled to herself as she read; with every word, it was clear this was a man who would try his best to make her happy. The letter confirmed that Isaac would be looking for her on the next company of emigrants to come over the mountains to Oregon in the fall. Throughout the next nine months, Annie would be on the road, living out of a wagon. Though she could try to send letters on ahead of her, it was more likely that she would have no other contact with her betrothed until she met him in person.

Provided she even made it to Oregon.

From all she was learning since the sisters had decided, she may have underestimated the obstacles between her and the west coast.

Through all of Louisa's doom-saying and Josie's preparations against any outcome, all of Margaret's helping beyond what she really should, Annie had laughed off their worry. It was only when she was alone in bed at night that she would admit to herself how frightened she was. Imagining the wide, dark, unknown expanse of North America, picturing all the dangers and possibilities between her past home and her future home was enough to make her stay in bed, safe and sound. But she couldn't do that. Somehow, Annie knew in her gut that the trip west would likely change her irrevocably.

At this point, she could only hope it would be a change she needed.

And so, one blustery afternoon in early January, Annie climbed into the Hudson family wagon that had been loaded high with the irreplaceable belongings—and three hens—that they could not live without and began her life-changing journey west to Oregon.

CHAPTER FIVE

There was nothing that annoyed Louisa more than when someone did not do their job properly. The journey from Virginia to Missouri had been uneventful, if longer than she had hoped. But at least in that time, she'd had no reason to complain too much. The porters at hotels, the landladies at boarding houses, most of everyone they had met in those twelve hundred miles had made their journey easier.

The bustling, disparate, crowded town of Independence, Missouri, was a different matter.

When they had been in town only a day, she had gone to Martin's Wagons to order the family's two wagons to be built. The wagon they had used to come west was already showing more wear than she was comfortable with. Louisa wanted a fresh and safe start, as well as more room for all the supplies she meant to purchase.

That very same afternoon, she had made the rounds to the livery to inquire about a team of oxen, to the general store to order the supplies they still needed, and to the seamstress to see if she could pick up any additional work for the remaining weeks they were in town. Louisa Hudson knew how to do her job, and making sure her family had everything they needed to get to Oregon was her job at this moment.

On the other hand, Eli, the clerk at the general store, did not seem to know how to do his job. After the Hudsons had been in Independence for two weeks, she had already visited the store ten times to confirm that all the items she wanted would be ready, would be available, would not be sold to someone else, and would be the price she had agreed to pay. There seemed to be only a fifty-fifty chance that Eli would confirm her questions to her satisfaction on any of her visits.

"I fail to see how this is a difficult question, young man," she said to him on her eleventh visit. "Either you do or you do not have a shipment of brown sugar coming soon. I would think that your employer, Mr. Hancock, would be eager to fill the orders of all the emigrants coming into town this spring."

"Yes, ma'am. He is, ma'am." Louisa could tell that the young clerk was a little bit afraid of her. He kept glancing to the other sales clerk for assistance, silently pleading to be rescued. "We sure hope it's coming, ma'am, but... well..."

"Well, what?"

He shrugged helplessly. "We'll be sure to let you know the minute we know, though, I think, all right?"

"You think," she repeated, then heaved a sigh. "It won't surprise you then, Eli, that I will almost certainly be back tomorrow to inquire again."

"I know," he said miserably.

She pretended not to notice the impertinence. If she let herself get sucked into training every inept clerk that crossed her path, she would never get anything else done. There were far bigger things to spend her energy on. Through the big front window of the shop, Louisa had just spotted a barrel-chested man walking by.

She had been looking for that man for a couple days already and wasn't about to miss this opportunity.

"Excuse me," she said to Eli, and was gone before she heard his response.

When Louisa stepped out of the store onto the boardwalk, she almost ran directly into a trio of young men and nearly into the thread of tobacco the middle one spit into the street. She gasped and pulled back, glaring at the man for his audacity.

"Excuse me, ma'am," he said, tipping his hat.

"Hrmph," she responded.

The other two laughed rudely at her.

But rather than engage, Louisa merely turned her back, going after the barrel-chested man she sought. She was a woman on a mission; she didn't have time for the polite pleasantries of strangers.

She stepped out into the street, avoiding the thickest mud as best she could to get a better look at the crowd that had already passed the store. She was sure the barrel-chested man had walked this way—she just needed to find him. With a deep breath, Louisa caught up her skirts and walked as fast as was reasonable down the dirt road.

There. She spotted him. He had stopped to speak to an older couple just past the next intersecting street.

Louisa hung back, not wanting to interrupt. This would have to be handled delicately. She needed something from this man and would suffer no failure. When she noticed that the group breaking up, Louisa went around them, stepped back up onto the boardwalk, and maneuvered herself to be directly in his path.

"Oh!" the man exclaimed. He had just said good-bye to his companions and turned to walk back, almost stepping right into Louisa. "I'm so sorry, ma'am. I must not have been paying attention."

"Oh, heavens," she simpered. He would likely never witness Louisa Hudson simpering ever again, but she thought it wise in this first introduction. "I assure you, the fault is all mine. I was just *dying* for a chance to speak to you, and I must have been over-eager."

"Is that so?" he asked good-naturedly. His bushy dark brown mustache was streaked with gray, and the smile beneath it was amused and a bit teasing. This was a man who, like Louisa, was used to being in charge and was generous in his leadership.

Louisa beamed up at the man. For all her prickles, she knew quite well how to be charming when she needed to be. "You wouldn't be George Mills, now would you?"

"Why, yes I am. What can I help you with, Missus...?"

"It's miss, actually," she said, taking his offered arm. "Miss Louisa Hudson. I'll walk with you if you don't mind, Mr. Mills. I don't want to take up too much of your time, and I hesitate to be a lady alone on the streets in a town like this."

"Right you are, Miss Hudson. I was just on my way

to see the blacksmith about replacing my tongs. Why don't you walk with me?"

"Why, now, how did you know that I've been meaning to see that man myself?"

The companionable grin that passed between them said more than any small talk would. George Mills burst out laughing.

"Miss Hudson, I can already tell that I'm about to give you whatever you ask for. My wife will tell you I'm a mite of a pushover, in fact. Why don't we just skip the pleasantries and get right to the heart of the matter?" With that, he placed his hand over hers where it was tucked into his elbow and led her down the crowded boardwalk.

She laughed in return. "I appreciate your candor, Mr. Mills. I can be direct. I've been hearing good things about yourself and Mr. Sullivan. My family—myself and three other women and a child—are planning on making our way to Oregon this summer, and I was hoping you would have room for us in your wagon train."

"I don't think there should be any problem with that. I will want to meet your brother first, or another Mr. Hudson, though, as we do any man joining the company. You never know what kind of ruffians could sneak in without proper vetting."

"There's no Mr. Hudson. I'm sorry, I thought I had said. Not unless you count my young nephew there. No, I'm sorry if I misled you, Mr. Mills, but my family is just me, my three sisters, and him. He's thirteen, and mature for his age, but really just a child yet."

He stopped walking. "Well, now, I'm not sure. I hesitate to take on a family who may be a burden on the rest of the company."

"I assure you, Mr. Mills, we will not be a burden. We have been on our own for years now, and made it this far without a male presence. If anything, our determination and independence would be a boon to your company."

There was a brief, awkward pause as George Mills seemed too stunned to respond. Then he burst out laughing, a hearty, warm chuckle of absolute joy and began walking down the boardwalk again.

"Well, Miss Hudson, I apologize for assuming. You and your sisters are more than welcome to join our wagon company. I confess myself to be quite interested in seeing how you ladies fare. I wouldn't dream of sticking my nose where it's not wanted. I have no doubt you are more than capable of driving a team, but if you need even a finger lifted in your assistance, you be sure to let me know."

"I'll do that, Mr. Mills. And I thank you. There aren't many men that would be able to look past their own person to let a woman fend for herself out here."

"Well, now, that's fine, as long as you understand no one expects you to fend for yourself. I spoke too hastily before. Why, you say the word, and I wager that by the end of the day, I could find a young man you could hire to drive your team all the way to Oregon for you."

"That won't be necessary." Louisa fought to keep the steel from her voice. She was forever being underesti-mated. "I'm sure I am grateful to you, but I aim to see that everything is taken care of myself."

"Just as you say," he said, nodding thoughtfully. "But you should know that as part of my wagon company, we do expect some measure of pitching in. Standing guard, helping out if someone gets injured. Everyone needs to pull their own weight, and that could mean aiding other families when needed. Will that be a problem with anyone in your family?"

"Oh, heavens, no," Louisa said with a light chuckle. "Annie goes along with whatever someone needs from her, and both Josie and Margaret practically live to take care of other people. You'll see, Mr. Mills. The Hudson family will be an asset to your company."

"Glad to hear it," he said as they reached the blacksmith shop. "Then consider yourself part of our little community. We'll send along word when we are closer to a leaving date, but be sure you get all your supplies lined up as quickly as possible."

She beamed at him as he gestured to follow her into the shop. With their wagon company settled, Louisa took great pleasure in ordering the tools they would need for their journey west. Everything seemed to be coming together, with only a few minor headaches. Though she never would have chosen to travel to Oregon on her own, now that they were on their way, she was well satisfied.

CHAPTER SIX

Annie opened the door to the telegraph office in Independence and stepped into the crowd of people waiting inside. Crammed elbow to elbow, nearly two dozen citizens were hoping to receive or send mail that day. With as many wagon companies as were expected to leave this town over the following spring weeks, it was no wonder so many people were looking for final communication with family back east.

The group seemed to be mostly women—mothers, daughters, matriarchs—all looking determined and harried. Each one must have a dozen other things to do that day; their expressions betrayed that their minds were elsewhere. Annie was sure she appeared the same. It seemed as though ever since her family had arrived in this far western town, this gateway to the frontier, the list of things Louisa had tasked her with got longer every day instead of shorter. Annie might never have thought to go if she had realized how much work it would take to get to Oregon.

As she waited in line to speak to the postmaster, the woman in front of her turned to look around the room. She caught Annie's eye and smiled shyly before turning back to face front. That smile jolted Annie out of her daydreams. It wasn't that the woman was scary or rude. It was that her skin was as dark as acorns.

Though Annie's family had never owned slaves, plenty of their neighbors had. They were an integral part of most communities in the south, but she had never been friends with a person from Africa. Annie had never seen a Black woman lift her head like this back in Virginia, and yet here in the west had looked Annie directly in the eye, as though there was nothing between them. Annie looked around to see if the woman was accompanying anyone, but she seemed to be on her own.

The whole situation was shocking to her, though not in an alarming way. It was new and different, and Annie had no idea how she should respond. This woman didn't seem to be enslaved, but Annie had no reference for how she should treat her otherwise.

Fortunately, in this case, the woman did not make an effort to speak to her, so Annie didn't have to decide. The dark woman minded her own business and moved ahead in the line to mail out her own letters. As she finished with her transaction and turned to leave, the strange woman with the warm brown skin smiled at Annie again.

Annie found herself smiling back. How nice to be in the west, where things like social expectations were less important. For the first time since leaving Virginia, Annie felt freedom in her choice. She—like this woman

—could be anything she wanted to be out here on the frontier.

"Next?" the older man behind the desk called out.

Annie stepped forward, a bright smile on her face. "I was wondering if anything had come for me. Annie Hudson?"

"General delivery?" he asked. He had already turned his back to her to check through the mail piled up around him.

"Yes, sir."

In silence, the man rapidly thumbed through a tall stack of envelopes. Some seemed crisp and new, but most were worn, battered, and clearly showed the damage they had taken from however many hundreds of miles they had traveled to reach Independence.

"Hudson. Here it is. Miss Annie Hudson? That you?"

He held the envelope out to her, and Annie's heart thumped when she recognized Isaac's slanted, spiky handwriting.

"Yes, that's me. Thank you," she murmured as she accepted the letter.

He nodded, but had already called "next" before Annie had a chance to move out of the way. A teenage girl with freckles spilled across her nose elbowed her way to the front of the line, seemingly heedless of Annie still standing there. Stepping to the front window so she had more light, Annie looked down on her prize.

There it was, in her hands. A letter addressed to Miss Annie Hudson, General Delivery, Independence, Missouri. That was her. This letter was for her. It had been so long since she had heard from Isaac. This man who she was preparing to spend her life with was constantly in her thoughts. Annie had spent all the months since leaving Virginia assuming that there would only be silence from her betrothed as she traveled, but he managed to get a letter here to her.

She was surprised to find that she didn't want to tear it open immediately; she wanted to make the letter last, to savor it a bit. Annie passed through the throng of waiting customers, back out onto the street, and turned north. Any thought of other errands she had meant to take care of had completely left her brain. All she could focus on was what Isaac had to say.

The crowd of bustling emigrants around her did little to distract Annie from thoughts of what was in that letter and what was waiting for her at the end of their journey.

Who was waiting for her.

Intellectually, Annie knew that she had really made her choice when she left Virginia. Even so, it was still possible that she could go back now. Back to the people she knew and the life she was used to. At some level, once Louisa had gotten on board the plan to emigrate west, all decision-making had been taken from Annie. She had just gone along with each choice, each one bringing them ever closer to Independence and now ever closer to Oregon.

She clutched the letter more tightly as she made her way up the street to their boarding house. Isaac Wheeler was a decent man. He was strong enough and motivated enough to get to Oregon in the first place. He was tender and compassionate enough to seek out someone to share his life with. Isaac would be enough for her. A life with him might not carry the passionate romance of her first love, but a life with a good man who cared about her could be enough.

Annie prayed that whatever was in this last letter to her would confirm this choice, especially since it felt as though the choice was somewhat Louisa's.

In this maze of thoughts, Annie reached home. The Hudsons had been staying at a small, respectable boarding house a few blocks from the main street of Independence. The place had only gotten more crowded since they had arrived a month ago, and Annie was unsurprised to find several people in the parlor, poring over the guidebook every emigrant knew by heart.

The trio of young Davis brothers and their mother had been at the boarding house since the Hudsons had arrived. More than once they had offered Louisa their help in driving their wagons to Oregon. Annie smiled at the memory of her older sister fully shutting down their offer after days of them hinting. The Hudsons needed no help from anyone, she told them. Annie imagined that Louisa would drive both the Hudson wagons herself if she could.

Annie was hanging her coat on the hooks by the front door when she heard her name.

"Oh, hello, Miss Hudson." Their landlady, Mrs. Case, had spotted Annie in the foyer. "Were you able to get what you needed?"

Annie looked at the still-sealed envelope clutched in her hand and then back up at the older woman. "Some. I may go out again this afternoon once I've had a rest."

Mrs. Case nodded. "Your sister-in-law is up there now. She just returned from shopping with Mrs. Montgomery. And I believe she was going to go out again soon with your nephew."

"Thank you," Annie said as she climbed the stairs. She had hoped for a moment alone to read over Isaac's letter, but being with Margaret was almost as good. She would respect Annie's privacy.

Upon arriving in Independence, the Hudsons had to hustle to find a place they could all stay. Many of the hotels were full to bursting, and private homes were opening up to boarders. They had lucked onto Mrs. Case's establishment, but the four women shared a crowded room, and Lawrence had been relegated to a cot in the attic. He never complained, though, the sweet boy. Annie felt a little guilty when she thought about all the hardships he and her sisters were going through for her.

When she opened the door to their room, Margaret was leaning over the washbasin, scrubbing at her hands. She looked up at her sister's entrance.

"And how was your day?" she asked cheerfully.

"Fine. Good."

Margaret nodded. She seemed to sense that Annie had nothing more she wanted to say at that moment, and she returned to scrubbing her hands. That was one thing that Annie appreciated about her sister-in-law; she always seemed so sensitive to other people's needs.

Annie had been sleeping on the far side of the far bed and made her way over there now. True, it felt at times as though she was relegating herself to the corner, but it also felt safe and secluded when she needed it.

Sitting down on the crazy quilt, Annie relaxed and finally let herself open the letter from Isaac.

"My dear Annie," it began. "I hope this letter finds you well. I hope this letter finds you at all. Thinking about you traveling across the continent on your way to me makes me afraid for you. But from everything you've told me, I believe that you—and Louisa—will be just fine.

"I want to thank you again for your courage and your willingness to go through this upcoming trial for my sake. I promise to spend the rest of my life making it up to you. I will do everything I can to make you happy and keep you safe. As soon as you arrive in Oregon, I will be there every day to take care of you and our life together.

"God willing, when you arrive in Oregon, your wedding gift will be here as well. I have ordered a piano to be shipped from New York. I know how much it hurt you to have to leave yours behind in Virginia. The new one arrives in San Francisco by ship at the end of the summer, and from there will be carted north to me. It is my hope that you will feel at home here and that this can be a small step toward that.

"Be safe, Annie. And God speed."

Annie closed her eyes and let out a sigh of relief. How blessed she was to have a man like this waiting for her in Oregon.

"Everything okay?" Margaret asked.

Annie looked up, smiled, and nodded. And how blessed she was to have a family like this accompanying her. For the first time, she was able to see past the strenuous journey and start to imagine how their life would be when they reached Oregon. Louisa would again start up her business. They would build a home together, learn anew what kind of vegetables they could grow easily in their garden. Lawrence would grow up with all the opportunities such an open land could afford him.

"Thank you, again, for coming," she said to Margaret, who turned back to her in surprise.

Margaret smiled. "I love you, Annie. And your sisters. This is exactly where God means me to be."

"I know, but... well, you can't deny it must have been quite a decision to pull Lawrence out of the life that he knew."

Margaret laughed. "Oh, I wouldn't worry about that boy adjusting too much. He's already tried to talk me into letting him run the farm on his own when we get there instead of boarding somewhere first. I think, as long as we give the boy enough space, he'll be just fine."

Annie thought about how tall Lawrence had seemed to her just the day before. Though barely into his teen years, he was already so strong, filling out the way his father had at that age. "If he's anything like Tom, I imagine he'll have you convinced by the time we get there."

"Oh, isn't that the truth? I find myself wishing Tom was still alive more and more lately. He would have loved this. And my poor boy wouldn't have to grow up without a father."

Annie knew all too well what it was like to long for someone who could never be there. But maybe the fresh start in Oregon would be as good for Margaret as Annie hoped it would be for her.

It wouldn't be long now. Louisa had found them a wagon company to join that would be leaving soon.

Though there were still the wagons themselves to be completed and the last of their supplies to purchase, they were so close to leaving for the west. Annie had everything she needed to start toward her new home.

She was ready.

CHAPTER SEVEN

It seemed as though the few weeks the Hudson family spent in Independence had flashed by in the blink of an eye. Every moment was crammed full of tasks, conversations, and hustling to get all the things ready that they needed to survive on the Oregon Trail for the next six months. Almost two thousand pounds of food, just to start with, not to mention every other item they might need when they arrived in Oregon to build their new home. Tools and blankets and shoes and compass and untold others. More than one man she had done business with tried to assure Louisa that the journey could only last as long as four months, but she was not one to take chances.

Through all that time, Louisa believed that everything would fall into place exactly as she needed it to. She was smart. She was prepared. She was by far the most capable person she knew. And she was doing more than anyone else to ensure her family's success. Even so, it was with no small feeling of relief when that April day finally arrived in which they were to leave Independence with the rest of the Sullivan-Mills wagon company.

The Hudson family had two brand new wagons built. The old, rickety vehicle that had gotten them as far as Independence could not be trusted to last much farther. Louisa would take no chances. When she received word that the new wagons were completed, the sisters packed into them all the family's worldly goods, all the personal effects, and all the supplies they would need for the next six months until they arrived in Oregon.

The whole family had made the visit to Martin's Wagons when Louisa was to pay for their purchases. Josie all but skipped down the street in her excitement. Margaret had almost made her son stay behind to continue his studies, but Louisa stepped in. The boy would be responsible for one of the wagons. He deserved to be there that first time.

Louisa's heart swelled with pride at all that her family had accomplished in such a short time—all that *she* had accomplished, really. She couldn't wait to show them the pristine, sturdy new wagons that would take them all the way to their new life in Oregon.

Martin's Wagons was one of two suppliers in Independence. With as much traffic as the town saw every spring, Jed Martin had his team working day and night to complete all the orders before the caravans left. Louisa led her family through the gate on the far side of the small, free-standing office building to the wide yard beyond. Everywhere she looked was a Conestoga wagon or sparse wagon frames in various states of being built. The smell of freshly cut lumber filled the air.

It took Louisa a good five minutes to get the attention of any of the men working, but soon Mr. Martin himself was leading the Hudsons to a pair of matched wagons that waited.

"So you see," Mr. Martin said expansively, "they are precisely as you ordered. I hope they are to your liking, Miss Hudson."

Louisa nodded, walking around the back of the one on the right to inspect the joints and look for gaps between the boards.

"You got any paint?" Lawrence asked the man. "Black paint."

"What on earth do you need paint for?" Louisa asked.

Lawrence pointed to one of the wagons parked on the other side of the yard. Stark black letters stood out against the white canvas, spelling out "CALIF OR BUST."

"We could do that," he said.

"Oh, no," Louisa said. "Absolutely not. I will not be advertising my own arrogance on the side of my home for the rest of the year."

"It doesn't have to be that," Lawrence said. "I could paint our name, or..." He looked around. "Or our city. Take some pride in where we come from, you know?"

"That's true," Margaret said, stepping in for her son. "That's a mighty nice idea, Lawrence."

"Can I?" he pleaded. "Please?"

"A lot of other folks are doing the same thing," Mr. Martin said. "And it could help other Virginians get to know you. Helps you be able to pick out your own wagon in a mess of 'em."

Louisa harrumphed, and looked again at the crowd

of finished and nearly finished wagons. Mr. Martin was telling the truth. She saw Bible verses, last names, cities, and declarations on maybe half of the canvas tops. Many people wanted to make their mark and help their own wagon stand out some.

Finally, she looked at Lawrence again and nodded.

Mr. Martin chuckled. "You can find some paint over the side of that shack there," he said as the boy dashed off.

"Just the city," Louisa called after him. "And just on one of them!"

She caught Annie and Margaret exchanging a look. But, she couldn't interpret it and, frankly, didn't have time to explain herself to them. Having the name of their city painted on the side of the wagon canvas would provide a much-needed anchor among the sea of other wagons. She already knew their family would stand out; she might as well have their wagon stand out too.

The morning they were to leave Independence, Louisa had her family up and out the door of the boarding house just after breakfast. Mrs. Case wished them well, along with the Davises and the Montgomerys who were also leaving with the same company. Soon the Hudsons found themselves in the caravan of wagons leaving the town in a few short hours. Louisa drove their lead wagon, where the women would be sleeping each night, and Lawrence drove the second wagon, filled to the brim with the bulk of their supplies for six months.

"Do you think he'll be all right?" Josie asked her oldest sister, craning her neck to see the wagon behind them.

"Of course he will be," Louisa assured her. "That boy

is the fastest learner I've ever met. You'll see. By the time we get to Oregon, he'll be leading this wagon train. He's a Hudson. And Hudsons get things done."

"All right, yes, fine, but right now, what matters is if he can drive a team of oxen by himself. He's only thirteen," Josie said patiently.

The two sisters were walking alongside their own team of oxen, just behind a family with three small children and just ahead of thirteen-year-old Lawrence driving the team hauling the Hudson family's second wagon. Behind him was a family of all boys; Margaret had reported that the father was a widower and was taking his sons for a new start in Oregon. Louisa had given Lawrence the space to learn, but she stayed prepared to take control again if she needed to.

"Almost fourteen," Louisa said. "Which reminds me... where did Margaret get off to? Is she not worried about her son?"

"Annie's keeping an eye on him. I think Margaret went off to make friends." Josie ended with a laugh. "There's no stopping her. All these new people around for her is like Christmas Day."

"Hm. Well, as long as she doesn't shirk her duties here."

"In my experience, Margaret always has more energy to do stuff around our home once she's gotten in her socializing for the day. Best to let her do what she does best. Besides," Josie continued, elbowing Louisa gently, "we always come out better for her friendships. Remember that time she organized the fundraiser to put a new roof on the parsonage?"

Louisa chuckled. "Just fifty cents from each family

because she knew every single family in town. You're right."

The caravan of wagons all leaving Independence on that gorgeous spring day was longer than Louisa had expected. Totaling something like fifty families, many of whom, like the Hudsons, drove more than one wagon. It was almost as if they were traveling with an entire town. Half the reason Louisa had so pursued George Mills's company was the fact that he had managed to convince an actual doctor to travel with them. But other than Dr. Martell and his wife, she didn't have much interest in the rest of their new neighbors.

It wasn't that Louisa disliked other people, of course. It was just that there were far more important things to worry about.

Like ensuring her hens stayed in their coop, on the wagon, where she could be sure they were safe.

During the months they traveled from Virginia to Missouri, Louisa attempted and discarded several different options for keeping the hens where they were supposed to be. When the family stayed with Mrs. Case, they were given a dedicated corner of the yard to pen them, safe from the local predators behind high fences and plenty of space to run around. Their landlady had been quite generous with them, requesting only the use of any eggs the hens might lay.

But in order to transport the three birds all the way to Oregon, a different arrangement would have to be made. Louisa was fairly certain—as much as she could be, at least—that she had predicted and eliminated any issues. But now as they were leaving Independence, those plans were put to the test. Each bird had been built a small cage that could be latched shut, and that would keep them in place while the wagon was in motion. Then—in theory, though Louisa would have to test it that night—when the wagon stopped for the night, she could corral the birds under one of the vehicles with a roll of burlap staked in the ground and pinned to the wagon's side. It wouldn't be pretty, but it would work.

And then Louisa and her family could have fresh eggs all the way to Oregon.

They had also brought their horse, Carrot, and three goats with them. Though she hoped to get milk from the goats as they traveled, as with the hens, Louisa knew not all animals handle stress well. They would just have to see how it went.

Such plans and considerations rattled around in her mind as she walked alongside her team of oxen. The trail out of Independence wasn't terribly long that first day; the goal was simply to get out of town and to the next water source. There was a campsite outside of the town where all the wagon companies were gathering, breaking off, and sorting themselves out.

They crossed outside the Independence border and traveled for several hours, Louisa leading the first wagon, Lawrence driving the second. Josie and Annie had helped as they could, keeping track of the animals, offering to take the reins, or bringing Louisa a canteen of water when the sun was beating down. But though she knew she should hand over responsibility some time along the trail, Louisa wanted to do it all herself this first day. She wanted to prove she could do it. She needed to prove that this journey was not a mistake.

By sunset, the wagon train had pulled into their first campsite, and Louisa was grateful. She kept a focused watch on the wagon in front of them, making sure to avoid any rocks or dips that may be along the path, and pulled their wagon into a space outside the existing grouping of wagons already settled. Lawrence pulled the wagon he led up next to the other, the two Hudson wagons sitting parallel in the fading light.

Louisa took a long breath. She still had many chores and steps to take before she could relax for the night, but she gave herself this first quiet moment on this first hectic day.

From where she stood, Louisa could only see the wagons closest and the very tops of trees maybe half a mile away. But, as she had been short her whole life, she was well used to doing what she had to do to get the view she needed. Catching her long skirt up with one hand and clasping the side of the wagon with the other, Louisa hoisted herself up to the seat. In two tall steps, she had gotten up high enough to see much more of the campsite where they would be staying.

Even in the twilight, she could see that the landscape all around was peppered with campfires, smoke rising into the violet sky. Though she had gotten a sense of how many emigrants would be heading to Oregon during the time they were in Independence, the sight of so many families all with the same goal in mind made Louisa catch her breath.

That sight was heightened by the sounds filling the air all around her. Another wagon full of giggling children pulled into a spot near her own, and she couldn't help but smile at the sound. The air was full of girls' laughter, men murmuring, mothers scolding, and from somewhere not far off, a fiddle playing a lively tune.

She wanted to get closer to the music, but Louisa hadn't even started on the chores they needed to do. Reluctantly, she climbed back down from the wagon and began to issue her instructions.

But when she looked around, she realized Lawrence had already gone.

"What are you doing?" Louisa asked Josie when she found her at the back of the wagon.

"Getting things for supper." She frowned. "I assumed you all were starving. I know I am, all that walking."

"Yes," Louisa said, a bit irritated. "What about the boy?"

"Lawrence went to fetch water," Margaret called back from where she had been seeing to the oxen. She murmured and pet one of their noses before turning back to Louisa. "I learned there's a spring by those trees over yonder."

"All right," said Louisa. "And where's Annie?"

"She went with him. We thought you'd want water for the animals too," said Josie.

"Oh. Well... then... that's fine."

"We're not helpless, you know," Josie murmured to her soothingly. "You don't have to take care of us at every turn."

"I'm not," Louisa said hotly "I'm not. I just... I just want to be sure. You know perfectly well none of us have ever done this before. We have no room for error."

"I know, Lou," she said. "We know. We'll be okay."

Louisa didn't respond, but busied herself helping Josie. She would need to reorganize the supply wagon once she had a better idea of what she would need each day. This would be a never-ending chore, but necessary. By the end of the night, Louisa was satisfied that everything that needed to be done had been done, and they'd be ready to begin again in the morning.

CHAPTER EIGHT

Annie rolled over to face the darkest corner she could find, hiding her eyes to try to catch just a few more moments of sleep. Her corn husk mattress rustled with every movement, so it was just as well her body was too tired to move much. After the previous day of walking so many miles, along with trying to calm Carrot and keep track of their goats, Annie was rather surprised she was even awake now.

"Up and at 'em," Louisa called through the opening in the wagon cover. "Lots to do today. Josie, you best hurry. Lawrence has already asked me twice about breakfast. He's liable to start himself any moment and burn our bacon."

Josie groaned, and the Hudsons sisters stirred awake from inside their sleeping wagon. There were two narrow cots along each side of the wagon, with two more bunks built above. As the youngest—and the spryest—Annie had been relegated to one of the top bunks and she remained curled up in bed as she heard the others waking around her.

Maybe it was the excitement of leaving Independence, or the noise of all their neighbors in the campsites nearby, but Annie hadn't gotten to sleep until late the night before. She felt as though she had just closed her eyes, and now here was Louisa waking them all again.

"How long do we have before we have to leave?" she asked groggily. Louisa was leaning into the wagon, making sure her sisters were following her instructions.

"We're not."

"What?" Margaret asked, taking up the line of questioning as she smoothed down her dress. "But didn't they want to start west as soon as possible?"

"No, we're staying here for another day," she said. "George Mills and William Sullivan decided we'll be on the trail tomorrow morning, instead. Apparently, there are still some families making their way out here from Independence." Louisa shook her head. "I don't know why they didn't prepare themselves properly. They should have known everyone else was ready to leave yesterday. The longer we wait to head to Oregon, the less grass there will be along the way for the oxen."

"Well, then, today will be a lovely rest for us," Margaret said resolutely, as she combed her hair back into its usual bun. Annie always admired her sister-in-law's determination to stay positive in the face of Louisa's pessimistic predictions.

"We don't have time to rest," Louisa said. "I want to get the other wagon repacked. Camilla and the girls are mighty agitated, and I think one of the hanging canteens was banging against their cages while we were on the trail yesterday."

"Will they be all right?" Josie asked.

"I'm sure they will," Louisa answered grimly. "I'll figure it out. But I need you, Josie, to make breakfast. Annie can help you. Margaret, once you're dressed, come help me unpack the other wagon. We've got to reassess where each item goes and repack it again before the end of the day. I don't want there to be any reason we are not the first ones ready to hit the trail tomorrow morning."

And with that, Louisa left them to their morning toiletries. Annie was grateful for the day of rest and aimed to take advantage of as much as she could. The first day of walking had been exhausting in and of itself, but being surrounded by so many strangers even more so. It seemed as though every time she turned around, there was a new smiling face and a name to remember.

All three of the other Hudson sisters had risen and were out of the wagon before Annie sat up. Though she was more or less used to traveling—having been on the road since Virginia—there was something about the constant walking, as well as the loading and unloading of the wagon, that exhausted her very bones. She stifled a yawn as she pinned back her hair and tied on a clean apron. Any dawdling would be noticed, and she didn't want to fight with Louisa about carrying her own weight.

When Annie climbed out of the wagon, Josie was already approaching, her arms full of fuel to build their campfire.

"Can you get us some more fresh water?" she asked upon seeing Annie. "Lawrence gave the bucket I had waiting to the animals." She shook her head with a smile. "We'll teach that boy. Just have to make him wait for his breakfast, and he'll learn right quick."

Annie nodded, yawned, and claimed the two empty buckets that hung from the wagon's underside. The night before had been a bit chaotic as they made their camp, but she had no trouble finding the spring again. Judging from the sun's position in the sky, it was still only just after dawn, but late enough that Annie encountered more than a dozen women and girls gathering their own water at the same time she was.

Some introduced themselves, some kept their heads down and their mouths shut. Annie found herself watching and listening more than anything else. There was a craving in her for friendship and companionship beyond her family. But this first day of meeting strangers felt like she was still understanding her place.

"Are you one of the Hudsons?" a voice called to her as she hauled her full bucket out of the spring.

Annie set it at her feet, wiped her wet hands on her apron, and turned to the voice. A tall, angular young woman in the black of mourning greeted her. She had warm brown eyes, round pink cheeks, and if Annie was not mistaken, was younger than she was.

"I am," Annie said with a returning smile. "Have we met? I'm sorry I can't place you at all."

"Oh, I guessed as much," she said with a dismissive wave and disarming smile. "But your sister Margaret talks all about you, so I feel like I already know you."

Annie laughed. "Yes, that sounds like Margaret. My name is Annie."

"Annie. So you're ... the youngest? The bride-to-be?"

Annie blushed but laughed. "She really does talk about me, doesn't she?"

"Only kind things, I assure you. My name is Rebecca. Or, I suppose, Mrs. Tenney."

"Tenney," Annie repeated. "I'm sorry, but that name doesn't sound familiar at all to me."

"That's probably because I'm the only one," the woman said. "Just me. My husband died before we even left Indiana, and I'm traveling with my parents and brother. The Stephenses."

"Mrs. Stephens, yes. I'm sure Margaret has mentioned her."

"My mother."

"I'm very sorry for your loss," Annie said somberly. "It must be very trying to be going through all of this without your husband, Mrs. Tenney."

"Please, call me Rebecca." Her eyes were bright. "Everyone calls me Mrs. Tenney, and it just makes me sad all over again each time."

"Forgive me," Annie said hastily. "Rebecca."

"I don't want to talk about me, or about the past," she said with brave cheerfulness. "I just wanted to introduce myself. From what Margaret has told me, I thought we might be friends. I used to play piano, too, you see."

"Did you? I miss it ever so much. But of course, it's completely impractical to haul one all the way across the continent."

Rebecca laughed. "I've only ever played our church's piano, so it's not as though I had any idea of bringing one to Oregon. Sometimes at night, though, I find my fingers playing a hymn against my knee when my mind is elsewhere."

"I was the piano teacher in our town." Annie shook her head. "Without one, I'm not sure how I will spend my time there. It's all so new!"

"There will always be something, I'm sure."

"You're right. Just like there's always some chore to do here." Annie gestured to the buckets she had set in the dirt at her feet. "My sister will be wanting these."

"Of course! Yes, well, it was lovely to meet you, and I do hope we can be friends."

"I hope so too," Annie said. She meant it, too. In Norfolk, she had a few dear, intimate friends, and she missed them terribly. Maybe it was time to start filling that gap. "Until then."

She smiled to herself as she hauled the full buckets back through the tall grass to where her wagons and campsite waited. There, in Lawrence's clear hand, she read "NORFOLK," like a beacon calling her.

A short walk later, Annie had reached her campsite again, where Josie presided over the campfire, adding a handful of twigs to raise the heat a bit. Annie set the full buckets down next to her sister.

"Annie!" Josie said. "There you are. Louisa has been looking for you."

"Oh, goodness," she said. "I was just... I got waylaid. I met Mrs. Tenney. It's so nice to make a friend outside our little circle."

Josie laughed. "That's what Margaret keeps saying. And that's precisely why Louisa is annoyed with her."

"Well, I don't aim to tell Louisa," Annie said with her

own laugh. She lifted one of the buckets of water and poured it carefully into the big pot Josie had set to warm. When she had stood up straight again, she realized Josie had been watching her carefully. "What?"

"I think you should."

"Should what?"

"Should tell Louisa."

"Oh, no, I don't think so—"

"I mean it, Annie. One of these days, you have got to actually tell her what you really think."

"I did! I have! Why do you think we're out here in Missouri, after all?"

Josie shook her head but smiled kindly. "Did you, though? Didn't Louisa make the decision for you?"

"Then I guess I shouldn't ruin my streak." Annie tried to say it flippantly, but the truth of Josie's words had struck her.

"Just think about it," Josie prodded. "She's your sister, and she loves you. Though Louisa isn't used to taking in other people's opinions, she does want you to be happy. You should tell her what you actually think once in a while."

Annie nodded. "I'll think about it."

"Good. You can think about it while you go get me more water."

"Yes, ma'am," Annie said. "And where's Lawrence? I want to tell him that his idea to paint on the canvas worked. I might never have found my way back to you all in this maze if it weren't for the letters guiding me."

The rest of the day in camp seemed to go by in a whirlwind. Louisa wanted Annie to be in four places at once, checking and rechecking, organizing and reorganizing, soothing the animals, and repairing the already torn canvas. It never seemed to end.

But by the time Annie tucked herself into her cot that night, she was starting to feel as though she had found her place again. This travel to Oregon would be temporary, but the friends she made along the way could be forever.

CHAPTER NINE

In spite of all the pressing need to start the journey west to Oregon, the Sullivan-Mills wagon company was still stalled out at their campsite into the late morning the following day. Whatever plans and arrangements each person had made, nothing seemed to be going right. Animals already hitched to their wagons pawed at the ground. Children who wanted to run and play were turning cranky as their mothers bid them to wait.

Louisa was livid. She glared in the general direction of the train captain, as though that made any difference, and mentally bemoaned the fact that she had to rely on a wagon train at all. With everything else in her life, Louisa had found that if she wanted something done right, she should do it herself.

The family was waiting. For what, they weren't sure. Josie had just finished putting away the breakfast things. Annie had gone with Margaret to gather their other animals—the horse and goats—while Louisa and Lawrence had harnessed the teams of oxen. She and

Josie stood by their draft animals, who munched on the little grass at their feet and waited patiently to be needed.

Louisa was anything but patient.

"What is the point in having a plan if no one sticks to it?" she muttered. "I've been ready since seven."

Josie made comforting noises but didn't answer her.

Louisa knew the answer herself anyway. She had long gotten used to the fact that no one she met was as committed as she was to getting a thing done.

"If I was a man..." she began under her breath.

If she was a man, to be truthful, much of her life would be different. She could even be a Senator by now. A rich landowner. A million other things that women had no access to. But at the very least, if Louisa had been born a man, she would be heading her own wagon company, and they would already be a day and a half farther west than they were now. They would have every safety measure in place, and every family under her supervision would be thriving.

She made a mental note to go over the food stores and ration where they could to make up the difference. Lawrence would still need as much sustenance as possible, growing boy that he was, but likely Annie or Josie—both petite and not driving a team of enormous animals—could do without a full portion as needed. That would be a decision for later, however. At the moment, all Louisa wanted was to get her wagons moving.

Louisa recognized a tall young man as the captain's son, Daniel Mills, riding through the camp, calling to the men and issuing directions. She watched as he stopped to talk to the families that would be in their wagon company. He had evidently been dispatched to give last-minute instructions and check that everyone was—finally, definitely—ready to leave. The last stragglers had arrived late last night, but now everything seemed to be falling into place.

As luck would have it, the Hudsons had spent the previous day camping next to two families who would be part of the Sullivan-Mills company. Other nearby families were waiting for different groups or waiting for other family to join them from back east, but the Hudsons' two immediate neighbors would continue to be that for the next stretch of their journey.

Margaret had reached out to all of the emigrants in their general area and had reported back names and details to her sisters. The Jameson family—the widower and his sons that Margaret had met—would be following behind them in the caravan as they all made their way west. It was Martin Jameson who had been playing the fiddle the first evening they were in camp, and when Annie learned that, her eyes had lit up. Louisa hadn't realized how much her sister must miss music until she had seen that expression.

To their other side, in the wagon the Hudsons would be following, was the Robinson family, with three children and who apparently had a spinster schoolteacher traveling with them. Margaret hadn't learned much more than that; the Robinsons' camp sounded a bit undisciplined and chaotic to Louisa, given her sister-in-law's description. But, Margaret had been thrilled to learn there was a schoolteacher in their company, talking on and on about Lawrence getting back into his education, getting caught up with other boys his age.

So, as they waited, Louisa stood next to her team of oxen, rein in hand, ready to set them into motion as soon as she saw that Buck Robinson in front of her had done the same with his own wagon. Daniel rode back up the length of the company's campsite toward his father's wagon at the lead, so Louisa had hope they would be moving soon. Any moment now, they should be heading westward.

"Let me get you something to eat," Josie said soothingly. "I can pull some dried apples or jerky out of the wagon while we're waiting."

Louisa heaved a sigh. Eating a meal of any kind felt like admitting defeat, like they weren't really going to be leaving that day. But Josie was right. There was nothing for it.

"All right," she relented grudgingly.

Later, she was grateful for the suggestion. Since the company had been so late when they finally pulled out of the campsite, the wagon at the lead did not let them stop for a mid-day meal. Instead, as they finally got the wheels turning and the wagon train underway, the sun climbed in the sky. As long as she was moving, Louisa was happy.

About early afternoon, however, the wagon in front of the Hudsons slowed to a stop.

Louisa didn't want to believe it at first. Just when they had gotten started, she was expected to stop again? She gasped as she reined her own team, slowing them to a stop just before she ran into the Robinsons. This was all more infuriating than she thought she could handle.

"What under the canopy is it now?" Louisa exclaimed, unconcerned about who overheard her.

"Josie, go on back, take the reins, and tell Lawrence to run on up ahead. If there's something we can do to speed this along or to offer assistance, we should do it. I don't want to be dawdling any longer than I have to."

She stood there, soothing her animals, as her nephew ran parallel to the trail up to the wagons ahead. The longer Louisa had to wait for an explanation, the crankier she got. She didn't even bother listening to Josie prattling on, trying to distract her from her frustration.

After less than ten minutes, Lawrence came running back to his aunt.

"Well?" Louisa prompted him.

He grimaced and took a few deep breaths, calming his heart. "It's bad," he said, shaking his head. "There's... There was an accident."

"What kind of accident? Why are we stopped?"

He shook his head again. "I couldn't see past the crowd, but it seems like a wagon turned over or got stuck, and the rest of the company has to detour around it."

Louisa groaned. "Well, as long as we are moving around it and not all stopping to gawk, I suppose that's the best we can hope for. Is everyone all right?"

He shook his head. "I don't know."

"Hmm," Louisa said, as she thought. "Well, go back to your team. Tell your mother and aunts what happened. I'm sure we'll get going any minute now."

But they didn't move. Not yet. Josie rejoined Louisa at their lead wagon, but her worried chatter grew more and more trying. Where her sister was always preparing for the worst-case scenario, Louisa held off her judgment until she saw quite how bad the situation was, even as she fumed.

"Lawrence said there was a crowd. It's likely that whatever the problem, it is in hand," Louisa reminded her. "As long as we keep moving west soon, I think we'll be all right."

Finally, after another twenty minutes, their wagon inched its way to the source of the delay. Louisa's stomach dropped when she saw the scene to the right of the trail— an accident had occurred. Somehow, a wagon had overturned, and a man was trapped under the heavy wheel, his family standing stricken nearby. Though many had stopped to help, it was clear at a glance that there was nothing to be done for the man. One tall young man directed the rest of the caravan around the wreckage to carry on down the trail.

Louisa took a deep breath and turned her gaze back on the road ahead of her. There was nothing she could do, and not delaying them any longer was her goal. She staunchly resisted staring at the disaster and instead kept putting one foot in front of another, not even looking when she heard the mournful cries of the two children. It was heartbreaking and, to be honest, frustrating. There was no doubt about that, but Louisa knew the best thing she could do was keep her wagon moving and get it out of the way. Her duty was clear.

Though the Sullivan-Mills wagon company had suffered through a horrific death of a member of their own, they never stopped moving. Under the heat of the spring sun, Louisa drove her team of oxen ever west, eyes looking ahead, step after step, leading her family toward their new life in Oregon.

Finally, after another several hours of walking, the wagon in front of her slowed again, pulling toward a campsite to the left of the trail. Louisa was quite tired from their first full day—almost full, she corrected herself—but rallied her strength to feed and water the animals, as well as issue instructions to her sisters.

"You just rest up," Josie told her after Louisa had given her specific instructions about what she was to cook for supper for all of them. "We all know our roles. Don't you worry about a thing."

Though Louisa was doubtful that all of them would be able to do everything she needed of them without more instruction, she nevertheless let herself sit a moment. Leaning against the back of their sleeping wagon, she watched as Lawrence lugged two full buckets of water back from the narrow creek they were camping by. As soon as he had set them down, he caught up the other two buckets to fill them as well.

She couldn't sit here shirking while he did that; Lawrence had had just as full a day as she had. Louisa got to her feet again and reached for the first full bucket of water.

Later, over supper, Louisa listened as her sisters discussed their first real day on the trail and the horror of the accident already befalling the company.

"The family's name was Buchanan," Margaret was saying. "Pastor Montgomery told me that Mrs. Buchanan has already hired a couple of the older boys to help drive her wagon west, rather than turn around and go back."

"Goodness, that's remarkable," Annie said. "What a

trial that must be for her. I wonder at a widow with two young children making such a decision."

"I'm going to go introduce myself in a couple days," Margaret continued. "Once she's had more time with her grief. The poor woman. It's all our duties as her neighbor to help her carry this load."

"Don't you be letting other people's problems keep you from tending to your own, though," Louisa said. She vaguely registered the shock on her sisters' faces before she continued. "I mean it. You all know. Josie has told us what the guidebook says enough times. This journey is going to take everything we have, and I won't be having you tiring yourself out for other people while your own family needs you more."

"Lou—" Josie began.

"No, you said that," Louisa insisted. "You made it very clear the dangers we were walking into."

"But we're still called to love our neighbors," Margaret said softly.

"Of course we are," Louisa said. "And what better way can we love these neighbors than by sticking to the path? You know that many of these families have only the barest of essentials to get them to Oregon. Dawdling for a day or neglecting your chores for *this* family just hurts everyone in the caravan in the long run."

She caught Josie and Annie exchanging confused looks.

"I'm just saying don't be sacrificing your own well-being for a virtual stranger," Louisa continued. "I've done everything to get this family the best chance at getting to Oregon. Finding the most respected company and captains, finding us a wagon train that includes a doctor, making sure that we have plenty of supplies to get us there. You've trusted my judgment thus far, haven't you? Trust me when I tell you not to take on the burdens of other people."

Louisa looked at her sisters—even Annie, who had remained quiet—and shook her head in disappointment. "You'll see," she said. "You'll wish you had listened to me."

With that, Louisa stood and crossed to the campfire, where she helped herself to another biscuit and spoonful of beans. This conversation was over.

CHAPTER TEN

Annie had spent her whole life listening to Louisa's declarations and inarguable pronouncements. There were only a couple ways to deal with her sister when she was like this, and one was to simply ignore her. Louisa couldn't stop Margaret if she tried, and the woman only ever pretended to listen to Louisa. When there was someone who needed to be cared for, Annie's sister-in-law was always the first to wade in. Once the company was on the trail again, Margaret continued her regular reaching out to the widow Buchanan. Annie even caught her absconding with a couple of the eggs Camilla and the other hens managed to lay in spite of the stress of their journey. Margaret had sworn her to secrecy—Louisa would have a fit if she knew. Annie was in no hurry to get in the middle of that.

Fortunately for the Sullivan-Mills wagon company, the Buchanan wagon accident was the only real tragedy for the first few weeks on the trail. Smaller mishaps peppered their days—horses throwing a shoe, children getting scrapes—but nothing insurmountable. Yes, there was exhaustion and stress, but everyone survived the abrupt change in their lifestyle. Progress each day was much more about getting used to the new changes.

Annie found herself noticing all the little ways living on the trail, her entire life in a wagon, was so markedly different from her life in Virginia. She was well used to scrubbing her laundry or helping peel potatoes; Annie had grown up with a long list of chores to do every day. It was not as though the Hudsons were particularly wealthy or that she was accustomed to a life of leisure. And yet, the constant walking under the heat of the April sun was far more draining than she had expected.

In Norfolk, Annie had spent her days alternating between helping Josie take care of their home and teaching piano to some of the children in town. It was strenuous in its own way, but nothing like this. Unlike her sisters, while they traveled west Annie didn't have many designated chores specific to her. Instead, she found herself running here and there, filling any role the other women needed her for. On any given day, that meant hitching a team of oxen, or scrubbing a pan, or mending a rip in Lawrence's best trousers.

In spite of all her physical exhaustion at being on her feet all day, Annie was proud of the work she was doing. Given that it was her own betrothal that brought the Hudsons west, Annie felt responsible for the health and happiness of every member of her family. The more she could take on herself, she would. If she could contribute to that by letting Margaret sleep in an extra twenty minutes or helping Josie spend less time with her hands in soapy water, she would do it. Never before in her relatively sheltered life had Annie felt so imminently satisfied with herself at the end of a long day of work.

Only three days into their trek, the train of wagons crossed into Indian territory. Though Annie couldn't know the exact moment that the native tribes became aware of the emigrants on their land, she somehow felt the shift in the air. Tensions throughout the company rose. During that first week, they heard more than one man raise his voice in argument around their campfires at night. Everyone seemed on edge.

Josie, deep in her guidebook research, told them such dangers as possible Indian attack would last virtually the entire rest of the way to Oregon, though from different tribes. Annie felt cold at the thought. A part of her was fascinated by the possibility of seeing a real live native out here on the plains. But there was a much bigger part of her that dreaded what danger she would be in if that happened. Though the warm glow of the campfires and the murmur of their neighbors' conversations helped Annie feel protected, the dark emptiness outside the cluster of wagons haunted her. Something deep within her told Annie that she could not relax her guard for a moment. Nothing about this journey could be taken for granted.

Annie had avoided conflict in her life as much as she could, and protecting herself from even facing an Indian was no different.

That first night after the wagon train had crossed into Indian territory, Louisa attended a meeting with the company leaders. All of the other families had sent a man, the head of their household, and Louisa insisted on representing the Hudsons as such. She returned to their campfire, delineating all the dangers and safety measures the men were putting into place. Any small slip and a member of their community would be at risk.

Each evening, when they reached their campsite, Louisa explained, the wagons would be pulled into a large circle. The wagon tongues would overlap to keep the vehicles as close as possible, and the hubs would be chained together to keep the circle secure. The livestock —cattle, horses, mules, and goats that the emigrants were driving across the plains—were corralled within the center of the circle. There was a wide-open area where they would hopefully stay safe and protected.

"Only men over the age of sixteen are required to stand guard," Louisa continued, with a glance at Lawrence.

At the same time, Annie looked at Margaret. The woman's relief that her son would not be at further risk was obvious on her face. But she knew that Louisa wasn't thinking about a mother's worry; she was only concerned with the safety of all of them. And if pushing her nephew to step up to that responsibility was part of that security, Louisa would do just that.

"Well, thank goodness there are so many men in this company to stand guard," Annie said. "I don't know what I'd do if faced with such an expectation."

"I'll say a prayer of gratitude every day for the men around here," Margaret said. "We'd never make it to Oregon without all these other folks."

"And it's smart to only take men over sixteen," Annie added, lightly, cautiously. Even this indirect disagreement with Louisa was risky. "So boys like Lawrence can keep learning and not be in too much risk."

"I don't know why you're worrying so much," Louisa said. "It's not as though any Indian tribe would dare come up against us."

Annie looked at her in disbelief. She opened her mouth to speak but couldn't quite put words to what she was feeling. There was something deep in her gut that belied Louisa's words. It wasn't anything she could truly articulate, but she still knew that her sister was wrong. How could she even think that?

In the lull, Lawrence and Margaret excused themselves. The boy was just like his mother and wanted to check in on a new friend he had made that day. As Josie was cleaning up the supper dishes, Annie found the words to contradict Louisa.

"I... I don't know if that's true," she said finally.

Louisa looked at her as though she had sprouted a second head. "What did you just say?"

"Never mind," Annie said, resigned.

"No, you tell me."

"It's nothing, Louisa." She looked at Josie, who offered her a sympathetic smile but didn't step in. Annie sighed. It was as though she could read Josie's mind, prodding her to actually tell Louisa what she was thinking for once.

"It's obviously not nothing. You disagree with me, though for the life of me, I can't think why. Why don't you have out with it, hmm? Enlighten me, oh wise one, about why you're right, and I'm wrong. Why is it that after everything I've done for you, you still question my judgment here? I know perfectly well that the men leading this company are fallible, as are all men, but I was part of that meeting to set security measures, and this is the best for all of us."

"I just... Louisa..." she pleaded, the sarcasm wounding her. "It doesn't matter."

"And besides," Louisa said, barreling over Annie's withdrawal, "I think it would be better if the boy *did* have to take on more responsibility. He's the man of the family now, and the more you meddling hens coddle him, the less he'll be able to handle as he grows into manhood."

Annie's mouth dropped open, surprised at such venom in her sister's voice. She was usually bossy, yes, but rarely so mean. She noticed Josie retreat, murmuring some excuse to go to the supply wagon. She wanted to call after her, to insist that Josie stand with her since it was her fault that she had thought to speak up in the first place. Instead, she looked back to Louisa. This fight had been a long time coming.

It was time for Annie to admit this to herself. Fighting with her sister—or, better said, being bullied by her sister—was at least part of the reason that accepting Isaac's proposal had been so tempting. Though Annie had never put it in such words to herself, she saw now that escaping from under her sister's thumb was part of the appeal. She had never stood up to Louisa, not ever. She never voiced her disagreement. Ever since she'd been old enough to register the thought, Annie had backed away from conflict and went along with whatever her sister had wanted.

Louisa always loved her, of course. Every decision she made for Annie was intended to be for her benefit. She had always meant well and tried to do the best thing for the whole family. Annie felt guilty for not being completely grateful. But, as she stood there under her oldest sister's glare, Annie knew Josie was right as well. She would never be happy if she didn't actually speak up for herself.

So, for the first time in she didn't know how long, Annie stood up straight, squared her shoulders, and looked Louisa in the eye. None of the rest of the family was nearby to back her up. It was just Annie and Louisa. She took a deep breath, hands tingling, aware of every inch of her body standing in the dirt beside their sleeping wagon.

"I think…" she began. "Well, I guess, I think it's not that easy." She finished with a noncommittal shrug. At the last moment, she had all but collapsed, unable to be defiant or even definite in her speech.

But even this tiny contradiction was enough to enrage Louisa. Maybe someone else would have had more of a discussion with her. Maybe someone else wouldn't have immediately reacted. But Louisa was never one to be accommodating, or even calm, if she thought someone was wrong.

"It *is* that easy," Louisa said. "You think you know better than me? You who accepted a proposal from some stranger on the other side of the continent? Who are you to insinuate such things?"

That stung. Annie wilted under her sister's criticism. She had suspected that Louisa looked down on her for her choice to go to Oregon, though she had never said so outright. Putting such a thing in words was more confrontation than she could manage.

Louisa continued railing at Annie, seemingly unaware that she was having a one-sided conversation.

"*I* went to the meeting with Mr. Mills and Mr. Sullivan. *I* am the one who heard all about their defensive strategy and all the tactics they are putting in place to keep us safe. I have been the one to take care of this family all along the way. And now you waltz in here with your thinking I'm wrong. Based on what? Nothing."

Annie had taken a step back, away from Louisa, away from the anger and the accusations. Nothing could be done to change Louisa's opinion, and Annie wasn't sure why she had even tried. She should never have let Josie talk her into this.

Louisa took a step toward her. Annie had never been actually afraid of her sister until this moment. But then, she had never actually said anything to provoke such anger in her either. All she wanted was for this horrible fight to be over, so she could have peace and rethink her choices about ever opening her mouth again.

Louisa glared at Annie, and neither woman spoke for a full minute. Annie looked down at her feet, willing her sister to stop, to walk away. But she knew Louisa had never been one to retreat from any challenge.

"Girls!"

Margaret's voice calling to them from outside the circle of light broke the stand-off. Annie lifted her head to look, hoping this would be a reprieve.

"Have you all had any of Mrs. Cole's dried cherries?" she asked as she approached.

Their sister-in-law's hands were outstretched, offering both of them a small piece of dark red dried fruit. When she got close enough, Margaret paused in her strides, blinked, and then looked from one to another.

"Am I interrupting something?"

"Not at all," Josie said, joining their cluster again. Annie wondered if she had just been watching from a distance. "I was just finishing cleaning up. Your timing is fortuitous."

"Lawrence should be back any moment," Margaret continued. "But Mrs. Cole offered me a piece of dried cherry to try, and I must say, it is just astounding. Try it. She claims they make an excellent pie. I might nudge Josie to go over to their camp to see if we can beg more."

"Oh my goodness," Josie said, mouth full of the fruit.

Annie, grateful for someone else to capture Louisa's attention, took the piece gratefully and watched as Louisa did too. Though she knew that Louisa would still never admit that she was wrong, Annie could at least hope that she would forget they had this fight at all. Agreeing and acquiescing and minimizing her own thoughts were the best tools Annie had for getting along with her oldest sister.

That night, after they crossed into Indian territory, after her fight with Louisa, Annie didn't sleep at all.

She tossed and turned in her cot, listening hard to the sounds of the prairie outside the canvas wagon top, worrying over what could be lurking in the dark beyond the glow of their campfires. It wasn't as though she didn't know what precautions they were taking; it was just that she was worried they weren't enough. She could never forget it was her own fault they were all out here in the first place.

CHAPTER ELEVEN

In spite of the stress and raising her voice, Louisa Hudson was not the type of woman to let someone else disagreeing with her ruin her night. Truth be told, she was not the type of woman to even acknowledge the point in disagreement. For all she cared, Annie could go right on thinking whatever she wanted—Louisa knew she was right.

She was right about all the safety precautions the men were taking, positive in the wisdom of her choice in wagon train leaders. She was right about Lawrence needing to step up to his responsibility as a man. And she was right about Annie not being able to do anything without Louisa there to hold her hand.

Why else had she torn up her entire life to escort Annie to Oregon? The girl had been moping around since her sweetheart had died years ago and never would have made a change if Louisa hadn't prodded her into it.

Louisa was confident in her decisions. She slept just as soundly in her narrow cot in the sleeping wagon as she had every other night since they left Independence. It was a dreamless, steadying sleep, even as her sister tossed and turned in her own cot. The next morning, Louisa was up, ready to leave camp before breakfast was finished. Annie could fret as much as she wanted, but all that did was reassure Louisa even more. She knew she was right. Annie was just giving in to her fear and uncertainty. The wagon company leaders had everything under control, as best they could. It was the leaders Louisa herself had sought out, after all. If her family just listened to her, Indians would never be a problem.

Besides, Annie would eventually see things Louisa's way. She always had before.

Breakfast was a quiet meal; while the bacon fried, Josie made coffee and brought a mugful to where Louisa was sitting against the far side of their wagon.

"You know she's just standing up for herself, right?" Josie asked quietly as Louisa blew on the coffee to cool it. "Just what you've always taught her to do."

"Well, I would think I have also taught her not to be foolish and worry about things that aren't going to happen."

Josie laughed. "You can't teach that. Some of us just need to look ahead to feel prepared. You might call it worrying, but Annie calls it helping."

Louisa rolled her eyes.

"Give her a chance, Lou," Josie insisted before she left to finish their breakfast.

From where she sat away from the rest of the family, Louisa watched Annie. She was sitting on the far side of the campfire, on an overturned bucket, warming her toes by the flames with her hands curled around her own coffee. Louisa tried to remember the last time Annie had disagreed with her and couldn't point to it. Yes, Annie's decision to write to that man in Oregon was made without consulting her oldest sister, but that was not the same as outright contradicting her.

These thoughts served only to make Louisa more determined to change Annie's thinking to her own. The trail to Oregon was not easy by any means, but scaring herself and stoking panic was simply not necessary. They had all embarked on this journey because of Annie, and now her younger sister was going to cause everyone else stress? Instead of listening to the wisdom of her older sister?

The very fact that Annie was still worrying over something that had been taken care of proved she needed Louisa to make her decisions for her.

As breakfast finished up and the other women packed up the wagons, Louisa and Lawrence hitched up both teams of oxen. When she saw her youngest sister turn back from the wagon, Louisa called out to her.

"Annie, could you come here please? I'd be mighty grateful for your help today," Louisa said, injecting a dollop of sarcasm into her request. "If you don't have anything more pressing, like target practice against the natives, for example, or fretting over the number of onions in the wagon, you could pitch in with driving the team. You know? The thing that *actually* would help move us toward Oregon?"

Annie flushed red but nodded. "Of course."

"It's essential that we all know how to do this," Louisa continued, more gently. "I know you've not much experience in handling livestock of this size, but..."

"I understand."

"I just don't want there to be any reason for the men of this company to doubt us or look down on us."

"I understand," Annie said again, more forcefully this time. "You're right, Louisa."

That was all she had wanted to hear. Louisa nodded brusquely. "Right, then. Just watch what I do this first morning. Listen to how I speak to them, but stay back at a safe distance for now."

They didn't have long to wait. Within minutes, the rest of the company was ready to roll out of camp. The calls and conversations from the campsites all around grew more animated as each family began their trek for the day. As the Robinsons' wagon moved forward, pulling into place on the trail, Louisa called to her own team and prodded them into action. The huge, two-thousand-pound animals leaned forward, straining in their harnesses as they set the heavy wagon rolling. Louisa was encouraging in her calls, getting the team moving, and setting them off for the day behind their neighbors.

Annie said nothing. She watched, she listened, and she fell into step, walking along the trail on the other side of the team from Louisa. But she didn't ask any questions or volunteer to take the reins at any time. Louisa grew irritated at her sister's passivity but continued with her training. Though Louisa occasionally explained to Annie what she was doing, the two sisters otherwise walked in silence.

In spite of the awkwardness between the sisters, the day seemed to pass quickly. Before she knew it, Louisa guided her wagon into the tight circle with her neighbors to camp for the evening.

"Right," she said to Annie, finally letting her exasperation get the better of her. "You take care of them now. Ask Lawrence if you need help."

With no further explanation, Louisa thrust the reins at her youngest sister and stomped away through the prairie grass. The wagon train had made camp near the bank of a narrow creek. Louisa reckoned she had more than done her part that day, both driving the team *and* teaching Annie, and she aimed to treat herself to a long, cool rest with her feet in the water before supper.

The sun was still just above the horizon when she reached the river. Many other women had already come to the banks before her, families nearer the front of the caravan, and had been in camp for ten or twenty minutes already. Not in the mood to be friendly or get in anyone's way, Louisa walked a few yards downstream and sat in the tall grass just on the edge of the water. The murmur of the other women's voices was a lovely background to her finally taking a break for the day.

Louisa unlaced her boots, stripped off her wool socks, and let out a long, slow breath of relief as she dipped her tired feet in the cool water.

"I hear that," a voice said behind her.

Louisa turned to see who had joined her—a Black woman, not much younger than Louisa herself, carrying two buckets, approached the bank of the creek from upstream. Frowning, Louisa tried to remember if she had ever seen this woman's face before.

"Are you..." she stammered, unsure of herself for once. "Are you a member of this... That is..."

The woman laughed. "I understand, ma'am. No disrespect, but I imagine you are wondering where I came from. I am part of your wagon company. My husband and me keep mostly to ourselves, though."

Louisa could imagine many reasons why that might be. "I'm sure. Well, I meant to come downstream to stay out of everyone's way, but I see you had the same thought."

The woman moved to the bank of the creek.

"My name is Louisa Hudson, by the way."

"Pleasure, Miss Hudson."

"Please call me Louisa. And what may I call you?" Louisa never failed to get irritated with such shallow small talk, but she had to remind herself that this woman couldn't possibly know what Louisa wanted from her. Whatever limitations and prejudice she had to deal with back east were likely to still show up in this community of travelers, too.

"Millie. Millie Franklin. My husband is Titus." She kept her eyes on the bucket slowly filling with water.

They remained in silence for another long moment before Louisa could think of something else to say. As much as she dearly loved to give advice, to guide those she met as she knew best, somehow that didn't feel quite right with this woman. For all Louisa know, Millie Franklin and her husband were owned by one of the other families in the wagon company. She wasn't quite sure how to proceed, not a common feeling for Louisa Hudson.

"Well, yes, then, it's a pleasure, Mrs. Franklin." Louisa got herself to her feet. She stood awkwardly for a moment before realizing she had to put her shoes back on. Sitting again, Louisa hurried into her socks and boots and left the woman to her chores, thoroughly distracted for a time from her conflict with her sister.

The following day, Louisa explicitly told Annie to help Lawrence. That would give her some time to be alone and, hopefully, quell her frustration.

"We'll reach the crossroads any time now," Josie said as she spooned out beans for each of their meals.

The company had stopped just after noon for a quick rest and bite, and Josie would not stop talking about what was coming up next in their journey. Both Louisa and Annie were in her hearing. Though Louisa was still frustrated with her youngest sister, Josie seemed to be doing her best to bridge the gap between them.

"Sometime today, I think. You'll see. We'll just be going along, and then the wagons up ahead will slow as everyone takes a gander." She grinned. "There's a sign at the junction and everything. It's the first big marker on the trail."

"What's the junction?" Lawrence asked.

"The trail junction. Where it splits. That's where we'll pass the sign that points the way to Oregon."

"And the other fork goes to California?"

Josie nodded. "That's right. Some folks are on their way to sunshine instead. But our company will carry on to Oregon."

"Huh," he said, quietly thinking. "Well, I guess there must be some good places in California, too, right, Aunt Josie?"

Louisa watched this conversation, and Lawrence's enthusiasm, fondly. The boy was growing into such an earnest, hard-working man. So like his father.

As the others continued talking, the thought of some folks choosing to emigrate to California instead of Oregon put Louisa in mind of what she would do when they finally reached the other coast. She had cash socked away, hidden deep in pockets and folded linens throughout the two wagons, but the saved money from the sale of their home wouldn't be enough. Even in worrying about it, she felt a little guilty. She had every reason to believe that she was far better off than the Franklins, as well as many of the other families in the company. But Louisa pushed that thought aside. She didn't have time to worry about everyone else. She had her sisters and nephew to take care of.

Later that afternoon, as she trudged along the trail next to her team of oxen, Louisa turned to Josie to voice her thoughts.

"I'm sure everything will work out, of course," Louisa said, "but it took me so long to build up the business in Virginia. I would hate for us to have to struggle any longer than necessary."

"You might mention this to Margaret. She's been doing so much with meeting the other women, our future neighbors, that she might be able to direct you to which could be potential customers for you."

"And which do not have two pennies to rub together," Louisa concluded. "Do you know how much they must have put into their wagon and all to travel west?"

"Well, yes. There's no doubt to be many poor farmers setting down stakes in the rich land of Willamette Valley. But I've seen at least a couple wagons full of bachelors heading west with us. I'd be flabbergasted if they know how to sew themselves new shirts. And if they don't have cash we can easily find services to trade for. Someone will have to dig our well, you know."

Louisa nodded. "That's perfect. That's exactly what I had in mind, but I thought I'd have more time away from these teams."

"You will," Josie assured her.

"Not if one of the others doesn't step up, I won't."

"Well, I'm sure Annie did her best. You just need to give her more time. You told her to help Lawrence today."

"Hmph," Louisa grunted. "It's not *that* hard."

"She's not like you."

"That's apparent."

"And would you rather be doing the laundry so she can be free to drive the team?"

Louisa couldn't help but grin at that. "You know perfectly well that washing clothes is my absolute least favorite thing to do. Sewing? Of course. Working tirelessly at the stubborn bacon stain, absolutely not."

"Well then," she said with satisfaction. "You do this all the time, Lou." Josie seemed to be the only person that could get away with scolding her. "You measure everyone else by your own ability, forgetting that she hasn't lived the same life as you. Be patient."

Louisa nodded, keeping her eyes on the horizon as they moved ever west. Her frustration with all the things she couldn't control ate at her, but she kept pressing on.

CHAPTER TWELVE

Annie had done her best. If Louisa thought she could learn to drive a team of two-thousand-pound oxen hauling an enormous wagon, she wanted to try. But she didn't have the skill or the personality to maneuver such strong creatures. Learning to drive a team of oxen had seemed simple before she had tried it. True, the stubbornness of the animals at times mirrored that of little Jimmy Raymond in Norfolk, whose grandmother had insisted learn to play music from a young age, but the authority Annie felt she could exert over each was far different.

She had spent an entire day walking alongside Louisa, studying how she interacted with the team and the words she used to guide them where she needed them to go. Annie marveled to see the firm grip her older sister had on the animals and the strength with which she bent them to her will.

Whatever she had done, however, had evidently not been enough for Louisa, and Annie was relieved when she wasn't called upon to demonstrate what she learned the next day.

"Is she mad, do you think?" Annie asked Margaret.

The pair was walking side by side in the prairie grass behind the Hudson goats.

The older woman had spent every day on the trail thus far keeping track of the trio of goats and the horse the Hudsons had brought west with them. Annie envied her this task sometimes. Margaret got to spend the day away from the dust kicked up by wagon wheels and wandered out in the plains alongside the caravan. Occasionally hours at a time went by without seeing her. At the end of the day, Margaret always returned to their campsite with stories about this family or that friend she had met through the course of her day.

But this day, Annie could still see Margaret walking parallel to the trail. As the sun began its slow setting in mid-afternoon, Annie picked up the hem of her skirt and stepped through the grass to walk alongside her sister-in-law.

"She's not mad," Margaret said. "You know she rarely gets truly mad. I think it's more frustration. Your sister has all these ideas about how everyone else should be and gets frustrated when reality doesn't meet her expectation."

"So I'm not meeting her expectations."

"Well, no, you're not, but I'm not sure you can. I'm not sure anyone can." They walked a few steps in silence before Margaret laughed. "I often think about how Louisa would have been as a wife."

Annie laughed at the thought. "Maybe we'll yet find out."

"Maybe. My mother was a bit like Louisa. My best advice? Just keep doing your best. You can't control how your sister thinks about you, so just make sure you're doing what you need to do for you."

It wasn't all that different from the advice Josie had given her, Annie realized. That same advice had backfired when she had disagreed with Louisa even a little bit.

"I suppose," Annie said thoughtfully.

Margaret reached out and took Annie's hand, squeezing it comfortingly. "And you just let me know how I can help."

"I know. Thank you."

Their conversation was interrupted by sounds of shouting in the caravan up ahead.

"What do you think is wrong?" Margaret asked. She dropped Annie's hand and hurried her steps closer to the commotion.

Even from this distance, they could see at least a half dozen men shooting rifles in the air.

"I think maybe," Annie said as she caught up to her sister, "they're celebrating?"

"Oh!" Margaret laughed, her eyes bright as she turned to look at Annie. "Celebrating! We've reached the fork in the trail. You can see—" She pointed into the distance. Annie squinted and could somewhat make out something on the side of the trail, maybe half a mile up ahead.

"Is that a sign?"

"I bet it's the sign to Oregon!" Margaret was practically bouncing up and down in her excitement. "The junction Josie told us about. We're on our way."

Annie smiled to herself as they continued their hike to the trail junction. When they finally came level with the sign, she allowed herself a short moment of gratitude that they had made it so far. In spite of whatever conflict she had with Louisa, Annie vowed to never take for granted everything her family was putting up with for her. It was dangerous, and it was difficult, and she was so grateful.

The day after they passed the trail junction—to as much celebration and fanfare as Josie had predicted—the Sullivan-Mills wagon company came to a shallow, rocky river. It was the first stream they had to cross, and though Annie watched the wagons ahead of them get through the gentle current just fine, she still worried.

The stream was shallow enough that several wagons could ford at once, so the Hudsons didn't have long to wait before their turn. Josie and Margaret worried about getting the animals to the other side, and Annie had her hands full helping Lawrence drive their second wagon across. Even with trying to tuck up the hems of her skirt, she was wet to her thighs, tired and hoarse from the effort of coaxing the huge animals.

But that nameless stream was a mere trickle compared to the great Kansas River that the company reached not long after. Everything Josie had learned from the guidebook about the Kansas River did not convey the full strength and monstrosity. They had crossed several streams in the days leading up to this behemoth, and Annie thought she was ready for the sight.

She was wrong.

As the wagons rolled over the low ridge, her breath

caught in her chest when she finally glimpsed the sheer size of the river and the undertaking it would be to cross it. From where they were, at higher ground, Annie saw half a dozen different wagon companies all funneling into a mass waiting to cross. More than a square mile filled with hundreds of white-topped wagons milled and inched forward, all moving toward the single place where the ferry crossed over.

The Kansas was several hundred feet wide in this spot. Though some other wagon companies were caulking their wagons and swimming their animals across, the men of the Sullivan-Mills company had agreed to ferry over. Two wagons, complete with live-stock and people, could be crossed at the same time before the ferry had to return to the first bank.

It was a slow process, and it was not cheap. But the captains had chosen the safest method to cross.

The Hudsons had to wait through till the afternoon of the second day for their turn on the ferry that would take their wagons across the wide Kansas River. Though she tried to occupy herself with watching the wagons safely to the other side, the waiting just made Annie more anxious. She spent most of the first day sitting on the swell of land that overlooked the river, as the ferry took family after family across. There were some mishaps—panicking animals and wagon wheels that weren't fully braked—but every person managed to get over the river safely.

When it was their turn, both Hudson wagons and all their animals were led onto the platform. Though it made Annie a bit nervous for all of their belongings to be concentrated on one crossing, instead of spread out over two, she didn't voice her concern. It wasn't her choice. She didn't relish having to explain her likely irrational fear to the men on hand to help each family with their crossing.

Lawrence and Louisa helped lead the teams onto the ferry. Daniel Mills and a couple other young men stayed nearby, helping to soothe and calm the animals. Margaret herded the family's goats and horse onto the ferry just behind the wagons while Annie hovered, trying to help as she could but in general feeling like she was in the way. She ended up against the far rail, helping Margaret keep the goats calm under the strain.

The ferrymen wedged pieces of wood under the wheels. These brakes would keep the wagons from rolling all over the platform and help keep it steady and balanced.

Annie held her breath as the ferrymen pushed off from the bank. They used long poles to push against the bottom of the river, against the current as much as possible to reach the other side. The water was faster than she had expected, and Annie gripped the rail hard to steady herself.

One of the poles got stuck. The man wielding it couldn't withdraw it from the mud fast enough to match the others, and the platform tipped slightly.

Annie gasped.

The oxen began to panic. Annie could see it happening and felt helpless to stop it. The lead oxen began to stamp and bray, loudly communicating their displeasure at being on the ferry at all. This was what Louisa had wanted help with, Annie thought. She had to step up for once and try to help. Those poor animals.

From where she stood against the ferry rail, Annie quickly gauged the distance to the oxen and hurried forward. As she moved toward the oxen, the platform under her feet tipped and bucked. She had trouble keeping her balance but kept moving.

"No!" Louisa shouted. "Don't— Stop, Annie!"

Annie froze, then looked up to see Louisa glaring at her, eyes wide. Standing still kept the weight distribution from moving any further.

"But—" Annie began.

"Don't move!" Louisa called, more gently this time, before turning back to help calm the enormous animals.

Just in that short moment, it was clear to Annie that Louisa didn't want her help. The animals were still panicking, but she didn't once look to her sister. She acted as though she could do it all on her own, and Annie would just be in the way.

Annie was mortified. What was the point of teaching her how to drive the team in the first place? The longer Annie stood there—as still as she could to not upset the balance any further—the more frustrated Annie got. All she wanted to do was what was expected, what her sister asked of her, and now it seemed as though that wasn't enough either.

As soon as the ferry slowed near the opposite bank, Annie leapt into the shallows. She could have waited; she didn't have to get wet to her hips. But she couldn't stand being near Louisa and her bossiness and her self-righteousness any longer. Better for Annie to deal with some measure of discomfort in her body than put up with more discomfort of her soul.

"Annie!" Margaret called after her.

She didn't turn or respond. Annie picked up her now-heavy skirts and waded awkwardly to the shore. It was shallow enough here that some of the children were playing and splashing at the water's edge just a bit upstream. She was perfectly safe, though cold, and relished the few moments alone she had.

Without Louisa in her immediate vicinity, at least she could be herself. Being alone allowed a few moments when she wasn't somehow letting her sister down. It seemed as though anything she tried to do was a disappointment to Louisa. It was all the more reason for her to just stay back and stay out of the way, she supposed.

The ferry reached the shore soon after. Annie stood in the grass and watched as Louisa and Lawrence led their teams and their oxen off of the ferry and up to where the campsite was stretched out across the plains. She followed behind, far enough back that Louisa couldn't ask her to do anything else. Annie knew she'd soon be back to following her older sister's every instruction, but just now, she needed a break. She found plenty to do helping Josie and Margaret with their individual duties.

As the sun set, Annie's dress had thoroughly dried, and she was mixing up biscuits for Josie. The final wagons were ferried across, so the Sullivan-Mills company could be rested and ready to continue west in the morning. Annie felt a dusting of flour across her right cheek and had reached to try to wipe it off on her sleeve when she heard a woman's voice calling over the prairie.

"Alexander!" she called. "Alexander McKinnon, it's supper time! Where are you?"

Annie smiled to herself, thinking about how much fun it must be to be a child on this trail. Her own childhood was rather stilted; her guardian, Louisa, was still growing up herself. She had been strict with Annie, not offering much freedom to explore or find her own way. But here, this Alexander fellow must have been given quite a lot of rein while his parents were busy ferrying across or setting up camp.

She had just settled the dough into one of the cast iron pans, starting to bake up a big batch of biscuits for the family, when a piercing wail was heard over all the chatter and laughter of the campsite. Annie held her breath. It was as though the entire company went silent, listening for the aftermath of that wail.

Without a word, Margaret left the campsite, wiping her hands on her apron as she strode off into the evening toward the sound. As Annie watched after her, she wondered what new tragedy had just fallen over the company. Maybe such freedom as the children had been given wasn't the wisest choice after all.

CHAPTER THIRTEEN

Louisa was still awake when Margaret returned to their wagons late that night with the word that little Alexander McKinnon had been discovered drowned in the shallows of the Kansas River. She had darted off as soon as they heard the scream and not returned for hours. The pastor and Mrs. Sullivan had taken the grieving mother in hand, and other mothers in the company had stepped up to help with the other children temporarily. It was a tragedy, and Louisa felt for the poor mother, but as with Buchanan's death, the emigrants couldn't stay put long. Fortunately, the community all working together was helping the family recover from it as smoothly as could be expected.

The following morning under the trees just outside the perimeter of the company's camp, a small funeral service was held, with most of the families in attendance. Louisa had unruly thoughts about how little time they could afford to delay, but she kept them to herself. She was not, after all, heartless. It must be heartbreaking for the McKinnons. She couldn't imagine having to leave behind the grave of someone in her family and prayed she wouldn't ever have to learn what that was like.

The service that Pastor Montgomery held over the small grave was moving and, blessedly, brief. When it was over, Louisa strode back to her own campsite. She didn't even realize she was walking alone until she was halfway back. Everyone else had stayed behind; each person gently offered the grieving family their condolences.

But soon, the wagon company headed west again, to Louisa's relief. Most of the families in the wagon company seemed dejected, beaten down by days driving wagons under the hot sun followed by cold and danger of crossing the Kansas River. The death of a child only added to the weight that every member of the wagon company carried with them. For Louisa, it all seemed to be the perfect reason to keep heading west. To many of their neighbors, however, it was all the more reason to rest.

The same evening, after they left the shores of the Kansas, Margaret returned to their campsite just before supper to report that at least a couple of the families were talking about turning back.

"Turning back?" Lawrence asked, alarmed. "Back east? By themselves? In the middle of the plains? Where will they go?"

"Independence," Louisa said grimly. "Maybe farther east after that, I'll bet. Your mother means those folks are talking about giving up. The cowards."

"Well, now," Margaret began. "I don't know about that. They're mighty tired, and it's not as though the traveling will get any easier now, will it? It must have been so hard to lose that young one, and many folks are petrified of losing their own children as well."

"But, what will they do about the Indians if they leave? How could they stay safe with just a small group?" Annie asked.

"That's probably why they won't go," Louisa groused. "Like I said... cowards."

"Which families?" Lawrence asked. "Not the Carters, is it?"

"No, not the Carters," Margaret said. "But even so, we do need to talk about how much time you've been spending with Jefferson Carter. You know I would much rather you use any extra time for your studies."

"Or any number of the tasks and repairs that need doing around here," Louisa interjected. "In my opinion, you would be much better off patching the crack in the side of the bunk than reading. Or messing about with this other boy."

"He is quite a bit older than you, dear," Margaret added.

"Only a couple years," Lawrence mumbled.

Louisa watched his reaction with interest. So that's where the boy had gotten off to every spare minute of the day. She turned her attention back to her supper as she thought over the option of turning back to Independence. There were far too many sacrifices she had personally made to get her family this far. It was inconceivable that she would be willing to give up now. And such determination was necessary as the wagon company continued their trek westward to Oregon.

In the days after the wagon company left the Kansas

River, the general mood of the emigrants was dour. Losing another of their community to death—and a child's death, at that—had everyone sticking a little closer to their campsite, being a little more careful, a little less cavalier. The pall that hung over the fifty families was oppressive.

The one bright spot in all of this was that after her failure on the ferry, Annie seemed more determined than ever to learn how to drive the team of oxen. The next morning, Annie was ready, standing near the team after breakfast, with a determined look on her face. Louisa hadn't asked her again to help, but neither did she turn her away. There were occasional afternoons that Margaret needed help with the goats or Lawrence with his team, but every day Annie was coming more into her own.

It surprised Louisa, she had to admit. She had never thought of Annie as being particularly strong or determined. The child had always needed Louisa to take care of her, after all. But if Annie wanted to take on more responsibility, she wasn't about to complain.

Throughout the morning, she could feel Annie watching her carefully. In the afternoon, Louisa drove the team on her own, while Annie switched to helping Lawrence. In her solitude, Louisa had been thinking over the first steps to take for her business when they reached Oregon and giving little thought to where she was going. Just one foot in front of the other, right behind the Robinsons. That was a benefit of being part of such a company, she thought. Though she hated having to put such leadership and decision making into the hands of others, and she certainly hated not going as quickly as she would have liked, she had to admit that it was nice to give her time to plan her future instead and simply give herself over to following.

She had known when she decided to give up her sewing business in Virginia that to build it up again on the opposite coast would take some grit, determination, and a bit of humility. It would require some actions that she had never taken before. Though she still had months before they reached Oregon, before she had to make any definite decisions, the sooner she began making her plans, the faster she would be able to make it all work in their new home.

It was while in this state of reverie that the sky opened up. Louisa had not been paying attention and had missed the thick gray clouds blotting out the sky that had swept in over the plains. Before she had a chance to dash to the wagon to collect her oilskin wrap, the top layer of her clothing was soaked. Within minutes she would be cold and wet through her petticoats.

"Gah!" she shouted in frustration.

Where was everyone else? Why hadn't someone seen the storm coming and brought her the wrap?

Louisa was just debating whether or not she could leave the oxen on their own—she thought not—while she went to the wagon, when Annie came darting up through the thickening mud. She held her own oilskin up over her head like a hood, with another in her free arm.

"It's a bit late for that," Louisa said, snatching the protection from her sister. She thrust the reins into Annie's hand while she quickly covered herself as best she could.

"I'm sorry," Annie gasped. "It was just so sudden. We didn't know—"

"You should have been paying better attention then, shouldn't you?" Louisa's sarcasm was always more biting when she was frustrated. And Annie always just took it without protest, which only frustrated Louisa further.

But then she saw her younger sister flinch when Louisa turned back to collect the reins again from her. Louisa set her teeth. She was sorry her sister seemed to be afraid of her, but she wasn't used to apologizing, and she wasn't sorry she had said something. The frustration of being forgotten and wet still coursed through her.

With the heavy oilskin wrapped around her shoulders to keep out the rain as best as possible, Louisa turned her back to her sister, calling to her team of oxen and continuing her plodding through the sludge.

The emigrants had two full days of pouring rain and the resultant mud. Mills and Sullivan pushed them forward. Though they only made five or six miles each of those days, at least that was more than none. Every mile west was a mile closer to rest. With Annie on hand to assist both of them, Louisa and Lawrence trudged through each step in the muddy trail, guiding their poor animals through pulling the thousands of pounds of wagon and supplies. The leather gloves Louisa wore kept her hands dry, but they were chilled to the bone, stiff at the end of the day with the effort of traveling just that little bit.

After several days of that mire, several days in which Louisa prodded her family forward through their complaints and discomfort, the dark gray clouds lifted. By mid-day, the sun had again made an appearance.

Louisa breathed a sigh of relief when the ray of sunshine cut across her. She lifted her face to the sky, letting the warmth rest on her cheeks for the first time in days.

Though the muddy trail persisted, the emigrants could at least start to dry their clothing, empty the buckets and start to warm up again. Louisa hung on to the reins of their lead wagon through the afternoon, relishing the chance to bake in the sunshine. The reappearance of the sun coincided with the company's arrival at a new campsite. As they made camp on the banks of a narrow river at sunset, Mr. Sullivan and Mr. Mills sent word around that they would rest here for a full day while the wagon train made repairs, collected water, and dried off.

When Lawrence heard they would wait here for a day, his face lit up like a candle flame, and his shoulders relaxed for the first time in days. Annie laughed out loud with the joy of it, and Josie merely closed her eyes contentedly.

Though Louisa always felt better when they were moving forward, the joy she saw on her family's face made the delay worth it. Grimly, she unharnessed her team and made sure the animals had the water they needed before she did anything else. Every other Hudson had already stripped out of their sopping wet clothes and were bustling about getting supper. Alone, Louisa climbed into the sleeping wagon to find something else to wear.

As she stood in the middle of the narrow space between the cots, Louisa realized there was something on her pillow. A clean, dry dress had been pulled out of the trunk where it had been stored and now lay waiting for her. Though it was difficult to unbutton what she was wearing with such cold fingers, Louisa eventually managed to get out of the cold, wet attire, stripping all the way down to her damp undergarments.

Debating only a moment, Louisa picked up the dry quilt from atop her own bed and climbed back out of the wagon. Josie was squatting by the fire, adding dried grass and a handful of sticks to prod the blaze bigger. Louisa closed the space to stand in the warmth, with her blanket wrapped around her shoulders for modesty.

"Thank you," she said, as she felt her toes begin to thaw. "Did you leave the dress out for me too?"

Josie shook her head, still eyeing the flames cautiously. "It was Annie. She thought she'd save you the time unpacking it since you had to manage the animals."

Standing again, Josie stepped back to stand next to Louisa and wrapped her arm around the older sister's waist.

"Supper in twenty minutes or so. You just rest and get warm. You've been working too hard."

Louisa only nodded, a bit overcome at what a nice change it was to be taken care of like this. Why didn't she let her sisters do this for her more often? She couldn't think why. Yawning, Louisa began to feel the exhaustion of the cold and the day's work creeping in.

CHAPTER FOURTEEN

Annie woke early the following morning in the cool darkness before the summer dawn. Just the glimpse of clear skies through the canvas opening put a smile on her face. A rush of gratitude washed over her when she thought of how little work she had in the day ahead of her, relatively speaking. It was as though even her body knew that when she slept; she stretched as she woke, feeling well-rested for the first time in weeks.

The previous several days—crossing the Kansas, the death of the child, the torrential rain—had been extremely trying. More so than she had expected. She'd forced herself to keep putting one foot in front of the other through a sheer act of will. But now the wagon company had a break and a full day to spend at this campsite alongside another soothing creek. Well, Annie reminded herself, as she climbed out of her cot, trying not to wake Margaret sleeping beneath her, not entirely a break. She would have plenty to do that day.

As part of the family's plan to come west, Louisa had decided that Annie was in charge of making sure all five of them had clean laundry at all times. It was not as though Annie minded scrubbing clothes all that much, but she chafed at the fact that it was just one more decision Louisa had made for her. There were other things she could have done, but this was what she was stuck with.

Even so, this would be the first chance Annie had in more than a week to do the Hudsons' laundry. Lawrence and Louisa alone had gotten unimaginably muddy as they had struggled to guide the oxen along the trail. Annie wanted to get an early start on the project, hopefully to give herself a relaxing afternoon. If she hustled, she could have all the water gathered and heated just before Josie was ready to start breakfast. Squinting into the early morning light, Annie grabbed two of the family's buckets and headed down to the water.

So many of the other emigrants had taken the chance for a slow morning. As Annie walked down to the stream, she smiled at the chirping of the morning birds that she wouldn't have heard later in the day. At that time of the morning, she almost had the place to herself, filling the buckets in relative quiet along the bubbling stream.

Only about an hour later, Annie had nearly completed her toiling to ready for the laundry. She made several trips to the water, gathered more wood and built their campfire, had the kettle boiling, and had carted out her laundry tub, now half-filled with hot water as the others woke.

"Goodness!" Josie said. She had just climbed out of

the wagon and was rubbing the sleep from her eyes. "It's barely dawn, Annie. Today was supposed to be a rest day. Didn't you want to sleep in?"

Annie laughed. "There's no resting on the trail. You know that."

"True." Josie smirked and then looked around. "Which I suppose means that I still have to make coffee."

"Yes, but I already brought you water." Annie pointed to a full bucket sitting near their wagon wheel.

"And built me a fire, I see. Well, then, no excuse, I suppose." Josie cheerfully got to work, heading back to their supply wagon to gather the food and pans she would need to make breakfast for five people.

Now that Josie was awake to keep an eye on the campfire, Annie could take their buckets back down to the stream and gather the rest of the water she would need. The sun had passed the horizon and created long shadows from the vehicles as she walked through camp to the clean water that ran nearby.

Later in the morning as it was, more of the emigrants were up and ready to start their day. Annie found herself in a cluster of women walking down to the water together. She watched the others surreptitiously, wondering if any of them would end up being a friend. Her sisters were wonderful, but Annie had left a lot behind in Virginia.

With two buckets full, Annie turned to head back up the trail and saw that a woman in all black had been watching her—Rebecca Tenney.

A nervous smile crossed Annie's face. "Were you... were you waiting for me?"

"Oh, no," Rebecca said dismissively. "No, I was just stalling." She laughed good-naturedly. "Don't tell my ma. She sent me down here to get water for the laundry, and I'm sure if it were up to her, I'd be done by now."

"That's what this is for," Annie admitted, looking down at the buckets in her hands.

"Then you understand." Rebecca heaved a sigh and bent to pick up her empty buckets as Annie moved out of her way. "And then once I'm done with the laundry, Ma wants us to come back down here and... Oh, actually. You should come!"

Annie frowned, confused. "Come where?"

Rebecca laughed again, leaving the buckets where they were, and put her hand over her eyes in embarrassment. "Goodness, where is my head today? Ma and I thought—well, actually, it was Ma's idea since I'm not sure she's ever taken a day off in her life."

"Sounds like my sister Louisa."

"Precisely. *You* know," Rebecca continued. "Ma got a bee in her bonnet that everyone else needed a treat. She thought it would be a nice thing for the *other* ladies if we come down here in the afternoon and have water heated here on the shore, so you all can take something of a comfortable bath. The river itself is still quite chilly, but at least you can wash your hair with something warm."

Annie blinked in surprise as the reality of what Rebecca was describing sunk in. "That sounds... That's mighty generous."

"That's Ma for you." Rebecca grinned. "Always thinking about how she can make your day more pleasant. Even if it means putting *me* to work. So you should come. Do it for her."

Annie laughed. "I'll see what I can do."

"Or maybe see if you can talk that tightly wound sister of yours into it at least."

"That might be difficult, but I'll try. If I don't see you, tell your mother thank you."

Rebecca smiled her good-bye as she bent to fill her buckets, and Annie made her way back to camp.

The rest of the morning, Annie was too caught up with breakfast and getting her laundry started to find a moment to tell Louisa about the treat down by the water. With all the mud of the past few days and the clothing and bedding of five people to see to, she just about wore out her arms in carrying the water to wash it all.

Just before midday, Louisa had finished the repairs to the wagon seat that she had been putting off. Annie thought she looked exhausted as she stood near the Hudsons' sleeping wagon, looking around their camp-site. She seemed lost without something immediate to occupy her. It was as though she wasn't quite sure how to spend her time without some chores that needed doing.

As Annie was watching Louisa, Margaret approached from the other side of camp where she had been dealing with her own responsibilities.

"Did you need any help with that?" she asked. "I've got the animals seen to and have some time."

She indicated the tub of laundry Annie was still working through. The top and sides of the wagon were draped with already clean trousers, shirts, and aprons, drying in the sun. They were at the far end of their supply wagon; Annie didn't think Louisa had realized she was watching.

"Actually," Annie said, lowering her voice so Louisa couldn't overhear her. "I wonder if you might help me with something else."

As Annie explained what she had in mind, Margaret's face lit up at the request, nodding enthusiastically.

"I know just what to do," she assured the youngest Hudson. "You know me. I can be just as stubborn as Louisa. I'll make sure she goes."

"Thank you."

Annie wanted to say more. She wanted to explain why she didn't feel up to inviting Louisa herself, why she wanted to stay hands-off with this request and enjoy her afternoon to herself. But no explanation was necessary. Margaret was right—she did know just what to do.

From where Annie was settled, she could watch and listen without interrupting. Throughout the conversation, Louisa remained where she was, seemingly rooted to the ground with no direction. She looked up when Margaret approached.

"You don't look too busy," she said. Annie could hear the grin in her tone. "I thought you might like to come down to the water with me."

"Water? Why ever for? I was just thinking about helping Annie with the laundry or seeing if Lawrence—"

"Oh, don't bother," Margaret interrupted dismissively. "Annie's just about done, and I told Lawrence he could spend the afternoon with one of the Davis boys."

"Well, all right, but I also wanted to repair a rip in Josie's bonnet while we're stopped for the day. I should do that before it gets dark."

"I think Josie was going to take care of that,"

Margaret said convincingly. For all Annie knew, the thought had never crossed Josie's mind, but that didn't matter at this moment. "We won't be gone that long, anyway."

"I don't understand why we would even need to go to the water. Do you need help hauling buckets for the goats?"

Margaret shook her head. "Nope! It's that the Stephens—well, Mrs. Stephens and her daughter, Mrs. Tenney—have dreamed up a bit of a treat for the hard-working women around here. All afternoon, they're gonna be heating up water so we can take a real proper bath. Or at least be able to wash our hair while staying warm. Doesn't that sound just like heaven?"

From this distance, Annie watched Louisa's face as her sister described what she had in mind for the rest of the day. It was like dawn breaking; the joy and expectation lit up Louisa's face. It had been weeks, at least since they had left the boarding house in Independence, since she had allowed herself a hot bath.

"Well, I don't know..." she began.

Annie willed Margaret to keep pushing.

"I'll get you back here well before supper."

"Before that, even," Louisa insisted. But Annie knew she was giving in. "I'll wash my hair, but that's it. No lounging about just being idle."

"Whatever you say," Margaret assured her, though Annie knew she might have her own ideas.

The two women ducked into the sleeping wagon to gather towels and toiletries. As Annie watched Louisa and Margaret make their way down to the water, she felt a small twinge of something. Some feeling that she hadn't given words to. She blinked rapidly, to try to make things clear, and turned back to the laundry that still needed to be seen to. As she knelt there in the dirt by the tub of hot water, Annie thought over her day, her week, and realized that what she had felt when she watched her sister leave was jealousy.

As soon as Annie had that thought, she dismissed it.

What did she have to be jealous about? Every member of her family had picked up their lives to join her on this life-altering move to Oregon. Any thought of complaint from her would be ridiculous. It would be ungrateful.

And yet...

Annie remembered the expression on Louisa's face when she realized she could go luxuriate in the water today. That had been a smile of relief that Annie hadn't seen since the previous fall, at least, since before she had taken charge of planning their move to Oregon. The last time Louisa had actually done something for herself was when she took an afternoon off from sewing for clients to hem new curtains for her home. It wasn't much of a break, even then.

It was as though Louisa was always so busy worrying that other people were doing what she thought best that she didn't stop to think what would be best for her. Undoubtedly, if Louisa had been the sister that Rebecca Tenney had told about the hot water, she would have come striding back to camp, insisting all the other three go while she remain behind and finish the chores.

So, yes, Annie could admit to herself that she envied the freedom her sister just afforded herself. But at the same time, she knew that Louisa deserved this treat as much as anyone did. It was Annie's own fault that she stayed behind completing the tasks that Louisa had decided she should do, rather than assert herself.

She continued to scrub away at the stubborn stain on Lawrence's cuff as she mulled it over.

CHAPTER FIFTEEN

Louisa's afternoon luxuriating in the water was wonderful, so much so she didn't feel as though she truly deserved it. True, she had been working hard, but not nearly hard enough to indulge in this. In fact, if it hadn't been for the practical aspect of having her hair washed, she might not have stayed as long as she did. She might have insisted that she had other things to do. But, as it was, Louisa was distracted.

While Margaret chatted away with Mrs. Stephens, Mrs. Cole, and the others, Louisa kept to herself. She realized later she had been watching for the Black woman, the possible-slave, who she had run into by the creek a week or so prior. It occurred to her that Millie Franklin was even more aloof than Louisa herself was. The woman never appeared that afternoon, but perhaps that was to be expected.

Eventually, Louisa and Margaret had gotten their fill, hair gleaming and clean in the afternoon sun. They dried off and made their way back to camp before supper.

Washing her hair in real warmth was a joy that Louisa carried with her for days. She began the next day energized to continue leading her family westward.

And she would need all the energy she could muster. The Sullivan-Mills wagon company planned to leave that creekside camp early the following morning, but this time weighed down with as much fresh water as they could carry. After that quiet campsite by the stream, the company wouldn't come across any other usable water for days. This meant the Hudsons would have to somehow find ways to cart enough water in their wagons to last several days for five people and all their animals.

"If we ration responsibly, it shouldn't be too hard," Louisa assured them, as the family packed up the following morning. "Lawrence, come help me lift this tub into the wagon."

She had it all worked out. The laundry tub would stay full of the fresh water they needed, as would all four of the buckets the family carried. They each had a canteen that could be filled, and she might even see how much water Josie's pans could hold, at least this first day. Then they could use that same water for cooking that evening. As Lawrence moved around crates in the supply wagon to make room for the tub to sit flat, Louisa calculated exactly how long they could stretch what they had.

"Is there really not any water at the next stop?" the boy asked, watching his aunt. The idea of having to ration his water seemed to be difficult for Lawrence to wrap his mind around. He had grown up in a town where that had never been a concern.

"Oh, there's water," she said, "but it'll kill you. Not fit for any of us or the animals. One drink would cramp your stomach. If we let the oxen drink their fill, they could die. So we have to be very careful, to make sure all this water lasts."

"Okay," he mumbled miserably.

"Lawrence," Margaret scolded. She had just approached from around the side of the wagon.

"I know," he insisted.

Louisa took one look at his defiant expression and frowned. This would never do.

"Go see to the goats. I'll call you when I need you again," Louisa said.

She and his mother watched the boy walk away, shoulders hunched up around his ears.

"I don't like saying it, Margaret, but that boy's attitude has gotten worse over the last few weeks. What happened to the bright, cheerful Lawrence who was so excited to go to Oregon?"

"Oh, I don't know," Margaret said. "He's gone through so much, it seems reasonable that he might be cranky now and again. He's only thirteen. The poor boy only just lost his father, and then we tore him away from his school and his home—"

"Yes, well, I lost my brother. You lost your husband. But you don't see us moping about or complaining, do you? No, I think we should take a stricter hand with him. Not let him run off to play with Jefferson Carter or Ralph Davis just because he's done with his chores for the day. That will make a man of him in no time."

"You think I should be *more* strict with Lawrence?"

Louisa heard the incredulity in Margaret's tone.

"Well, I'm happy to take on that task if you prefer it, of course. I'm sure we can find a man in the company somewhere who could use another pair of hands. Free labor in exchange for keeping him occupied. In fact, Lawrence might be able to learn some useful skills, blacksmithing or whatnot, if he had more structure in his life."

"More structure," Margaret repeated.

"Yes. What the boy needs—"

"I'm quite aware of what the boy needs, Louisa," she said quietly. "He is my son after all."

Louisa was surprised by the coldness in her sister-in-law's tone. "Of course, I only meant that I'm happy to take on some of that responsibility if you would like."

"No. Thank you. I'd rather not."

With that, she spun on her heel and headed off to Louisa-didn't-know-where. She felt a bit put out that her offer to help had been so rebuffed but consoled herself with the fact that Margaret would surely see her side eventually. And hopefully not before it was too late.

The tension between the sisters lasted a couple days. Margaret was cheerful and chatty with the other two but only acknowledged Louisa when she absolutely had to. Louisa was wise enough to not bring up Lawrence's behavior again for now. She would have another opportunity, and in the meantime, the boy's mother would come around to her way of thinking.

Not long after this fight, the wagon company reached the banks of the Platte River. Louisa had been leading her team on her own, thinking over the various families that Margaret and the others had befriended and wondering if any of them might take Lawrence under their wing. Approximately late morning, Louisa led her oxen up the trail, up a low ridge. The Robinsons in the wagon ahead of her had already begun the gradual descent into the valley, but Louisa halted her team briefly at the top to take in the view.

The trail curled up onto a low ridge, and from where she stood, Louisa could see across the green valley that had been cut through the middle by a shallow, wide river. They had reached the Platte River. They knew from Josie's reading of the guidebook, and indeed from what Louisa herself could see from this vantage, the trail they followed ran parallel to the Platte for days. Eventually the trail would cross the shallow water, and Louisa would need to lead her team through. She couldn't see the crossing from here but knew it was shallow enough that there was no need for a ferry, and they could simply wade across.

Louisa set her jaw and called to her team, leading the wagon over the ridge down into the valley behind the rest of the company.

A few days later, when it was time for the company to cross the wide, shallow Platte River, Louisa was determined that they wouldn't have any of the chaos that had happened at the Kansas. It would be far safer than the tilting platform over strong currents, but it wasn't without risks. Many of the wagons could cross at the same time since it was merely a question of stepping into the water. The family's wait to get to the water's edge was short, though they were near the back of the caravan. Louisa spent the entire waiting time giving the others directions for what they needed to do to get everything to the other side.

"You're sure I can't help—" Annie began, as their wagon crept closer to the shore.

"No, no," Louisa said impatiently for the fourth time. "I need you to do what I have instructed. I'm fine on my own. Help Margaret with the animals. Lord knows what will happen if those goats get out of her control. We don't want to be chasing them downstream or collecting their little bodies from underfoot."

Annie seemed dejected, but Louisa gave her one last bright smile before turning her attention to the team of oxen. The water was shallow enough here that she could walk the team across, just as she had walked the team across the plains and through many more narrow streams. She would have to go slowly, careful to avoid rocks and not get stuck in the mud. She would also have to get wet, but Louisa Hudson was perfectly capable of doing both those things on her own.

Her team took a bit of coaxing—they didn't want to get wet, no matter Louisa's comfort with it—but eventually, she had led all four enormous animals into the shallow water. The slow current coursed around their legs. Louisa encouraged them along, step by step, into the middle of the river. She looked over her shoulder and realized she didn't see any other member of her family.

"Lawrence," she called to the boy once they reached the water. "I want you where I can see you." She waved her arm down, indicating he should bring his wagon alongside hers to cross the water. "Slowly now."

Annie hovered on Lawrence's other side, close enough to come to his aid if needed. But at least she was doing as she had been told; she carried one of their smaller goats in her arms. Louisa looked farther back and saw Margaret leading their horse across. Josie was nowhere to be found, however. Where could she have gotten to? She was supposed to be helping her sister-in-law as well.

Craning her neck to see around the teams farther downstream, Louisa grew frustrated at her sister's behavior. Josie knew better.

In her distraction, Louisa lost track of where she was stepping. Her right foot slipped, sliding down the stone deeper into the water. Her ankle turned as she tried to regain her balance. But her left foot hadn't gained its own purchase yet, and Louisa stumbled forward into the river, dropping the reins as she did.

"No!" she said, on her knees in the river.

The oxen saw their window to escape this horrible situation. Two of them tried backing up, while one tried to pull the others upstream and the last made for the far bank. Louisa had to roll over into the shallow water, getting wet from head to toe to stay safely out of their hooves. Once moved, she scrambled to her feet —as best she could in sopping dress and hurt ankle— and moved slowly, gently toward her team to calm them.

The reins Louisa had used to guide them dangled in the water. She hurried to catch them up lest they get caught in the animals' legs or in some river weeds. She almost fell again in her haste and learned quickly to not put too much weight on her ankle. It would heal and be fine, but now was not the time to get hurt again.

She looked around again one last time for someone, for help, but in the end, she was able to get control over her team on her own. After what seemed like an interminable amount of time, Louisa stumbled up the bank of the river, her team and wagon following meekly behind her. She found her family and, exhausted, drove her wagon toward where they waited.

"Goodness!" Annie exclaimed when she saw her oldest sister, soaking wet, bedraggled, hair half down and hanging in thick wet strands around her face. "What happened to you?"

Louisa just shook her head, too tired to speak.

She sat on the lip of one of their wagons and set to work wringing out her dress. "I'll just be a minute," she assured anyone near enough to hear her. "I know we can't stay."

"We can stay long enough for you to get your bearings at least," Annie said. She had appeared at Louisa's elbow.

Louisa nodded.

Annie put a hand on her shoulder and squeezed gently. "You just call if you need something," she said before heading to where Josie was trying to calm the team of oxen.

Louisa was grateful to be left alone while she calmed her own racing heart. She needed time to reckon with the fact that she had made a mistake. Not that she would have admitted such to her sisters. Even just forming those words in her own mind had her defensive. But maybe she should have accepted Annie's help when it was offered and not tried to do everything herself.

Maybe.

Maybe she couldn't make something true simply through her own force of will. Though it had taken all these many weeks that they had been on the trail, Louisa had to admit that traveling to Oregon might actually be a bit more dangerous, a bit more trying than she had planned on.

Maybe she couldn't actually do it all on her own.

From where Louisa sat outside the ring of the campfire, she watched her sisters. Josie joked with Lawrence while Margaret was a few steps away talking to the schoolteacher traveling with the Robinsons. What was her name?

Louisa realized she had no idea. She had been so focused on getting her family to Oregon safely and efficiently, she hadn't taken the time to pay attention to anything else. She hadn't said more than four words to anyone outside of her family. The stress and fear were making Louisa turn more and more inward, resulting, in this case, in her not accepting help when it may have been wise.

Annie, on the other hand, was blossoming out here on the trail. She would likely never be as decisive or determined as Louisa was, but she was coming into herself in her own way. From where Louisa sat, she watched as Annie inserted herself into Josie and Lawrence's conversation. Though she couldn't hear what was being said, the smile on Annie's face warmed Louisa.

Though not as much as a fire would.

Louisa stood. The hem of her dress was still damp, and she felt a deep desire to be with her sisters. Her scare of the afternoon had rattled her, and the comforting circle of family, of women who loved her in spite of her mistakes, would be a balm.

"The next part of the trail is going to be rough," Josie was saying as Louisa approached. "I read that more wheels break on the next few miles than anywhere else on the trail."

"Well then, we will just have to go slowly and be careful," Annie said matter-of-factly.

Louisa snorted. "Because we're not careful any other time?"

The women went quiet around the circle, other than the muffled swishing of Josie's dishwater. Louisa recognized immediately that she had been too harsh—yet another result of her not accepting help before. Now she was tired and cranky and lashing out at her family.

"Come sit down," Annie said softly, offering Louisa her spot closest to the fire.

"Anyway," she continued, changing the subject, "I just... I wanted to say thank you for all you did today." Louisa pretended not to see the expression shared between Annie and Josie; she fixed her eyes on her youngest sister. "We all worked together, and I think we know how to do it better the next time."

Annie offered Louisa a small smile, as though she knew this was as close as the older woman might ever get to admitting she was wrong.

CHAPTER SIXTEEN

Once they had crossed the Platte River, Captain Mills didn't stop the caravan. If a family needed to rest after getting through the water, they could, but the company as a whole continued on. The Hudsons, and any other family that had to pause on the other side of the river, had enough time to catch up to their company before supper when the wagon train made camp. Gaps in the circle stood here and there, waiting for the stragglers to settle themselves in for the night.

They kept pushing on, through the exhaustion and the injuries. The following day, after supper, the tell-tale cry of Martin Jameson's fiddle carried over the otherwise quiet evening. The emigrants needed that injection of joy and peace. As before, there in the middle of the secure circle of wagons a small bonfire had been built, and the half dozen musicians were beginning to gather. That time-tested invitation to the young folks in the company floated through the air, calling them all to the dance.

Annie stood outside the warm light of the Hudsons' campfire and watched as the dancers began to gather. Though the youngest of the Hudson girls, she still felt a bit too old to join them and was content to watch from afar. She had an idea there was some not-insubstantial courting going on under their parents' noses and smiled to herself at the memory of her own betrothal, the music of the dance mingling with her memories.

She and John had been going together for years, since she was old enough to know what love was. Since that very first Sunday School picnic in which he brought her a piece of his mother's apple pie before it was all gone. Their courtship had been slow and sweet, based on a deep friendship and security that Annie had so missed after her parents had died.

For her eighteenth birthday, John had arranged with Louisa to have his whole family over for a Sunday supper. There, in the midst of everyone who loved them best, John had promised to love Annie forever and asked for her hand in marriage. It had been so simple, and yet it was precisely what she would have asked for. All she wanted was him.

"I hope they don't keep that up too late," Louisa muttered as she passed behind Annie.

The comment brought Annie back to the present, back to the reality of her exhaustion and the long day. Crossing through the Platte River that day before had been more tiring than she had expected, and the rocky terrain they had to cross tomorrow morning would be no better.

In fact, the trail the following day was one of the worst stretches they would have to endure.

Annie went to bed well before the musicians broke up. Despite the late night around camp, each wagon was packed and heading west by early morning. At the front of the caravan, George Mills paused to consider his path around the impediments, but then bravely, slowly, led the way. When the Hudsons reached the field of stone, the bright morning light glinted off of every piece of metal in sight, indeed off of some of the smoother rocks that littered the terrain as well. The Hudson girls watched as Buck Robinson cautiously led his team through a narrow gap in the boulders that stretched for a mile in every direction.

Annie had never seen anything like such a landscape. How had so many stones come to be scattered all over this stretch of the countryside? It was as though the very earth had spit them up. As she watched, the wagons ahead of them paused, jostled, at times had to drive a wheel or two directly over a rock that couldn't be otherwise avoided. It would be slow going all day, and each family would be lucky if there were no injuries or accidents.

"Seems mighty difficult for a person to do on their own," she ventured, glancing at Louisa to see if her sister had heard her.

She didn't try to offer her help again. Anything more direct would have left Annie stung by her sister lashing out. She had only seen Louisa's wounded pride once before—when the naval officer she had been engaged to married another woman not long after Louisa broke off their betrothal. Louisa had simmered in a fury for more than two weeks after that.

So now, Annie just stayed back and waited to be

asked for. But, instead, Louisa gritted her teeth in frustration and set to do it all herself. This was nothing like the soft, rolling hills of Virginia, nothing like what she was used to. She felt bad to see Louisa and Lawrence struggling but grateful that she was not one in charge of the wagons. How did the men manage to make the sharp turns necessary to go around the boulders? How could they stand the stress and strain of rolling the wagons' wheels over the rocks they couldn't avoid?

Somehow, the lead wagons found a path between the small boulders and the deep ruts and helped each member of the caravan guide their own vehicles through. In spite of everyone working together, however, three different wagons broke down while trying to cross the rugged terrain. The company was delayed as the men worked to repair them so the caravan could continue.

The work was frantic—heating the necessary tools, scavenging the necessary wood. In most cases, the repair was merely a stop-gap, the wagon barely hanging together long enough to get to their next campsite.

As she watched, Annie wondered how it could be enough. The next campsite was at the bottom of the next chasm, down a steep, narrow trail. It would take all of the company's muscle and ingenuity to keep the wagons safe.

The trail had been cut into the edge of the rock. The wagons and livestock were led slowly, cautiously, down into the gorge, foot by precarious foot. The descent was so steep that Louisa and Lawrence, with the help of a couple of the Jameson boys, chained their wagon wheels to keep them from rolling out of control.

Only the most sick and infirm rode inside the

wagons on the journey down into the canyon. Annie, Margaret, and Josie waited out of the way until most of the wagons had started their way down before walking behind with Carrot and the other Hudson animals. Annie felt like her feet might slip from underneath her any moment.

"I just hate to see such pressure put on a boy of that age," Margaret said. "I know this is not the first time I've said that I wish Tom was here, but…"

She trailed off, and Annie and Josie murmured supportively. It didn't need to be said. If Tom were moving to Oregon with them, Lawrence could have a chance for a boyhood a little while longer. He could go off with Jefferson Carter or Junior Sullivan, tagging along with the older boys and their fun, instead of constantly having to do all the most strenuous manual labor for the Hudsons.

"It'll be different when we get there," Josie assured her. "Louisa will have her new business to set up and won't have as much time to nit-pick and manage every single piece of our lives. You all can board for a year or so somewhere, and Lawrence won't be responsible for every single thing. It will work out."

"I hope you're right."

Annie said nothing. She was too busy thinking over how disinclined Louisa seemed to listen to what the boy's mother wanted for him. The poor child, to be pulled in so many directions.

Their hike to the bottom of the canyon wasn't terribly long. To Annie, it was a relief to finally feel like they were walking on level ground again. But before they could seek out their wagons and make camp, Annie realized that waiting at the bottom of the trail stood an older woman Annie recognized by sight, though she hadn't said more than a few words to her. It was the wife of the wagon company captain, looking for *her*.

"Mrs. Mills?" Annie said. "Goodness. Is there... is everything all right?"

"Miss Hudson," Mrs. Mills said, lighting up when she spotted her. "I wonder if I could ask a favor of you."

"Of course, ma'am."

Josie and Margaret took off with the animals without more than a curious look over their shoulder. Mrs. Mills must have plenty of more important things to manage. What did she need Annie for?

"Were you waiting for me?" Annie asked.

"Oh, yes, but not long. Don't worry."

Annie smiled. Why she had been waiting was far more pressing than worrying how long she had been waiting.

"Is everything all right?" she asked again.

"Yes, thank you. But I had hoped I could ask a favor of you. I've been thinking about some of the ways the needs of this company could be filled, but I know I can't do it alone. Could I persuade you to help me host a quilting circle? I thought one of these days that we stay in camp for longer than just an evening would be a good opportunity."

Annie was so surprised she couldn't respond right away. "I... what?"

"There are so many families in this community who simply did not come prepared for a six-month overland journey, and I want to do something for them. I am sure there are other families, like your own, that can spare a few hours, and maybe a little fabric to help put together a quilt for a child who might need it."

"But, a quilting circle? Me?"

The more Mrs. Mills explained it, the more confused Annie was. How did anyone in the camp have time for that? How did the wife of one of the company captains not understand that? Furthermore, why would she think of Annie to help organize?

Not one of those questions would Annie utter out loud, however. She wouldn't want Mrs. Mills to think she was arguing with her.

"I know now is not a good time, but there will be a number of campsites later in the journey that will work. My husband won't keep us moving every minute of every day. We'll have time to spread the word to the ladies and gather supplies. I think you would be perfect for this, so I hope you'll consider it."

"Oh." Annie tried to smile and hide her confusion. "Yes, I'll think about it. I'll have to talk to my sisters, of course, and make sure they don't have need of me."

"Certainly." Mrs. Mills placed her hand gently on Annie's arm. "Talk to them and just let me know."

After that strange conversation, Annie was in a bit of a daze before she could find her family again. The space was not large; the width of the canyon maybe only as long as a city block, just wide enough to contain the safety of the wagon circle. As she struggled to get her bearings, Annie looked up to the top of the ridge towering above her. Somewhere out there was a tribe of Indians. Several tribes. Maybe keeping an eye on the emigrants as they passed through the land. Who knew what they saw of the wagon train without themselves being seen.

She shook herself out of it and looked for the "NORFOLK" painted on the side of their wagon canvas. They were on the closer side of the circle, with a campfire already started. If Annie hurried, she might still be of some use to Josie as she cooked. As she got closer, she realized they had a visitor.

A tall teenage boy Annie recognized as Junior Sullivan stood in the circle of campfire light, his hands stuffed in his pockets. As his father was one of the captains, he was often sent on errands just like this.

"We'll be here for a couple nights," he was saying as she approached. "There should be plenty of water and grass for the animals to fill up on, and then we can leave day after tomorrow. And if you need anything, my father is happy to help as needed."

He tipped his hat in good-bye as he trudged on to the Robinsons' camp.

They had supper soon after, and Annie felt dizzy at the buzz of conversation. It had been such a long, tiring day. She was grateful that the company had stopped to make camp for the night and sought out some space to think. Annie ducked away from her campfire and crossed to the outside of the wagon circle. There was something about the exhaustion and stress of the day, coupled with the request from Mrs. Mills that made her heedless of any potential danger, out here on the open plains, outside of the protection of her community. A band of Indians could come riding up and kidnap her, and Annie wouldn't be able to stop them.

But wasn't that what most of this journey had been,

she thought to herself. She wouldn't have come west if she hadn't become acquainted with Isaac. If she was honest with herself, she might not have come west at all if her sisters hadn't helped make it happen. And now that they were spending every day struggling and merely surviving, she felt caught up in innumerable forces she could not control.

Thirst, hunger, sickness, Indians. Every day was another twenty-four hours in which Annie—and everyone in the company—had to deal with circumstance after circumstance they could not control.

Annie stopped, brushing her palms across the tops of the prairie grass that stretched all around her to the horizon. The stars were just beginning to make themselves seen. Nearly six months had passed since they had left Virginia, and yet the stars still felt familiar. The constellations were the same ones she had grown up learning about, the same steady stories that graced the heavens above them.

Alexander McKinnon was dead. Wagon wheels had broken, animals gone without water. The trials and tribulations would keep coming at them as they crossed the continent toward Oregon.

And through it all, Annie could be as steady as the stars themselves.

She turned to look back at the campsite she had left behind and watched as her family gathered around the fire. Josie was just finishing the dishes, Louisa taking off her shoes to rub at her ankles. And Annie made a resolution to herself.

Some things were inevitable. Some things they would

have to suffer through. She knew enough that she couldn't dispute that.

But not everything. They had not been put on this earth to merely endure.

Annie would not be a leaf floating down the river with the current. She would be a stone in the river bottom. She may be worn down. She may be pushed along. But she would resist, and she would make the water flow around her instead.

CHAPTER SEVENTEEN

The following morning, Louisa woke with a sense of overwhelm. She had stayed up too late last night, watching for Annie. There they were in the middle of the continent, their camp the only civilization for miles, and her sister had just wandered away into the darkness outside the circle of wagons, with no weapon or word about where she was going.

"You've got to trust her," Josie had said, while Louisa paced worriedly. "She can take care of herself."

"Maybe," Louisa muttered.

What that girl had been doing out in the darkness, Louisa had no idea. After all that Louisa had gone through to get her this far, now Annie was just off on her own, risking everything.

When eventually Annie had come back long after dark, quietly climbing into the sleeping wagon seemingly without regard to how she had made her sisters fret, Louisa was too anxious and high-strung to go to bed herself. She lay in her cot in the dark, watching Annie crawl into her own bed, and fuming. She had stayed up even later, thinking about all the many hundreds—nearly thousands—of miles they still had to travel and about all the chores and things that could be done the following day.

Living on the Oregon Trail for the summer was really no different than her days had been in Norfolk. She always had at least half a dozen things she could be getting done.

When dawn broke again on yet another day living out of this wagon, and Louisa Hudson was already exhausted at the thought.

But she had never, ever, been one to shirk her duty.

And so, mind whirring with lists and plans, Louisa pulled herself to a sitting position. With Josie's bunk above her, she had to sit forward, leaning into the narrow aisle between the cots. Her boots had been tucked under her bed the night before; her dress and apron hung on a hook just to the side. Margaret had already risen for the day, and Louisa didn't make much effort to stay quiet as she dressed.

By the time she had smoothed back her hair and pinned it up, Annie was also sitting, stretching in the little space she had under the top of the canopy. Louisa said nothing. She didn't trust herself not to sound angry. After the failure she had suffered fording the Platte, Louisa was too depleted to be patient.

So, instead, she moved forward with her day, starting by collecting pails of water for the oxen. After three trips back and forth with the buckets, the rest of her sisters were up for the day.

"Ha!"

Josie's jubilant voice came sailing out from behind the supply wagon. Louisa turned to look, curious at what could have prompted such joy.

"Eggs!" she called as she came around the corner.

Her hands were full of more eggs than Louisa had seen at one time since they had left Virginia. Five at once. Josie must not have had a chance to check yesterday, or possibly the day before. Even at home, when the birds were happy and calm, they never laid more than one each daily. Since they had been relegated to the narrow cages and the jostling wagon, Camilla and the other hens had been vocal in their discomfort. Days would go by when they were unable to produce at all.

But now five eggs!

"Five," Louisa said, just to confirm she wasn't seeing things. "Five eggs this morning. We all can have one."

"It's a miracle," Josie averred. "God must have known we'd be staying in camp today."

Louisa laughed at that thought. Her theology was sound, and she read her Bible faithfully, but she had never ascribed to the idea that the Lord paid attention to every little detail of their lives. It was all the more reason for Louisa herself to stay so vigilant.

Nevertheless, if this was indeed a miracle from above, Louisa would be happy to indulge. They hadn't had a fresh egg in at least a week, and that was used for a pastry Josie baked for all of them to share.

Later, as they were sitting down to their precious breakfast, a visitor appeared.

"Ladies!" Pastor Montgomery approached the Hudson wagons, hat in hand. "Misses Hudson, I hope I'm not interrupting."

Louisa quickly swallowed her bite of egg and biscuit and rose to greet him. "Pastor, welcome. Good morning. Would you like some coffee?"

"Oh, no, thank you." He paused. "Is that... do you all have eggs?"

It seemed from his tone that this was more of a sense of wonder than any desire to share in their food, but Josie stepped right up. She'd have to give up her own breakfast, but maybe the sacrifice was worth it to help support a man of God.

"It is. Louisa's hens have been laying real well the last few days. Here. We have just enough for you, too."

He had seemed like he was going to deflect her offer but gave in rather quickly as she offered him a plate with a fresh, hot biscuit and a fried egg. As far as Louisa knew, they were the only family in this caravan that had brought chickens with them. Fresh eggs were a luxury that every person missed.

"Oh, go on then," he said with a grin.

"What brings you by, Pastor?" Louisa said as she offered him a seat.

He took the tin plate from Josie carefully and used the side of his fork to cut into the fried egg. Once he had taken a bite, he moaned a tiny bit with pleasure. Louisa caught the pleased smile on Josie's face, knowing she had made one more person happy with her cooking.

"Pastor?" Louisa prompted again.

"Oh!" Pastor Montgomery blushed a little, chewed hurriedly, and swallowed. "Yes. I'll be holding a church service tonight. I thought there are probably a lot of folks who miss worshiping with their community. There's a spot by the stream, up against the side of the canyon. I've already gotten the okay from the captains if you want to join us after supper. Half-past seven? Should give us enough time before sunset."

"Oh, my yes," Josie said. "Goodness, you're right. I *have* missed that."

"I think someone told me you used to sing in your church choir?"

Josie looked at Annie. "Actually, we both did. Annie used to play the piano sometimes, too."

"Well, in that case," he said, "I hope you'll both come and sing loud. My wife— Well, it might just be me up there tonight, and I could use the support." He grinned and took another bite of his egg.

"This is the first one that you've done, isn't it?" Annie asked.

He nodded. "I didn't feel like I could take from the time and attention of anyone while we were still getting our feet under us. But after the last week or so..." He trailed off, shaking his head at the memory. "Maybe the word of God is exactly what we all need."

The pastor stayed only a few minutes longer—long enough to finish his breakfast—before saying his good-byes and heading on to the next wagon in the circle. Louisa hadn't participated much in the conversation; she had been too busy thinking about what he had said. Could she afford to take the time to go to a worship service that night? She knew she was saved. She had no qualms on that score. Maybe her time would be better served resting for another full day on the trail tomorrow, or she could even repair the hem of her dress that had gotten snagged a few days back.

God wouldn't miss her.

Louisa spent most of the day thinking about it. After supper, as she nibbled on the johnnycakes that Josie had made, she made her decision. Annie and Josie sat on either side of the campfire, chatting amiably. Margaret stood a couple yards away, watching the animals that passed through the center of the circle of wagons as they wandered. Lawrence was lounging between the two rear wheels, under the sleeping wagon.

"Are you all still going to see what Pastor Montgomery is doing?" Louisa asked.

"Oh yes!" Josie said. "I can't wait. Especially if there's singing. I've missed it so much. We should probably leave soon, I'm thinking."

"I'm not sure I care to go to the church service," Louisa said. "Frankly, my soul is saved, and my time would be better spent thinking over our journey tomorrow."

They didn't try to force her, and it was only after they had left that Louisa realized that Lawrence had stayed behind as well.

"You're not going?"

He shook his head.

"Your mother's not making you?" she teased.

He snorted a laugh. "No. She's..." He paused and crawled out from under the wagon before he continued. "I think she's trying to give me a break or something." Lawrence sat on an upturned bucket not far from where Louisa sat. "She keeps encouraging me to go to bed or eat more food. A couple days ago, she even offered to help me drive the wagon." He chuckled.

"She loves you very much," Louisa said.

"Yeah. She does. I just wish her idea of a break

meant letting me go hunting with Junior Sullivan or to the Schmidts one night with Jefferson."

Louisa's ears perked up. "The Schmidts? Why do you want to go there?" It wasn't until the words were out of her mouth that she realized she had little idea who that family was. She had kept to herself too much, relying on Margaret to make the connections they needed.

"Oh... it's just some fellas. They... It's all a bunch of brothers, so they are maybe a little more uncouth than Mother would want me spending time with."

"I'm sure if your mother says no, she must have a good reason."

"Yeah." Lawrence sighed. "Why aren't you going to church tonight? I thought all old people liked church."

Louisa laughed. "Do I seem that old to you?"

He shrugged.

"Well, I suppose old people like rest too," she said. "Truthfully... and I haven't told your mother or aunts this... I'm starting to feel the weight of the trail pulling on me. It's rough going, isn't it?"

He nodded and sat up a little straighter. In his expression, Louisa saw her own brother, Lawrence's father. She saw his determination and his frankness.

"You still glad you came?" she asked.

"I think so. I guess I didn't know it would be so hard, though, or that folks would die."

"I thought I knew how hard it would be, and I was wrong. Maybe the Oregon Trail is just the kind of thing you have to do anyway."

"Yeah, maybe."

She stood up and took a deep breath. "Now, because you and I have such a long, hard day ahead of us, we should take advantage of this early night and get some rest, don't you think?"

He looked wistfully over his shoulder, toward where Louisa thought the Carter wagon might be. But when he looked back at her, he was nodding cheerfully. Before she climbed into the wagon to sleep, she saw Lawrence spreading out his own bedroll under the wagon.

The next morning, Louisa was glad she had given herself a break. Maybe she would actually do it more often. Washing her hair that afternoon had been rather pleasant, after all. She woke just after dawn feeling refreshed and energetic, ready to keep making progress west. In no time, she had her team harnessed, had drunk her coffee, and followed the Robinson wagon back onto the trail. After leaving the camp at the bottom of the canyon, the Sullivan-Mills wagon company climbed a slow incline back up to the high prairie.

The sky above was clear and blue. The sun was hot and direct. And Louisa thought only about the travel ahead.

CHAPTER EIGHTEEN

After leaving the camp at the bottom of the canyon, Annie felt ready for another long stretch of hard trail. The sun beat down overhead, but she had been rested, and had plenty of water, and felt like she could endure just about anything. She was ready. They pushed onward for several monotonous days, the Great Plains stretching in all directions.

They were well into June now, and the spring flowers were beginning to fade. Without the pops of color throughout the surrounding meadow, each day felt even more like all the other ones. Annie felt a kind of comfort in the sameness, knowing what she needed to be doing, and where she would be that day.

One morning, however, that sameness ended. After a quick breakfast and packing up again, the Hudsons waited for Captain Mills to lead the caravan along the trail for the day.

And then they waited longer, the sun climbing in the sky.

They should be leaving any moment.

Annie started to feel anxious as more time passed without any word or motion.

Everything was packed up and ready to go, but for some reason a full hour had gone by, and no one was moving. Since the Hudson wagon was near the back of the caravan, they had no knowledge of any decisions made at the head.

As the morning wore on, Louisa grew more and more irritated.

"Why aren't we leaving?" Louisa asked anyone within earshot. "We don't have time to waste just standing around."

"I'll see," Annie said, and walked off purposefully before anyone could object.

She passed the Robinsons, who looked just as bewildered as she did. As she kept moving up the caravan, she continued until she saw a small crowd gathered around the Van Anda wagon. Though Annie had not yet met them, she recognized the heavily pregnant woman, leaning against the back of her wagon, talking to half a dozen neighbors in a circle around her.

Annie approached and overheard Mrs. Van Anda say the name "Sullivan," as she joined the circle.

"Is that where the doctor went?" Tom Jameson asked.

"Where?" Annie asked. "Is that why we haven't left yet?"

Mrs. Van Anda sat forward, eager to reveal the news. "Doctor and Mrs. Martell were called to the Sullivan camp just before we were supposed to leave. Seems the little one, what's his name?"

"Jeremiah," someone offered.

"That's right. Jeremiah has been taken ill. Mrs. Sullivan suspected measles, but I ain't seen the doctor come back yet to confirm it."

"Measles," Annie repeated under her breath.

The Hudson girls had all had measles when they were young. Annie could only remember flashes of that time. She had only been eight years old, but her parents had still been alive and most of Annie's memories of that period were of an overwhelming sense of dread. She looked toward where she thought the Sullivan wagon was, as though she'd be able to see the looming creature of the measles overtaking them.

"What will happen?" she asked.

"Depends," Tom Jameson said with a shrug. "By all rights, for the protection of everyone else, we should leave them behind. We can't have that spreading around the camp."

"But William Sullivan is the captain!"

"Right. So, there's no telling what they'll decide," he finished. "But if one of my boys gets sick, I don't know what I'll do."

"I just hope we get moving soon," Tabitha Gilroy said. "I don't know that my food stores can stand to take any more time than we absolutely have to. I've sent Sean out hunting twice in the last week, and he hasn't come back with anything more than a couple prairie chickens."

Before anyone else could add their own experience, the booming voice of Daniel Mills cut through the air.

"All right, everyone. We're leaving in ten minutes! Ten minutes!"

Annie looked up to see him riding his horse through

the camps of all those still in place. In a short moment, he was gone.

"Well, I guess we have our answer," Mrs. Van Anda said. She struggled with her balance and finally turned to Annie. "Give us a hand, would you?"

She reached out with both hands to help the pregnant woman to a standing position, holding her up until she had regained her balance.

"Will you be all right?"

"Oh, yes, honey. Just one more day like the last. You go on back to your family. We got ten minutes."

Annie hated to leave her, but the oldest Van Anda girl appeared to help her mother, so all seemed to be in hand.

That day seemed to stretch on forever. Although they continued moving west, as fast as they could to make up time lost that morning, to Annie, it seemed like time had stopped. All she could think about was that poor sick boy and how frightened his mother must be. Her mind was elsewhere, and Annie was actually a mite surprised when the Robinsons' wagon in front of them slowed. The caravan was led to the right of the trail, toward a copse of trees that signaled a water source and campsite. As the Hudsons pulled their own wagons into the circle for the night, Annie looked up at the sky. They still had hours before sunset. Why were they already making camp?

"It seems early, doesn't it?" Louisa said when she noticed Annie's gaze.

"I'm worried."

Without waiting for Louisa's response, Annie hurried to take the reins from Lawrence.

"Go, run ahead, see what you can find out. Why we're stopping already," she told him. "I'll take care of this team, but we will have no peace if she doesn't have answers."

"Aunt Louisa?" he said with a grin.

Annie only chuckled and prodded him along.

He nodded and ran off toward where the company captains' wagons would be and where he could ask an adult who might know what happened.

Unhitching the team on her own and getting them water was more work than she had remembered, especially since she was distracted. Annie kept glancing toward the other side of the wagon circle, toward where Lawrence had run off. With the news they had learned that morning, it seemed as though things could only have gotten worse.

It wasn't long before his gangly figure was again striding toward their camp. Annie set the bucket of water down at the feet of the oxen team, letting them fend for themselves until she had learned the worst.

Margaret, Josie, and Louisa gathered just behind Annie, waiting the interminable moments before Lawrence was close enough to relay the news.

"It's Jeremiah Sullivan," he said grimly. "He..." Lawrence looked down and took a moment to clear his throat before looking up again. "He died. This afternoon, I guess."

"Oh!" Annie felt like all her breath left her body. Though they had heard that he was sick, the shock of yet another member of their company—a child at that— dying was more than she was prepared for. How could they stand it? "Oh, his poor mother."

Margaret let out a choking sob and reached for her own son. Lawrence closed the distance between them and allowed himself to be hugged more tightly than he had in months.

Annie stood stock-still in a daze. How much more would they have to lose? They were not even halfway to Oregon and already the trials seemed to be destroying them. She could barely remember why they were going there in the first place, under the weight of so much stress.

She and Josie prepared the family's supper in silence, each alone in their own thoughts. The rest of the evening was quiet and subdued; Annie could not stop thinking about that poor family.

The following morning, the company was delayed in leaving so the Sullivan family could hold their funeral for Jeremiah. There was a part of Annie that didn't want to attend, that couldn't handle more heartbreak, the death of another child. But, with all that she had been through since receiving Isaac's proposal, she was learning that ignoring something wouldn't make it go away. She couldn't just sit back and let life pass her by.

And maybe paying her respects to the family of one of the leaders of this wagon train was the best place to start.

The Hudsons again shared another meal in silence, before making their way together to where a small crowd was gathering outside the camp. A shallow grave, a few feet off the trail, had been dug. It shocked Annie to see how that vibrant boy could fit in such a tiny space.

When a dozen or so families had gathered, George Mills gave the pastor a nod. Pastor Montgomery prayed over the boy, prayed over his family, that they might have peace. His eulogy hoped for calm for the company and safety from further illness.

As Pastor Montgomery praised young Jeremiah Sullivan for his kindness and his joy, Annie felt the weight of grief fall over her. She hadn't even met the child properly but already missed him. Across the circle of mourners, with every phrase and intonation from the pastor, the pall of depression seemed to fall more and more. Annie wasn't the only one wishing they could have stopped this somehow.

Though the funeral service didn't last long, the mourning that pervaded the company would.

Pastor Montgomery finished his closing prayer. Captain Sullivan and his older son Junior filled the small grave with loose dirt. The boy's mother and sisters stood nearby, each crying into their handkerchief. Soon the father and brother piled heavy stones on top of the grave. It was to deter predators, Annie realized, to keep the body from being disturbed.

Annie turned away, heart pounding. She couldn't watch any more.

The rest of her family had already started making their way back to camp. The animals still had to be hitched up, the campfire put out. When Annie reached their wagons, Louisa asked her to make sure the hens had been loaded safely.

"Hurry up, please. We have to go," Louisa said. "We can't linger."

"We still have time," Josie said admonishingly. "A boy died. We can give his mother—"

"We don't have much time. Not after the delays the

last few days. We need to be able to get over the Blue Mountains before the snow. That could be as early as September, I've heard."

Even the death of a child couldn't stop the company's relentless progress toward Oregon. Ten minutes after the last stone had been placed on Jeremiah Sullivan's grave, the wheels of the lead wagon began to roll.

Annie spent her morning walking parallel to the trail, close enough to hear Louisa if she should call for her, but far enough away to have some solitude with her thoughts as she grappled with the seemingly never-ending heartbreak of traveling on the Oregon Trail.

CHAPTER NINETEEN

The blazing sun beat down on Louisa as she led her family, their teams of oxen and two wagons ever westward. While it seemed a blessing to not have another large river to cross, or a canyon to traverse, having day after day of the same terrain only made the journey seem longer. Louisa had nothing to look forward to every day except step after step to slowly cross the continent with her two wagons.

The heat was unending; Louisa felt as though she was constantly wearing clothing damp with her own sweat. The neckline chafed after days of not drying properly in between the heavy manual labor she did each day. Annie offered to take some of the load from her, to try again to lead the wagons, but Louisa needed to do it herself. She felt like she needed to be sure she was always doing as much as she could to protect her family and get them to Oregon. She honestly did not know how she would spend her time if she didn't have this responsibility on her hands.

And so, day after day, night after night, just behind the Robinsons' wagon, Louisa walked, arms straining and voice hoarse from guiding her team of oxen. At the end of each day, she could see the strain on her sisters' faces, but she was already doing all she could. She led their wagons and gathered the water and fuel when there was any to be had. She gave up sleep to make sure that their vehicles were in shape for the next stretch of miles. She gave up food to make sure her growing nephew had enough.

For days on end, they trudged through what seemed like a wide platter of prairie grass. Flat plains stretched in all directions, without even a hill to break the monotony. From dawn until dusk, the emigrants marched westward, marking time only with the rumbling of their stomachs or the falling asleep as soon as their head touched the pillow.

What trees had been in this sparse landscape had long ago been picked clean, and Josie had to make do with using well-dried buffalo chips for fuel for the fire. She managed to perfect the efficiency of her cooking, saving as much time as she could to make the little fuel they had last. Louisa soon grew used to eating cold beans with her cold biscuit, neither even warmed up from the day prior.

Every day seemed the same. After burying the Sullivan boy, Louisa felt even more determined to make sure every member of her family got to Oregon safely. She found herself constantly checking to make sure Lawrence had enough water or that Margaret hadn't hurt herself while keeping track of their goats. If she could have, Louisa would have insisted that Annie stay within her sight at all times, whether she was an adult of twenty-five or not. The more she let herself think about it, the more Louisa felt as though if she just tried hard enough, she could keep every one of them safe.

With this mindset, Louisa set off into the prairie grasses one evening to collect more dried buffalo chips. Both Josie and Annie had volunteered to go, but Louisa preferred that they stay inside the protective circle of wagons, instead of wandering out into the wild open, where anything could hurt them. She had heard talk about snakes, or wolves, even. Instead, with a rifle slung over her shoulder just in case, Louisa headed off on her own and would hear no argument against it.

So many wagon companies had already passed this way that summer. So much of the available fuel had already been collected and burned up. Louisa had to venture farther and farther out to find enough buffalo chips for her family to use. She pulled up the corners of her apron, using its broad surface as a pouch to carry them in. Because the grass was so high—almost to her hips—Louisa had to go slowly, looking carefully at the dirt under her with every step.

As the spring turned into summer, the days grew longer and longer. The sweat on her brow was drying in the evening breeze, and Louisa wanted nothing more than to finish this chore so she could get back to camp and wash her face. She tried to keep her thoughts on the cold trails they would have to travail in the mountains. Maybe when they got that far west, she could remember the heat and sunshine of this day to warm her.

Louisa was interrupted in her thoughts by a quiet voice.

"Oh! Excuse me, ma'am!"

Louisa looked up to see that... slave? Former slave? Freeman? She wasn't just quite sure what to call her. Though the Hudsons had never owned any servants, she'd still grown up in Virginia, after all, and had more than her share of interactions with the darker race that populated the servants' quarters and kitchens of her neighbors. Even so, she had never met a freeman, not owned by another.

She cleared her throat, stalling, trying to decide how to respond.

"Did you need help with that?" the woman asked, gesturing to the full load that Louisa carried in her apron.

"Oh, goodness, you scared me." Louisa hung her head, trying to quiet her heart. "So much tall grass out here I didn't see you at all, Mrs. Franklin. What are you doing out here?"

"Same thing you are, I imagine," she said, gesturing to Louisa's apron. "You seem to be having better luck than me. You sure you don't need help carrying any of it?"

There was a small moment when Louisa almost took her up on the offer. She was so tired and so hot. But she had gotten this far taking care of her family; she could do a little while longer. This woman was not her servant.

"Oh, thank you, but I think I have it handled. I wouldn't want to take any of your time if you're doing the same thing."

Mrs. Franklin nodded. She looked as though she wanted to say something more but changed her mind. The two women worked side by side quietly for a minute. Though she did have almost more than she could carry, Louisa kept seeing one more piece, took one more step. The more fuel she gathered now, the less she would have to gather later or in the morning, so she would keep going as long as she was physically able to.

The longer they worked in silence, the more questions Louisa had, things she had been wondering about Millie Franklin and her husband since they had met a couple weeks prior. Namely, what on earth were they even doing traveling to Oregon? She figured her sisters might think it rude, but Louisa wanted to know.

"Do you mind if I ask you a question?" Louisa had learned that most people did not appreciate her directness, so she tried to soften it when she remembered to.

"Um, well. Certainly."

"Are you..." Now that she had come to it, she didn't know what to say, how to word it. "Are you... is someone directing your trip to Oregon? Someone making you go?"

Mrs. Franklin offered a small, polite smile. "Are you asking if I am someone's property?"

"Well, yes, I suppose I am. I'm sorry, I just—"

She waved a hand, dismissing Louisa's excuses. "I get that question all the time, most often far more hostile. That's a big part of why we are going to Oregon in the first place."

Louisa waited, curious what she would say. All thoughts of why she was out in the open prairie were forgotten completely. She couldn't recall if she had ever had an honest conversation with a person like her before.

The Black woman sighed as she began. "My husband Titus and I used to belong to a lawyer, Mr. Tyler, in

Atlanta. He was getting on in years, his wife died, and after he retired, he sold off much of the others that he had owned for so long."

"But you and your husband stayed?"

She grimaced slightly. "He didn't sell us, if that's what you're asking. By the end, though, Titus and me were doing everything that needed doing in that home. Not even excepting cleaning the old man's bedpan. He had a son, Beau Tyler, who lived up in Alexandria and only came down to visit every few years or so. For a long time, it was just me, Titus, and old Mr. Tyler.

"When he died, last summer, we were so scared. We didn't know the younger Mr. Tyler at all and were sure he'd just have the whole estate liquidated, and we'd be separated. I'm sure I don't need to tell you... the thought of being torn from your only family, the only person that loves you. Well, we had some mighty rough nights, I can tell you."

"But, you're here now. What happened?"

Mrs. Franklin sighed again, a soft smile resting on her face. "I don't know. I can't rightly say what put the idea in his head, or if maybe it was his father's idea. I just don't know. All I know is that young Mr. Tyler came down to Atlanta himself to handle things after his father's death, and he... He freed us." She shrugged apologetically. "It was... It was overwhelming and petrifying and wonderful. He even gave us some starting money; he suggested Oregon, where there would be fewer people who look down on freedmen. He helped make sure we got out of Georgia safely. I had only ever seen him a couple times before that, and I'll never see him again, but I'm grateful to him. He saw that we were people and that we deserved a chance to build a life same as anyone."

She trailed off at the end of this speech, as though afraid she had said too much.

"I'm sorry." Mrs. Franklin looked down, embarrassed. "I didn't mean to get so emotional. I just... I haven't told anyone that story before." She looked up, directly at Louisa. "We have to be very careful what people we trust, you understand. We can't take anything for granted. Not anything."

Louisa nodded. "I understand," she said, though in truth she wasn't sure she did. "I'm just... I'm full of questions and wish I could talk to this Mr. Tyler of yours. To find out what he was thinking."

Louisa thought she saw a flash of anger cross Mrs. Franklin's face, but it disappeared quickly.

"I'm just grateful he did. We've got our fresh start and our whole future ahead of us, and I'm quite pleased with how it's all turned out so far. But, I don't want to keep you any longer, Miss Hudson. I hope you have a good night."

The Black woman turned and darted off through the grass to her own wagon before Louisa could respond. She was shaken; it seemed as though she had offended the woman somehow but couldn't say why. And on top of that, she was marveling at how far the Franklins had gotten on their own. They had lived their whole lives, up to that, point having decisions made for them and being given instructions for everything they did. And yet somehow, they managed without it now.

They weren't just managing. Mrs. Franklin had seemed genuinely happy.

Louisa looked back toward the circle of wagons, toward the family that she had been trying so hard to protect from every danger or even inconvenience. Was it possible that they, too, would bloom with more freedom?

She shook her head at herself; all she could think about was how she would feel if she dropped her vigilance and they were in danger. With her apron full of fuel for their campfire, she walked back through the grass.

CHAPTER TWENTY

"Annie!" Josie called. In the chill of dawn, she was bent over the start of the campfire, coaxing the spark to life. "Can you check on the hens for me? We haven't had a fresh egg in a couple days."

Annie was pulled out of her reverie. She had been admiring the way the sun refracted in the dew on the prairie grass, stretching out as far as she could see. They were now about three hundred miles into their journey, three hundred miles closer to Isaac and her future.

"Of course," she said, cheerfully.

She made her way to the family's second wagon, where their trio of hens had been cooped overnight. Though there had been some trouble at the beginning of their journey, getting the netting to stay put, by now all the kinks had been worked out. They had a smooth system, and the three birds had a safe and quiet place to stretch their legs each night. There were three small boxes that were moved from the wagon bed to underneath and between the wagon wheels each night when they stopped. They got their fill of insects that lived in the tall grass, and Camilla and the other hens had the comfort and safety they needed.

In spite of all the family's efforts to coddle them, though, the hens seemed too stressed to produce the daily eggs they had been accustomed to back home. This made each egg they did lay even more precious. The sisters never knew if there would be one. Annie found herself holding her breath in anticipation as she pushed back the netting to check their nests.

The hens protested half-heartedly, clucking at Annie as she entered their domain. But they were too interested in feasting on the bugs hopping at their feet to pay much attention to her. After a quick search, Annie discovered that two of the girls had laid eggs that morning. She gasped in delight. Two at once was a luxury they had not had in weeks.

As she returned to Josie, eggs in hand, she noticed that Lawrence was still curled up in his bedroll under the other wagon. He had both arms up and over his head, as though trying to block out any light or sounds. As though he would somehow be permitted to sleep in. As though there wasn't already a mountain of work to get to this early in the morning.

Annie chuckled to herself. She wouldn't be the one to wake him, but she certainly didn't envy Margaret her job in doing so.

"Two this morning," Annie said as she handed over the eggs.

Josie's face lit up. "Two! Maybe I'll save them for baking. I was fixing to make my whirligig the next time we stopped long enough."

"I'm sure Lawrence would love that," Annie responded.

"Lawrence has never failed to love each and every mouthful of anything I put in front of him," Josie said with a laugh.

"Thank you, Aunt Josie." The boy's voice floated out from under the wagon.

"So, you *are* up," Annie said. "You know your aunt Louisa will have your hide if you don't have the oxen watered before we have to go."

"I know, I know," he muttered, crawling out from his sleeping place.

He stood, stretched, and let out a long sigh. Annie marveled at how much he had grown in the few months since they had left Virginia. Why, he was almost fourteen, now. They would have to remember to plan something for his birthday.

"Coffee's ready," Josie called out. "Breakfast in just a few minutes."

Annie set to work pulling the plates and utensils out of the grub box for their breakfast, so Josie could focus on not burning the johnnycakes. This long on the trail, they had most meals down to a quick routine. Even without her having to say so, Annie knew Josie would bake up some extra biscuits for them to eat with supper before putting the campfire out.

Ten minutes later, breakfast was cooked, and all the Hudsons sat or squatted around their campfire, eating contentedly.

"Who was that I saw you talking to last night?" Margaret asked.

Annie looked up to see that she was speaking to

Louisa. Louisa always seemed so focused on getting chores done and making miles across the plains that she rarely left their camp. Had she made a new friend?

"When?"

"Last night. When you were out collecting buffalo chips. I saw you talking to another woman."

"Oh…" Louisa chewed slowly and swallowed her bite of bacon before answering. "That was Mrs. Franklin."

All of the other women waited for more information, but Louisa didn't volunteer any.

Finally, after a full minute of silence, Margaret prompted. "Honey? You know that…" She sounded apologetic as though she hated to be the one to point this out. "Well, she's Black."

"I know that," Louisa said defensively as Annie's eyes darted back to her oldest sister. "You think I'm blind?"

"Well, no, but I just wonder if… Well, we wouldn't want to get mixed up in some runaway's business, would we?"

Louisa frowned. "She's not a runaway."

"How can you be sure?"

"She told me," Louisa insisted. "And I believe her. She and her husband were given their freedom when their old master died, and they thought a fresh start would be easier than staying put."

Annie and Margaret exchanged a glance; she could see the worry all over her sister-in-law's face. She never shied from defying Louisa when the occasion warranted, and in this case, Margaret could very well consider her sister-in-law's actions dangerous to the family.

"So, she's…?"

"She's free, not a runaway," Louisa said, pointedly.

"And, as a matter of fact, she's quite happy, she says. But I don't see that it's any of our business, do you?"

Annie shut her mouth abruptly.

"Goodness, Louisa," Margaret said. "We were just asking questions."

"And I'm just answering them. I don't know any more than that. It's not my job to figure out a stranger's life."

A cold quiet fell over the group.

Annie caught Margaret's eye and shook her head. Maybe there was something more there, but now was probably not the time to push it. She didn't know what to think. Or what to say. Hearing Louisa decline from having an opinion about someone else's life in and of itself was a surprise. What could be going on in her head?

Lawrence—thirteen years old and confident as ever —had no qualms about changing the subject.

"Miss Atkins is doing more lessons this week. Tonight. Can I go, Mother?"

Margaret looked at her son for a long moment, as though trying to register what he had said amidst the discussion of the Franklins. "Miss Atkins?"

"Yeah, the schoolteacher that's riding west with the Robinsons. She's been doing lessons for all the school-age children. Some in the morning for the little ones, and in the afternoon for my age. On the days we're stopped in camp, at least. I promise I'll still get all my chores done. It won't interfere. But can I go?"

Margaret glanced at Louisa. "Why don't we talk about this later?"

"But why? It's just... reading and stuff. You keep telling me that my education is important and how I need to know how to add up figures and things when I run a farm. Wouldn't Father have wanted me to go? You're the one who said—"

"Enough, Lawrence," Margaret interrupted gently.

Annie had spent this exchange watching Louisa's expression, but whatever her oldest sister was thinking was a mystery. Keeping quiet and not offering her advice unsolicited was completely out of character for her. But for whatever reason, her thoughts seemed to be elsewhere.

Throughout the rest of that day, the Sullivan-Mills wagon company continued westward, and Annie walked with Lawrence as he led the family's second wagon. She was proud of him for so staunchly asking for what he wanted. Where did a child of his age learn such a thing? Certainly not from her example.

He was bubbling over with enthusiasm about the books that Miss Atkins was going to help them read and how he was glad he had talked his mother into bringing some of his father's books to Oregon.

"You're really excited about those lessons?" she asked him. "I guess I just didn't realize it was so important to you."

He looked at her in surprise. "Of course! I feel like I don't know *anything*. When we get to Oregon, I'll be too busy setting up our farm and building a house to do it then." He shrugged. "I don't know. Maybe it's not that important. I know that's what Aunt Louisa thinks, anyway. But I want to do it."

"Your dad used to read a lot," Annie said softly.

"I know. One of the things he wanted was for me to

go to a university. That's probably not likely now, but at least I can do more than just a few years of school."

"Do you want this badly enough to not go playing with your friends? I thought Ralph Davis was going to teach you some card game."

He frowned, confused. "You mean that I won't have time to do both."

"Maybe. Likely Aunt Louisa already has a long list of chores she wants you to do. You might have to choose between the lessons and the playing."

"Well, sure. Yeah. Okay. Maybe it's like that new friend that Aunt Louisa made. What's her name?"

"Mrs. Franklin?"

"Yeah. Didn't Aunt Louisa say that she seemed really happy now? I guess… I mean, yeah, the lessons are work, but it's work that I want to do." He shrugged. "If I don't play cards with Ralph, it's not the end of the world."

Annie smiled at her nephew. "How did you get so smart?"

He blushed. "Besides," he continued, "you'll do Aunt Louisa's chores for me, won't you?"

"Very funny," she said, grinning. "I can't even finish all the chores she has set aside for me."

What Louisa had said about the Black woman had stuck in her mind, however. When they stopped that night for camp, Annie kept her eyes out for Mrs. Franklin. Louisa's reaction—defensive, dismissive—had piqued her curiosity. Even after she had brought back water for Josie's cooking, Annie went back to the spring, just in case. But she never saw the other woman.

CHAPTER TWENTY-ONE

Day after day followed in which Louisa could only focus on the miles ahead of her. The mornings were the same. The evenings were the same. Even most of the terrain they covered was the same each and every day. And Louisa walked all of it, reins in hand, calling to and guiding her team of oxen.

As she walked, Louisa took advantage of the quiet as best she could. The air was full of the rumbling of the wagon wheels over the dirt, the laughter of the children playing in the fields on either side of the trail, the calling of the men driving their teams, and any number of other joyful sounds. But to Louisa, these hours of solitude as she drove the wagon away from the sisters and the needs of her family were as quiet as she would ever get.

The hot, monotonous days continued until Louisa felt as though she might lose her mind. She was dedicated and focused, more so than many people, but even she was getting tired of the same days full of sweat and exhaustion with no change in sight. The only break in the long, seemingly unending stretch of prairie was the occasional detritus left behind by previous emigrants, cast to the side of the trail.

Folks had been traveling west along this route for almost twenty years, and it was clear from some of the things left behind that not all of them were as well prepared as Louisa was. Many of the Americans who headed west from their well-appointed and comfortable homes in the eastern cities didn't seem to realize that they couldn't take the comforts of civilization with them.

The wagons they had built were enormous, and the oxen pulling them were immensely strong, but even those animals had limits. When a family had to bring along thousands of pounds of food just to keep everyone fed, there wasn't much space left over for the family heirlooms, though people did seem to try.

Every few miles, the trail carried Louisa past a piece like a discarded wardrobe, tipped over on its side with the door hinges all but rusted off. The next day she would notice, ten feet off the trail, set up straight and tall as though it had been carefully set aside, a solid oak chest. The painted lid was faded and peeling after so many months in the harsh outdoors. Grass continued to grow up around the furniture, heedless of the symbols of civilization that had been hauled into this wilderness.

But furniture wasn't the only thing that had been left behind. The wagon caravan drove past the carcasses of animals that had died in their trip west—first one, and then more and more frequently. Oxen, mules, and even a pig had likely dropped where they were left, with wolves and vultures soon upon them.

But none of these small remains along the trail were quite as exciting as when the first hint of Courthouse Rock appeared on the horizon.

"Do you see it?" Josie called out as she ran toward Louisa.

"See what?" Louisa squinted into the afternoon sun at where her sister pointed.

"It's only just... Well, you have to know what you're looking for, I suppose, but right there, you can just make out Courthouse Rock."

"Goodness, finally. I would have hoped we'd reach there before now."

"There's still probably a couple days yet. But, you'll see. We'll keep heading directly to it."

And so they did. The enormous, granite stone, named after the courthouse in the county seat in Missouri, loomed over the travelers for miles as they went. It was the first of many, which blessedly opened up a whole new part of the country, finally breaking the harsh flatness of the plains. The journey west was full of signposts just like this, letting the emigrants learn just how far they had come and celebrate every mile.

A couple days following Courthouse Rock, the tall shape of a granite spire appeared on the horizon. As they got closer, Louisa could see that the spire towered over a round rock, making the entire structure look not unlike what it was named for—Chimney Rock. The monument towered over them, drawing the winding caravan toward it for miles. The landscape all around offered examples of the kind of natural sights most of the emigrants had never seen back east. It was impossible not to be awed when the caravan camped at Scott's Bluff overnight.

Not half an hour after the wagons had been pulled into a circle and chained securely for the evening, Lawrence came running back to camp.

"Where've you been?" Louisa asked him.

"The animals got their water," he said. "I was just—"

"I wanted you to help me check the wheels this afternoon," she said. "You can't just go running off whenever you feel like it."

"Are the wheels broken?"

"Well, no, but that's why we need to check them every so often. To head off any cracks or damage."

He blanched and looked over her shoulder. "Is my mother around?"

"She would agree with me, Lawrence."

He looked around as though hoping to be rescued from this scolding.

"I'll ask you again. Where were you?"

"I just— Ralph said he had something to show me, and then I ran into Jefferson who said he and his brother were going to try to climb up the bluff after supper, and I came back immediately, to make sure it was okay that I went. I didn't know you wanted me to check the wheels. I would have stayed if something had been broken. I never shirk my chores, Aunt Louisa. Really, I don't. I just wanted to see what Ralph needed."

"Hmmm," she murmured. She wanted to be fair; it was true that he never avoided or put off the things he knew he was supposed to do. Maybe he was telling the truth, though she still didn't trust this Jefferson boy.

As she was considering this, her attention was caught

by a figure walking several yards behind Lawrence. It was Mr. Franklin, the husband, that freed slave. He didn't even glance at the Hudsons on his way to his destination, but his wife's words sprang unbidden to Louisa's mind, and she recalled how happy she had been with the simple option of being able to make her own choices.

"Well," she said with a sigh. "I still need you to help me. I want to go over all the wheels together. But after that, I won't stop you. Whatever your mother says is okay."

He hadn't gone three steps toward looking for his mother when Louisa regretted what she had said. How could she be sure that Lawrence would choose to do what he most needed to do? She remembered one time a couple years ago when the boy had skipped school to go fishing with a couple friends. Tom and Margaret had punished him when they found out, of course, but Louisa couldn't stop thinking about what such a choice had indicated about the boy's character.

But, that was three years ago, she reminded herself. Maybe things were better now. Maybe she had been able to instill a sense of responsibility into Lawrence in the meantime.

The question was, could Louisa herself finally let go? She wanted to help the boy grow into the man she knew would make his father proud, but so much of that depended on Lawrence doing what she thought best. Could she trust the child to do that?

That evening, after he had helped her, Lawrence made his excuses and went off with Jefferson, promising to to be careful.

"You said that was okay?" Louisa asked Margaret, indicating her son's disappearing figure.

"Of course. The boy finished his chores. He can't get into too much trouble. And he needs to spread his wings sometime. He's going to have fun for once." Margaret laughed. "Boys need to let go once in a while."

"I suppose."

But the rest of the night, Louisa stewed over the decision, only finally relaxing when Lawrence had returned and crawled into bed for the night.

In the days after the wagon company left the shadow of Scott's Bluff, Louisa watched Lawrence's behavior closely. There were certainly instances when she worried about him getting enough sleep or making enough time to do the chores she requested of him, but nothing too terrible happened.

Maybe she should continue to give him space.

There was a commotion up ahead, and the wagon in front of the Hudsons slowed. Louisa frowned, wondering what was holding them up. They had left Scott's Bluff only the day before and weren't due to make their next camp for hours yet.

"I hope it's not another accident," Josie said.

Within minutes, however, they had learned. Daniel Mills, the wagon company's oldest son, was riding down the length of the train calling for the men to circle up.

"Making camp right here," he yelled out to everyone in earshot. "Grab your guns, men! There's buffalo on the horizon! Ten minutes."

"Buffalo!" Josie said with a gasp of delight. "Think of it."

Louisa did think of it. She thought about how good a

steak would be, or fresh jerky, as she led their team to the makeshift campsite the other settlers were starting to form. As with every other stop, the wagons were pulled into a circle, with the livestock in the middle.

"Well, I suppose it will be nice to have an afternoon off," Annie said, looking around at the women beginning to make camp.

"I've never once bemoaned not having a man in our party until now," Margaret said. "Lawrence is no shot at all, and I can't imagine any of these men giving up much that they worked hard for."

"Isn't this why you made friends with them?" Josie teased.

Margaret laughed. "Friends with their *wives* and mothers, also whom won't easily give up a side of meat. Oh well. We'll have a quiet afternoon at least."

"Hang that," Louisa said with determination. "I'll go."

"You?" Annie said with a gasp. "When's the last time you went hunting?"

"Well, I'll allow it's been a while, but at least I've been. More than any of you all can say."

"Maybe we should send Lawrence," Margaret was saying as Louisa strode off toward the wagons.

She climbed into the back of the wagon to hunt up the family's rifle. They hadn't had much call to use it, but it should still work just fine.

"You're serious," Annie said in amazement when Louisa emerged again.

"Of course I am. Worst case, I come back empty-handed."

"No," Josie said, stepping in front of her. "Worst

case, you die. You could get thrown from the horse or get shot or any number of things."

"I'll be fine," Louisa said, brushing past her. "Margaret, could you saddle up Carrot for me?"

Five minutes later, everything was as set as it was going to be. Margaret had hastily prepared the horse, while Louisa had gathered what weapons she thought she needed. She had little idea what to expect from such an outing, but she knew without a doubt that with this, as with everything else, her family needed her.

Louisa mounted Carrot, rested her rifle across the pommel in front of her, and rode off to the north with the men leaving for the hunt. She had every faith that she would return from the hunt with enough meat to feed the family for days.

CHAPTER TWENTY-TWO

As soon as Annie watched her oldest sister ride off with the men of the company to hunt a buffalo, she felt herself soften. It had been a good many days since they had actually had *time* on this journey—time to catch up on chores, or nap, or just time to think. Though it somehow felt unnatural, like there was something else she should be doing, Annie resolved to spend this afternoon giving herself a break. She was grateful Louisa had been so eager to go on the hunt, and Annie could stay behind without looking over her shoulder every moment.

For that was precisely what Annie wanted to do that afternoon: rest. If Louisa was there, Annie would feel compelled to continue finding chores to do, to go along with whatever her older sister decided was best for her. But right now, what Annie thought would be best for her was a quiet afternoon in the shade of the wagon. It was so seldom that she actually listened to what *she* needed that she spent a good ten minutes dithering about it.

Margaret and Josie had already set upon their preferred activities. Josie was starting up a batch of biscuits while Margaret was venturing into the prairie to gather fresh grass to dry for her mattress. Both of those things Annie should help with. There were any number of other things Annie should help with.

But Annie was tired of 'should.'

The first thing she would do was collect cool water from the nearby spring. Then, she could let her tired, calloused feet soak while she brushed out and braided her hair. Her long, golden-brown mane was a veritable rats' nest, and it would feel so good to clean up a bit.

Half an hour later, she was lugging her bucket of water back to her campsite. Annie debated whether or not to pull out the laundry tub for her soaking and if she wanted to go collect more water.

Before she could even take her shoes off, Annie was distracted by a whooping noise in the distance. Her first reaction was, of all things, to be frustrated. She had been looking forward to a quiet afternoon, maybe spend some time alone or chatting with Rebecca. A few hours of a break with nothing expected of her were precisely what her soul needed this day.

But that flash of frustration almost immediately gave way to terror.

She suddenly knew what that whooping sound was. Though she had never heard it before, it had haunted her dreams and her fears. It was the sound of the unknown and of the wild. It was the sound of her family falling under attack.

Half a breath later, Annie heard what initially sounded like thunder, a low rumbling growing ever louder. All around her, the other women seemed to slowly become aware of the same sounds that Annie was hearing. They all turned breathlessly toward the sound, just as Annie realized that the low rhythm underlying the piercing yells was the sound of dozens of horses riding hard in their direction.

"No," she said to herself.

Without a thought, Annie let her instinct be her guide. She turned on her heel and bolted toward her campsite, where Margaret was just starting on washing some of the family's laundry, and Josie was slicing up bacon to cook.

"Where's Lawrence?" Annie asked desperately.

Margaret looked up and seemed to hear the noise of the attackers for the first time. She went pale.

"Lawrence Hudson," she screamed toward the center of the circle.

"What do we do?" Josie asked in a panic.

Annie couldn't remember the last time she had found Josie without a plan. She was always even more prepared than Louisa was. Annie stared at her sister blankly for what felt like an eternity, all the while hearing the whoops and hooves thundering closer.

"Annie!" Josie screamed as she grabbed her by the shoulders and shook her.

That woke her up. Her sister needed her. Her family needed her. The entire community of emigrants needed her, never more so than in this moment when they were under attack, and nearly all the men had left the camp.

"Where's the rifle?" she asked Josie. "Louisa would not have taken both. There's another one somewhere, and we have to find it. Check the sleeping wagon, and I'll check the other."

Josie nodded brusquely and set off at a run.

"Margaret, find your son," Annie said, feeling helpless, as though she actually needed to tell her sister that. "When you do, go to the sleeping wagon. We'll be safer there. They won't come after the mattresses."

As soon as her sisters set off, Annie felt a cold wave jar her. She paused, frozen to her spot. What was she about to do? Could they survive this?

That was too long to delay. Annie forced herself into action, running to the family's supply wagon. In a few quick steps, she had climbed up and into the wagon, where boxes, sacks, and barrels were all piled around the perimeter. With a sense of dismay, Annie realized she had not been in here for weeks. She had no idea where anything was. She had just gone along with Louisa being in charge of everything, and now that she needed a rifle and ammunition, Annie had no clue where to start.

In the muted quiet inside the wagon, the sounds of the warriors approaching seemed far away. If she wanted to, she could lull herself into a sense of security; she could pretend those shouts were of rambunctious children.

"Focus, Annie," she whispered to herself.

She made fists with both her hands, clenched her teeth, and forced herself to look carefully at the space all around her. Standing in the center, as much as possible, Annie rotated slowly, eyes poring over every inch, every crevice, looking for where Louisa might have tucked the rifle.

Letting out a sob of frustration, Annie realized she

had made a full turn and still not seen it. How much longer could she stay separated from her sisters? Maybe she should grab a pan or something else heavy to use for a weapon.

She hung her head, dejected, then resolved to look once more.

As she raised her head, the first thing Annie's eyes lay on was the muzzle of the rifle. It had been wrapped in a blanket, though the end stuck out, and tucked between bags of beans near the end of the wagon. When Annie reached the spot, she was relieved to find that several boxes of ammunition had been tucked under it too.

Thank goodness. She had everything she needed and hurried back to the sleeping wagon just as the first native warriors breached the circle of wagons.

"Get in here!" Josie hissed at Annie as she climbed into the wagon. "Get down."

The three women and one boy crouched silently, petrified far back in the dark recesses of the wagon. Though they couldn't see what was happening outside the canvas cover, the yells and shots made Annie's imagination run wild.

Josie gasped. When Annie looked at her questioningly, she just pointed at her ear, and then out of the wagon, instructing her to listen.

Annie listened.

It was horse hooves. And they were drawing closer.

So close, the horse and rider must be just on the other side of the canvas.

Annie's hands shook, and she gripped the rifle tighter.

They heard the horse pause outside the opening of their wagon before continuing on to the supply wagon.

This was it. There wasn't anything they could do.

But Annie couldn't stay still and not know what was happening. She stood from where they had been hiding in the corner and crept to the opening in the canvas. Staying as out of sight as she could, she peeked through the small gap to check on their attackers.

He had reached the supply wagon, dismounted, and disappeared behind it, past where she could easily see from her vantage point.

"What is he doing?" Margaret whispered.

"Shh!" Josie admonished.

Annie was wondering the same thing. There was some part of her that knew that whatever flour or trinket the man took from them could be replaced. A side of bacon wasn't worth their lives. In spite of all this logic, she couldn't help but feel deep down that there was *something* she could do.

As they watched, the Indian came back out of their supply wagon with his hands full. Annie stared, unbelieving. She couldn't believe this possibility hadn't occurred to her.

He held Camilla. She watched as he wedged the hen under one arm and then reached into the wagon for more.

"No!" she screamed. "No!"

Annie was frantic, hysterical at the thought of losing the family's chickens. It was the one thing that really made this whole venture feel normal. The native trying to loot their supplies would not be allowed to take that from her.

As she went to leave, her sisters tried to pull her back. But she was too angry, too determined. In a fog of fury, Annie disentangled her arms from their clutches and climbed out of the wagon.

"No!" With every defiance, Annie screamed louder. She drew even closer to him, stopping some twenty feet away, but the warrior seemed unconcerned. She had no idea if the man understood English, but his condescending smirk told her he cared not at all what she said, whatever came out of her mouth.

Annie saw no other recourse. She took careful aim and fired the gun, letting out a yelp of surprise at the kickback as she did so.

Though all the Hudsons had been trained to shoot as they grew up, Annie'd had no reason to handle a gun for years. Her lack of experience showed in her shooting now. She had deliberately aimed low, hoping to injure him in the leg or foot. But by avoiding the mass of his body, she had only succeeded in missing him completely.

A small cloud of dirt kicked up a full foot behind him, where the bullet dug in.

But it was enough. It showed the looter she was serious.

He dropped Camilla, and then, deftly, swiftly, almost before Annie realized what was happening, he had ducked into the supply wagon, grabbed two sacks of what they later learned was cornmeal, and was gone again.

"No!" Annie screamed again as he darted off, but this time with far less conviction. He was already leaving. She had won. A tide had turned, and all the natives seemed to be retreating the way they came, albeit now weighed down with food, clothing, and other supplies they had stolen from the travelers.

As Annie began to catch her breath again, the feelings from all five of her senses washed over her in a wave. She realized in surprise that she was crying and used her sleeve to wipe her face, heedless of whatever dirt or dust was now streaked across her cheek. The sounds of sobs and yells floated across the circle of wagons. It was very likely that everyone had lost something; everyone had been attacked. She prayed no one had been injured, though if somehow they had been able to avoid that, it would be a miracle.

"Annie!"

She turned to see Josie running toward her after leaving the cover of the family's other wagon. The sisters threw their arms around each other, sobbing with relief.

"Are you all right?" Josie asked, pulling back and looking Annie all over. "We heard the gunshot..."

Annie shook her head, then nodded. "I'm fine. Just... scared." Her voice shook. Her hands felt numb. She needed to sit down. "Are you all right?"

Josie nodded but didn't take her eyes off her sister. "How did you do that?"

She opened her mouth to answer but didn't have any words. Shaking her head helplessly, Annie just shrugged. "I just..." She shook her head again. "I have no idea."

Josie laughed, releasing tension that had been building for the last hour. "I always knew you had it in you. We just had to come to the middle of the continent to find it."

"What do you mean?"

"Oh..." She waved a hand dismissively. "You know.

Louisa is always going on about how you couldn't say boo to a goose. Why do you think she went to such lengths to get us on this trail in the first place? She never really thought you would do it on your own."

"Really?" Annie was stunned.

"Yes, but, honey, you know how Louisa is. I wouldn't think anything of it."

Annie nodded, but she knew she would think only of this for days. Her own sister didn't believe in her.

But Josie had been right—Annie did have it in her. Even now, she wasn't quite sure where she had found the courage to walk right up to that native, but she had done it. Her. Annie Hudson had fought off a warrior, bent on stealing their supplies.

She wasn't at all certain she would be able to do it again, but for now, it was enough.

Margaret and Lawrence found them then, and Annie went through the motions of again assuring that she was all right, that she hadn't been hurt. Once her sister-in-law was convinced, she went to find anyone else who might need help.

"I'm going to go see Mrs. Martell," Margaret said, "if I can find her. I have a suspicion she might need a second pair of hands or four after that attack."

Annie watched her go, then collapsed to the dirt as the weight of what she had been through finally hit her.

CHAPTER TWENTY-THREE

Louisa felt a small smile playing on her face. Her heart was still thumping after the excitement of her day. She had done it—she had done what she had set out to do and now was returning to camp having provided for her family. The afternoon sun was slowly setting as Louisa rode back to camp. She was in the middle of the crowd of men who had all gone out to hunt the buffalo and was more than a little pleased with how she had performed. It had been a much more difficult, but also more exhilarating, adventure than she ever would have guessed. The first hurdle, however, had been to convince the men that they needed to take her seriously.

When she had appeared on her horse, rifle ready, at the outer edge of the hunters, she endured many scathing looks, muttered insults, and more than one outright condescending suggestion that she make her way back home to the comfort and safety of the camp. Louisa was prepared for this, of course, and had politely insisted that, no, she was right where she intended to be and would be joining them as they went after the buffalo herd.

Samuel Findley, the right hand of Captain George Mills, had stepped into the discussion that was quickly growing more heated.

"Now, Miss Hudson, we understand your desire, of course, but we can't be looking after you while taking down the beasts. It's just not safe. Ben will make sure you get back all right."

His oldest son, Benjamin, stood at hand, ready to escort her back.

Strangely, it was Titus Franklin—the former slave and husband of Millie—that was the first to defend Louisa. She would have thought he wouldn't want to antagonize the other men if he could at all avoid it. Maybe his wife had told him about her, or maybe he was just used to being an outsider himself, but when Samuel Findley started making noises about Louisa heading back, it was Titus who vouched for her to continue on.

Louisa had burned with indignation that her ability would be doubted, but she knew better than to open her mouth. Of course, Samuel Findley had no idea what a woman was capable of, let alone what Louisa Hudson was capable of. He had likely spent his whole life sheltering his wife and daughters and never gave them a chance. All Louisa was asking for was a chance. With Titus there to tell the other men he'd be responsible for her safety, there was grumbling, but they let her stay.

Louisa knew they were more set on going after the buffalo before it was too late than spend time fighting with her any longer, but she'd take what she could get.

"I'm mighty appreciative, Mr. Franklin," Louisa said

quietly as the two trailed the rest of the group, "but I'm perfectly capable of taking care of myself."

"I don't doubt that, Miss Hudson," he responded with a respectful nod. "That's why I told them you'd be just fine."

"But—"

"This way, they'll leave us both alone."

She caught his conspiratorial smile and smiled back. He was one of the very few men in Louisa's acquaintance who did not immediately underestimate her. She didn't quite know how to take it.

"You don't even know me."

"I know enough," he said. "My wife told me you all had chatted, and I hear other things."

"Things about me?" Louisa had hardly interacted with anyone outside her family. What kinds of stories were making the rounds?

"Nothing bad, ma'am. I apologize if I alarmed you. But it's not lost on any of these fellas that you're the woman in charge of bringing your whole family to Oregon. There's no question you must be a mighty strong woman. And that tends to make some folks uncomfortable."

She thought about that for a moment before responding. It was nice to know that she was admired by some outside her family, though she didn't really need the validation. But at the same time, she knew how contentious some men could get, especially if they felt threatened.

"Thank you," she said finally. "And thank you for vouching for me. Maybe we ought to show them what they're missing out on."

He chuckled. "Miss Hudson, don't you be getting me in trouble now."

Between the two of them—and the occasional assistance of the other men, once they saw that Louisa wouldn't be holding them back—Louisa and Titus managed just fine on the hunt. They avoided drawing unnecessary attention to themselves while still making their contribution in bringing down the beasts. Louisa was perfectly confident that she more than deserved the share of the spoils that she was bringing home.

Now, at the end of the long and exhausting day, Louisa was riding alongside many of her neighbors, chatting amiably with almost fifteen pounds of meat slung across her saddle ready to be salted and dried. She was quite proud of herself, and rightly so. When her family saw what she had done, what she was bringing home for them, their praise and admiration would be justified and more than welcome.

"Well, I guess Carrot will be glad to be back to camp," she said to Titus as they approached the wagons. "He hasn't had to hustle like that since Virginia."

Titus laughed. "Your horse's name is Carrot?"

"He likes carrots," she responded with a shrug. "His original name was Julius Caesar when we got him a few years ago, but that's a bit of a mouthful. Annie started calling him Carrot as a joke, saying he was like to turn into one for all he ate. Got into a basket of freshly picked carrots once when we weren't looking."

Titus laughed again. "Sounds like a smart fella."

"Smarter than his own good, I'd say."

But she was too distracted to continue. They had reached the farthest perimeter of the campsite, the men ahead of her were slowing. It was clear that something was wrong. She gasped when she realized there was a gap in the circle of wagons, as though they had been pulled apart, leaving the camp exposed. Where she had expected a calm quiet and the soothing smell of supper simmering over campfires, here there was a measure of chaos. She heard bustling, action, calling out and women hurrying from one side of the circle of wagons to another.

She heard the heart-wrenching wail of someone grieving.

"What happened?" she said under her breath.

But there was no one nearby to answer her. Titus merely tipped his hat in good-bye and rode off to his own wagon. The rest of the men had already broken up their group, each heading to find his family and ensure they were safe. Louisa looked around quickly, trying to ascertain what she was heading into, as she urged Carrot through the breach, across the open circle to the two Hudson wagons. A quick glance as she approached assured her that everyone seemed all right. Maybe scared or stressed, but she would have to find out more.

"What happened?" she called to her sisters as she dismounted.

Margaret darted forward and crushed Louisa in a hug. As she pulled away, she took the horse's reins from her. "We're safe," she assured Louisa. "No one got hurt."

"But what happened?" she asked again, exasperated. "Will no one tell me?"

"There was an attack," Josie said from her seat on the rear lip of the sleeping wagon. "No one got hurt, but... They must have been watching. They must have seen you all leave the camp and took their chance. It was so fast. It was…" She shook her head, remembering. "They must do this all the time, to all the companies crossing through their land."

"Who?" Louisa asked. "Indians?"

Josie nodded. Louisa was stunned. She searched her sisters' expressions, looking for some sign, some clue of what they needed next. Louisa had gone off to the hunt thinking that was the best way she could take care of her family, but it was clear she had been needed here as well.

"I never should have gone," she said. "I'm so sorry. I should have been here. I should have protected you. What was I thinking?"

"We're all fine," Margaret assured her, coming back to the circle around their campfire. "We made off a lot better than some of the other families, in fact. Mrs. Montgomery might have broken an ankle. The Mills family had at least a dozen of their cattle stolen. We just lost a few of our supplies. We're all fine, Louisa, really."

"But… how?"

Josie grinned and looked at their youngest sister before responding. "Annie, actually."

Louisa laughed in astounded relief. "No. What? Really? Annie?"

She looked at her younger sister—really looked at her—for the first time since she had returned from the hunt. Annie did have a certain glow to her, a presence that she hadn't had before.

Louisa crossed the campfire to where Annie was sitting on the lip of the wagon, outside the circle of light, outside the attention and conversation. She looked up at Louisa as she approached, seeming bashful. She certainly wasn't used to such attention.

"Did you, really?" Louisa asked. "You took care of all of them when I couldn't? When I wasn't here?"

"I only did what any of you all would have done. It's nothing special."

Louisa could see that such praise was making Annie uncomfortable, and the last thing she wanted was for her sister to regret her actions. She merely put a hand on her shoulder, squeezed lightly, then turned back to the campfire.

"Well, you'll all have to tell me all about it while I prepare the buffalo meat I brought back!"

"Buffalo!" Josie exclaimed.

With that, all discussion of Annie's heroics were set to the side temporarily. Louisa could get one of the others to give her details outside of Annie's hearing. It was just as well—Louisa needed a moment to reconcile the idea she had of her sister with this new, ferocious, determined version. Here she had thought that Annie would be nothing without her, a passive bystander, and then the first time she's away, her baby sister stepped up.

Her sisters continued chatting away, telling Louisa all about what she had missed.

"That New York girl, what's her name? Miss Harper?" Josie said. "She faced down one of them too. I'd wager we'll be hearing lots of stories of these women all finding their courage over the next few days. And so many others were injured."

Louisa looked hard at Annie, who was blushing. Who would have ever thought her baby sister had the gumption? She opened her mouth to say something, to scold her for her heedlessness, or insist that she let Louisa handle anything like that in the future. How could her sister have put herself in such danger?

But when she saw the admiration on her other sisters' faces, Louisa instead decided that maybe this moment warranted letting Annie have the spotlight.

Louisa closed her mouth again, sat back, and listened to their stories about the day.

CHAPTER TWENTY-FOUR

Annie had so been looking forward to a quiet, peaceful afternoon, but that didn't happen. Instead, she somehow found herself armed and defending their wagons from an indigenous warrior bent on stealing all their supplies. The Indian attack on the camp had turned everything into turmoil. She didn't even have a moment alone, let alone a moment of quiet.

When the Indians arrived in camp, everything had happened so fast. Now that it was all over, Annie felt like her memories deceived her. Had she really confronted one of the scariest warriors on the plains? Had she really defended the family from attack? Anyone who knew her back in Norfolk would never have guessed that quiet, accommodating Annie Hudson had such resolve in her. Yet here she was, accepting the praise and thanks of her sisters for protecting them.

When Louisa returned from the hunt, Annie realized all over again the magnitude of what she had accomplished in scaring off that attacker. Josie and Margaret would not stop talking about how brave she had been and how proud they were of her. It was far from Annie's personality to step into conflict at all, and yet she had chosen this moment to do so.

Once or twice, Annie caught an expression cross Louisa's face that made her steel herself for a fight. She was far too aware of her older sister's control over her life and over all her choices. What must Louisa be thinking?

When the stories were shared, and Louisa was more settled, the first thing Josie did was slice off several thick, fatty pieces of buffalo meat to cook for the family's dinner.

"And you two get the biggest pieces," she told Annie and Louisa. When she noticed Lawrence's dejected face, she laughed. "There is *plenty*, Lawrence. I promise you'll be fine."

"Tell us how the hunt went," Annie insisted, eager to get some of the attention off of herself.

"Well, you'll never guess," she began, before launching into an amusing tale of how she had had to argue her way to even be included on the hunt, recalling how Titus Franklin had to vouch for her until finally, the other men had just given up.

The way Louisa told the story made her sisters appreciate the meat she had brought home even more. Such effort had gone into providing for them.

The rest of the evening, Annie demurred from telling the same story again from her point of view. It was enough that she had done it; the memory of actually approaching the man and firing the gun seemed more than she could handle at the moment. She still felt anxious thinking about the danger she had been in. Fortunately, her sisters seemed to recognize this and left her alone.

More than once, Annie felt Louisa's eyes on her, but the scolding and subtle criticism that she expected never came.

"Will you let me practice shooting more now after this?" Lawrence asked his mother. "I could have done that too."

Annie had totally forgotten about the boy. In her mind, when everything was happening, he had been a child that needed to be protected. But now, hearing him ask Margaret for more ways to help, she realized it must have been so hard for him.

Lawrence was having to grow up so quickly, between his father dying and his traveling west. Annie was sure that in his mind, this attack on the camp was a ready-made opportunity for him to be a man, and he had been thwarted.

"We'll have to see, dear," Margaret said. "I don't see why not, but let's not talk about it tonight."

"When, then?"

Both Josie and Louisa looked surprised at his reaction; Louisa seemed to be debating with herself over whether or not to intervene.

"Lawrence," Margaret said, "please do not speak to me in that tone."

He looked chastened.

"I will let you practice shooting more, and I will be very proud of you when you bring home meat for supper the way your aunt did. I'm not trying to keep any of that from you. But when I say we'll talk about it later, I need you to accept that. Do you understand me?"

Annie and Josie exchanged amused smiles. Sometimes Lawrence seemed older than his years, but other times his petulance came through. He was such a good boy, and Annie always admired her sister-in-law. It must be so difficult to raise a boy of that age without his father around. But whatever she was doing seemed to be working.

Lawrence nodded grumpily but didn't argue back. He took several bites of his buffalo steak and seemed to perk up again soon.

Annie went to bed that night with her belly full and her mind in a bit of a haze. Flashes of moments flitted through her brain one after another as she tried to understand her actions. Annie was certain she wouldn't sleep a wink, but as soon as she lay back in her cot, the energy and adrenaline of the day completely drained away. The next thing she knew, Margaret was gently shaking her awake as the morning sun peeked through the flaps of canvas.

"We've got to go," she said gently as Annie rubbed her eyes. "Captain Mills wants us away from this place as soon as possible, just in case the Indians think about coming back. We thought we'd let you sleep a little, but come eat breakfast so Josie can put the dishes away."

Annie nodded blearily. She still felt like she could sleep for another day, but that was a luxury none of them could afford now. The longer the company stayed here, the more time their attackers had to return and finish the looting and ransacking they hadn't been able to do yesterday.

And Annie didn't know if she could handle such action again.

She climbed down from her cot and hastily brushed her hair before pinning it up again. The laundry she had thought to do yesterday afternoon never even got started, so she pulled on her least soiled dress and apron and climbed out of the wagon. As soon as her two feet were on the ground, Josie handed her a hot cup of coffee.

"There's a biscuit and bacon in a towel for you over there." She indicated one of the overturned buckets by the campfire. "You have time to eat, but just barely."

Before Annie could respond, her sister was off again, carrying the cleaned pan and empty buckets to their supply wagon. Margaret was herding up their animals—including the chickens Annie had saved—and Lawrence and Louisa were hitching up the oxen. Annie had only a few moments before the whole company would head out.

She chewed slowly on her breakfast as she watched the bustle all around her. After the excitement of the previous day, Annie still felt a bit foggy. She hadn't quite gotten her bearings, but she knew she was far from the most affected member of the company. She had this one brief moment, and then she would need to step into her responsibility as she had every other day.

Louisa hurried past her to collect something from the supply wagon, but on her way back to the team, she paused and looked down at where Annie was sitting on the overturned bucket.

Annie couldn't read her expression. It seemed... was gentle the right word? She was so unused to seeing such vulnerability on her oldest sister's face that she almost didn't recognize it.

"Yes?" she prompted when Louisa still said nothing.

Louisa blinked, smiled wider, and then leaned down to kiss Annie on the top of the head. The latter was so bewildered at her sister's behavior that she burst out laughing.

"What was that for?"

"You know," Louisa said. "I'm just... I'm seeing you in a new light, is all."

With that enigmatic declaration, Louisa continued on to her team of oxen and left Annie to her breakfast. She was slightly unnerved—Louisa was never demonstrative in her affection. Her idea of loving her family mostly involved arranging for the roof to be replaced or driving a team of oxen across the continent. Annie couldn't remember the last time her sister had touched her affectionately.

But she wasn't about to complain. If there was one thing this journey was teaching her, it was that all of her family could change. Nothing was fixed, not even the night sky. The stars she saw tonight would be different in six months.

With a deep breath, Annie stood up, gathered the empty bucket to tuck away in the wagon, and finished the last few bites of her breakfast. She was as ready as she would ever be for the next leg of their journey west.

Not ten minutes later, the first of the Mills' family wagons led the way out of the campsite, back onto the trail. The Findley family was not far behind and before long it was the Hudsons' turn to take their place in the long string of vehicles rolling along the trail. Annie stood back in the grass, out of the way while Louisa and Lawrence got their teams moving. As soon as they had settled into a rhythm, Annie darted on ahead until she was walking beside Louisa. The security of her oldest sister was exactly what Annie needed this day.

The company had several days of travel ahead of them, but they would soon reach Fort Laramie, a protection against more attacking forces and possibly replacing the supplies so many family members had lost.

CHAPTER TWENTY-FIVE

Louisa walked along the trail, reins in hand, next to the hulking oxen that had been her companions since they had left Independence. Their hot breath on her neck had become part of the background of her journey. Their muscles twitched under their hides as they ambled along the ruts in the dirt. She wasn't always on her own with the animals; occasionally, Annie walked beside her as she led the team of oxen westward to Fort Laramie. When alone, however, Louisa found herself thinking more and more about the courage Annie had shown in her defense of the family. She was grateful, yes, as she had told her sister. But she was also furious.

She was angry that it had happened at all, to begin with. She was angry that Annie had put herself in that position. But the more she thought about it, the more Louisa wondered if her anger should be directed at herself. Anger that she had failed or that she had left her sisters so at risk.

Louisa Hudson had never been one to look inward or

second-guess her actions. Doing so now was quite unsettling for her. She threw herself even more into work to make up for such thoughts, stuffing her feelings down where they could not distract her. There would be no shirking under her watch.

On the day following the attack, word spread of the injuries other families in the wagon company had suffered. Though Louisa was already burdened by the tasks and the people she was responsible for, she reminded herself that helping those who needed it was part of her duty as well. George Mills had said as much when they had discussed the Hudsons joining this wagon company, and she hadn't yet done her part.

But, at the same time, Louisa barely knew any of them. She had kept her head down, working hard for so long, there were few faces she recognized and even fewer names.

She did her best, though. Louisa Hudson never did anything less than her best. She had seen how Pastor Montgomery had made himself available to so many other members of the company. The man was constantly in service to others, sometimes with little thought to what he needed himself. Now with his wife laid up with a hurt ankle, Louisa worried that she wouldn't be able to manage on her own. Truth be told, now that Annie had shown what she was capable of, Louisa herself felt a bit superfluous. Maybe she needed to prove that she was still the capable, necessary member of the family that she had always thought herself to be.

So, more than once, she handed her own team over to Lawrence after the company had made camp. With her own team taken care of, she hurried to the Montgomerys' to see what help she could offer them. Seeing Mrs. Montgomery's face light up as she limped over to Louisa was a balm to her ego. She knew she was motivated by the gratitude and clear need that Mrs. Montgomery showed, but Louisa also knew that she was, in fact, doing good. It wasn't all for show or credit.

That assuaged her conscience a little bit.

But even with these little gestures, Louisa was still looking forward to their arrival at Fort Laramie. She'd be happy when they arrived, and she could buy more supplies for her family and at least prove to herself that she was needed. Captains Mills and Sullivan had already made it known that they would spend half a day at that site. Louisa felt like running the rest of the way to the fort; the hope of purchasing cotton for a new dress or more dried fruit carried her the final miles.

The days of monotony and mere survival stretched on over the miles before Fort Laramie, punctuated by the last of the buffalo meat and helping a neighbor. But soon, the small dot on the horizon began to take shape as they slowly made their way across the flat plains. Though it was difficult to see it clearly around the rest of the wagon train ahead of her, Louisa kept her eyes on the walls of the fort, counting down the hours until they reached it.

Fort Laramie had been called a crossroads of the west, a place where Americans could rest, refresh, and continue on their chosen path through the wilderness of North America. Louisa, for one, was grateful that the United States Army had purchased the fort almost two decades earlier from the original traders who had initially built it on where the Laramie and North Platte rivers meet. Though Annie's actions defending the family had made Louisa feel more secure than she would have expected, the additional protection of Army soldiers only added to that.

The attack on the wagon company could have been debilitating. The boon of the buffalo meat had been a necessary gift that lifted the spirits of everyone in the wagon company after such an attack. Some families had been so ransacked that they had picked coffee beans out of the dirt to use anyhow. The thought that they could hopefully replenish some of their foodstuffs and supplies was what pushed many of the emigrants every day. But, thanks to Annie and her quick-thinking, the Hudsons still had most of their supplies.

After days of keeping her eyes on the fort, by mid-afternoon, the first of the Sullivan-Mills wagons reached the shadow of the fort walls. Everyone seemed in a hurry to make camp, losing no time establishing their circle of wagons for the night. The faster they were settled, the more time they would have in the safety of the fort and the company of soldiers.

Annie hurried to help Louisa unhitch the team. She and Lawrence took care of the animals as Louisa climbed into the family's sleeping wagon to pull out her purse full of money that she had kept hidden. This was all of the funds she had made from the sale of her business, their house, and furniture. This was all that they had to start their new life in Oregon. Louisa would protect this money with everything she had.

She tucked it deep into her dress, climbed out of the wagon, and made her way to the supply wagon. Even with just a quick glance around, it was clear that their food stores had been quite depleted since they had left Independence. The last thing Louisa wanted to do was to have to ration the family's food; hopefully, there would be plenty at the fort to sustain them.

When she climbed out of that wagon, she called out to her sisters still setting up camp.

"I'm headed to the fort now. Any last requests before I go?" Louisa asked. "It looks like everyone I've seen walking away from the fort has had their arms full of supplies. There might be quite the selection."

"Do you think?" Josie said. "Truthfully, Lou, I'll take more of anything. Whatever they have, I can use. Lawrence has been growing so much, I worry about that boy. We just need to get more food in him."

Margaret nodded. "I have half a mind to butcher a goat one of these days."

"No, no," Louisa said. "We need to put that off as long as we can. I'm sure there will be plenty of options at the fort. I'll go now. Before too many others make their way." She smoothed down the front of her dress.

"Do you want help?" Josie asked.

Louisa shook her head. "I'll send Lawrence back for whatever I can't carry."

What she left unsaid was that she didn't want to have to balance anyone else's opinion or requests when they saw what the options were. Louisa could manage. She always had before.

She walked slowly toward the front gate of the fort, right past at least a dozen Indian huts that had been built right up to the wall. Louisa felt more curious than scared, however, as she peered at the brown faces of the women who watched her from their doorways. She spotted at least one army coat and realized that these native women must be the wives of some of the soldiers. They were nothing like the wild attackers that had stormed the emigrants' camp a few days prior. From the stories her sisters had told, Louisa was expecting less control, more of a feeling of danger.

There was a guard tower at each corner of the outer wall of the fort, with soldiers looking down across the plains, and across the visitors, with an eye out for danger. This was one of the safest places in all of the west, Louisa reckoned, and so passed by the Indian women with more of a sense of calm than she might have otherwise.

As Louisa crossed through the gate into the parade area in the center of the fort, her breath caught. After so many months of feeling cut off from the rest of humanity, here they were meeting with strangers for the first time. In addition to the members of the Sullivan-Mills company, it seemed as though at least three or four other large wagon companies had stopped at Fort Laramie that day. Everywhere she looked, Louisa saw evidence of hardship and long weeks on the trail.

Men shuffled by, stoop-shouldered, as though the weight of the world had descended upon them. Women hustled past her, eyes bright and eager as they sought the very thing to best care for their children. A small boy accidentally ran right into Louisa's legs, as he laughingly ran from another boy. More Indians, calmly walking in pairs, fur traders laden with their wares, Mexican settlers, more soldiers. Each one of these people had left a more familiar, more secure home somewhere else, seeking a new life in the American West. Maybe it was for a financial opportunity, maybe it was escaping an unfortunate life, but Louisa realized as she looked around that all of these people had that one thing in common.

And whichever it was, moving toward something better or moving away from something worse, Louisa knew that every one of them was at least as determined as she was.

She wove her way through the square to the large storeroom in the center of the fort. The doorway was crowded, but Louisa soon squeezed herself in. The room had tall ceilings, with shelves lining the walls nearly to the top. Stacks of boxes and barrels stood in organized rows through the middle of the store. Though some of the items, like jerky, had been depleted, there was still plenty of most of it.

She wandered, wide-eyed, looking at the selection the fort managed to keep stocked. Josie had drilled into her head all the supplies they had and what they were most likely to run out of. Fortunately, the Hudsons had only lost a minimal amount of their foodstuffs in the Indian attack, but there was still plenty more that they could stand to have replaced. Louisa herself needed a new dress, for starters. She had underestimated how much the fabric would wear down under the sweating and constant walking that driving the team of oxen necessitated.

While she was shopping, many other women from the Sullivan-Mills wagon company entered as well. Louisa recognized most of them by sight but realized that she knew hardly any of their names. Only Mrs. Montgomery and a couple others had Louisa even spoken to in the months since they had left Independence. She had been too busy working and instilling discipline in the rest of her family to take any part in the social aspect of their trip west.

But what else could she do, she asked herself as she chose the fabric that she needed, and she loaded up on beans that would hopefully fill Lawrence's stomach. She needed to get them all to Oregon and could worry about making friends once she got there.

After feeling like she had lost her footing by being away during the Indian attack when Louisa returned to her camp and her family with her arms full of so many of the food and other items they needed, she once again felt like herself. She once again felt like the provider and protector and guide that they all needed.

CHAPTER TWENTY-SIX

After days of exhaustion trudging across the plains following the danger and excitement of the attack on the camp, arriving at Fort Laramie felt to Annie like letting her breath out after holding it for too long. They made their camp quickly before Louisa hurried off to the traders and supplies to see what she could purchase for the rest of the journey. Her oldest sister seemed intent on hustling, getting everything done that she could squeeze into the few hours they had here before dark.

But all Annie wanted to do was rest. She wanted to climb back into the dim wagon, into bed, and pull a quilt over her. The reality of the pain, the death, and the tension of the previous couple of months was catching up with her. She felt on the verge of tears every day and had to hide it from Louisa lest she be fussed over even more.

But she couldn't rest. Not yet. There was always another chore to do, always another thing on her list that Louisa expected her to take care of.

With a sigh, she pushed down her feelings of hopelessness and went to the river to collect water. Since she hadn't gotten the laundry done on the day of the Indian attack, it *had* to be done today. Once the water was collected and heated—through several trips to the river—Annie dug through the mess in their sleeping wagon, collecting the soiled clothing and towels. Even at a glance, she could see this would be a big project.

While Louisa attended to the family's shopping, Annie set about to wash every single piece of clothing the family had. She would get it all done, and then maybe she could have a break. But first, it needed to get done. Camping along the shores of a substantial river was a resource they wouldn't have again for a week or more.

It seemed like Louisa had been gone no time at all when she returned, arms full with two bags of rice and a bolt of fabric. As she crossed directly to the supply wagon to store what she had bought, she called out to Lawrence with instructions.

"Go on back to the fort, and see Mr. Rosenfeldt at the store. He'll give you the rest of the goods I purchased. I believe they're all in a big crate together, so if you can't carry it on your own, come back and ask your friend Jefferson or Ralph or someone else to help you."

"I got it, Aunt Louisa. I'll make sure it happens."

"And if Mr. Rosenfeldt gives you any trouble, you come right back here to me."

Annie would never know what it was about Louisa's overbearing directness that finally drove her to contradict her older sister. Maybe it was just the accumulation of so much weariness, or maybe it was the sullen expression on her nephew's face at being so managed. What-ever the cause, Annie found that she couldn't let this end with Louisa dampening the boy's spirit.

"Louisa," Annie said softly, "let him handle it. He can."

Louisa looked at her in surprise before sighing. "Fine, yes, okay. Go ahead, Lawrence."

He grinned and ran off to the fort without another word.

"I didn't need you telling me how to handle Lawrence, you know," Louisa said when he had gone. "I was simply reminding him of his responsibility and his options should anything go awry."

"Well, yes, I— I know," Annie said with a stutter. "I know."

She almost stopped there. Practically every other conversation Annie had ever had with her sister would have stopped there. But something was changing in Annie, and this tiny little inconsequential disagreement could be her first step toward changing their relation-ship. If she could confront an Indian attacking them, she could certainly disagree with Louisa, she reminded herself.

"I know what you were trying to do," she said, "but maybe it's time to let him do it himself."

Louisa narrowed her eyes at her. "What do you mean? Are you saying that a thirteen-year-old child doesn't need adults looking after him? That we should just let him run wild?"

"No, of course not. No. I'm only saying that we'll never know if he is learning the lessons we're trying to teach him if we don't give him the space to show us. What does Margaret say about it?"

"I... Well..." Louisa looked thoughtful. "I don't know. I haven't asked her."

Annie felt like she had said enough. Decisions about how to raise Lawrence Hudson should be made by his mother above all else.

"And maybe you could—" Annie couldn't believe she was saying this "—could give the rest of us some space as well?" She cringed at the look of betrayal on Louisa's face, but it was too late to take it back now.

"Excuse me? Give *you* space? You mean, space like the entire great plains and western frontier?"

The sarcasm was biting, but Annie knew she should have expected it.

"I'm sorry, I didn't mean that. I just..."

"What, then? What did you mean? While I am slaving over getting everything done and focusing on every single detail to make sure we all get there safely, what *space* is it that you think you need?"

This was it. This was Annie's chance. Louisa was, or at least seemed to be, listening to her.

"I need you to trust me," she said simply.

There was a pause while Louisa tried to register her response.

"I do trust you."

"To a point. But, Louisa... I'm twenty-five years old, and you didn't even trust me to make my own decision about where I wanted to live."

There was more, goodness knew. Annie could list several dozen examples of Louisa managing her life to the smallest detail, but maybe this one big one would be enough.

The expression on Louisa's face was one of confusion, indignation, and hurt. She opened her mouth but said nothing as she retreated a couple of steps.

"I don't know what you're talking about," she said finally, before turning her back on Annie and returning to the supply wagon.

She watched her older sister go, dismayed at Louisa's reaction but also surprised at her own. Josie had told her more than once that she needed to tell Louisa more of what she thought. Annie had been telling herself that, as well. Why had now been the time that she felt like she could do it?

Annie returned to her laundry, scrubbing out the dirt that had settled in all of the seams and hems of everything they wore. Margaret and Josie had both gone off somewhere, and with Louisa rustling about in the wagon, Annie found herself alone. Humming to herself, she thought back to the unexpected kiss that Louisa had dropped on the top of her head after the attack by the native warriors. Everything had been a bit of a blur since that day; Annie hadn't let herself think about it. But now that she had been so honest with Louisa, she wondered if that day had affected her more than she realized. Or wanted to admit.

Though it had been several days, she had put off writing to Isaac about the attack on the campground. Annie knew, of course, that by the time he read the letters, she would already be safely by his side, but the idea of putting her fear into words made her procrastinate.

Maybe it was time, she thought, as she wrung out the water from one of Josie's aprons.

And now she could also tell him about standing up to her sister.

"Got any time to do some of that for me?

Annie looked up from her laundry tub to see Rebecca Tenney approach the Hudsons' camp.

She grinned. "Depends. Is your laundry as absolutely dust-choked as ours is? I thought the days that we had to walk through the mud were bad, but the thin layer of fine dust just gets everywhere."

"Oh, don't tell me that." Rebecca sat in the grass across from Annie. "I was supposed to be doing our laundry today too."

"And if you don't do it today…"

"I know. I *know*." She grinned. "Ma keeps reminding me. I almost want to go to the fort to get what I need to make more frocks rather than wash what we already have."

Annie laughed, but that reminded her of a more somber topic. "Were you able to get the supplies you needed at the fort? You lost so much."

In the days since the attack, Annie had done her best to offer comfort to the friends and neighbors who had been hit worse than they. Rebecca's family lost so much food; if they hadn't had the buffalo meat, they might have had to beg from others for charity.

Rebecca nodded. "Pa bought what he could. Quite a bit, I think, but I'm not sure he had enough money for everything that we lost. I suppose I may just have to do without sugar until we get to Oregon." She smiled cheerfully, but Annie wasn't so sure.

"I just keep reminding myself it could have been so much worse."

"I know!" Rebecca leaned forward excitedly. "You must have been so scared. I can't believe you did what you did."

"I've been thinking about that, actually." She paused in her scrubbing. "I can't really believe I did it either. It seems like I must be remembering it wrong or…"

"Or maybe you're stronger than you think," Rebecca finished for her.

"I don't know about that," she protested, though her earlier conversation with Louisa left the lingering thought.

"Or maybe it's just that traveling across the entire continent has made you stronger."

Annie looked at her friend, a small smile on her lips. "Maybe."

"And, of course," Rebecca said, standing again, "traveling across the entire continent means laundry. I had better go start mine before Ma comes looking for me."

She left Annie alone again with her thoughts. Maybe Rebecca was right. Maybe Annie was a stronger person than she had been in Virginia.

Before they left Fort Laramie, the Hudson family and everyone else in their company had to prepare for yet another long stretch of miles on the trail without any fresh water sources. Annie and Margaret filled their barrels and superfluous pots and everything they could get their hands on with water. They were getting better at this. As a matter of fact, and Annie found she could go longer without water than she would have expected.

Early the next morning, the Sullivan-Mills company set off, leaving the fort behind them.

During this part of the journey, while the company was rationing their water, Annie found that she had few responsibilities. Her usual tasks of laundry and cleaning needed to be suspended until they were sure they had enough water for food and for their thirst. It was far more important that the oxen who were hauling their life westward had the water they needed than that Josie was able to wear an apron without stains.

Maybe it was Rebecca's vote of confidence, or maybe it was her growing skill with the oxen, but Annie found herself with moments of genuine pride in herself, more than she had felt in so long.

CHAPTER TWENTY-SEVEN

Louisa Hudson didn't mind monotony. Or, rather, she told herself that she didn't mind it. And, for her, such discipline was almost as strong as the truth. She had plenty of experience placing stitch after stitch in a bride's new trousseau or a businessman's new best suit. Doing the same thing over and over again was always just forward progress, in Louisa's mind, so she never had much to complain about.

That was precisely how she viewed the Oregon Trail. After being on the move for so many weeks—more than two months now—every day felt the same. Every meal felt the same. Sewing a new dress for herself and having a slightly different color to wear was the one thing that made some days feel differently from other days.

But, all of it was forward motion. Literally, every step she took brought her closer to her goal. As long as the wagon train kept moving.

Every day, it kept moving.

Until one afternoon, Louisa was pulled out of her

thoughts when the distance between her and the Robinsons' wagon shrunk.

Louisa groaned out loud when she realized the wagon train wasn't just slowing—it was stopping. They couldn't afford to stop. They still had five miles to make that day. She sighed as her lead ox stamped her feet in the dust of the trail.

"I know," she murmured. "I'm frustrated too."

All forward progress had completely halted. There wasn't much she could do. It was either wait here or go see what had happened and help if she could. Louisa was confident enough in her own ability to assume that there was a possibility she *could* help.

"Annie," she called. Her sister was usually within earshot, if not in Louisa's line of sight. "Annie!"

A few short moments later, Annie was by her side, face flushed from running. "Are you all right?"

"I'm fine, but something ahead is not. I won't have a moment's peace if I don't do *something*."

Annie grinned. "Give me the reins."

"I knew you'd understand."

Without even a thank you, Louisa went to seek answers. She strode on, purposefully, as quickly as her short legs would take her. Passing family after family who were merely looking ahead and waiting for someone else to tell them what to do, Louisa felt like she was one of the few people in this wagon company who had any gumption left. As she walked to the side of the trail, around the halted and dejected travelers, she couldn't help but be taken aback by some of their expressions. The days of heat and little water had been hard on all of them, but Louisa seemed to have fared better than most.

Maybe she was heartier. Or maybe it was just that she had decided that the only way to get through this immense struggle was to stay positive, to keep looking forward.

She passed maybe a dozen or more wagons before finally spotting someone who looked awake, someone who looked as though they knew what was going on. Louisa approached an older woman, speaking to her husband, who still had his mules' reins wrapped around his hand.

"Did you see what happened?" Louisa asked, interrupting them. This could be a matter of survival. It did not do to stand on ceremony.

The woman nodded grimly. "One of the oxen fell."

"Fell?"

"Just collapsed, I'm afraid. Must be the heat or exhaustion. Maybe not enough water, since we've been rationing. The poor Gladwell family now have to carry on with just three."

"Goodness," Louisa said. "How terrible for them! How will they manage?"

"I suspect we'll see a chest or piece of furniture on the side of the trail, or they might be able to borrow a cow from the Mills or the Duncans or someone. Not that a cow can replace the strength of an ox, of course. They can't put too much strain on the rest of their team if they're going to make it all the way to Oregon."

"Certainly," Louisa said. She made a mental note to check on her own team more carefully. "Well, I appreciate the information. I don't want to take up any more of your time. It's just that we're way back in the train and often don't get news until long after the fact."

Her husband jumped in. "I'm Dr. Martell," he said, offering his hand to shake. "And you're Miss Louisa Hudson, are you not? You and your family have the chickens?"

Louisa smiled, pleased in spite of herself. "Why... Yes, yes I am. I'm honored that you should have heard of me. You of all people. I keep telling my sisters how lucky we are to have a doctor in our company."

"Well, my dear," he said, "let us hope that you never have reason to call me, hmmm?"

"Sisters?" his wife said. "Oh! Yes, Hudsons. Your sister Margaret has been quite kind. I remember now. No men in your party, is there?"

"Goodness," Louisa said with a self-conscious laugh. "I had no idea we were so well known."

"My dear, something tells me you are used to doing the uncommon," Mrs. Martell said with a wink. "Of course people are going to pay attention when four women are perfectly capable of taking care of themselves in circumstances when some men would fail. Frankly, I'm surprised you're not more used to it."

Louisa smiled again, gratified to have earned the praise and admiration of this couple. They were older than her by almost a generation, and there was something in their demeanor that reminded Louisa of her parents. Her sisters had been too young to remember much about their parents, but they'd had the same genial, welcoming air that the Martells did. Maybe when they all got to Oregon, Louisa could find the time to better befriend this couple.

As she made her way back to her own wagon, Louisa thought about what they had said. She had always been so adamant about taking care of her sisters that she hadn't thought about what it might mean for them to take care of themselves.

"Well?" Annie called when she saw her sister approaching. "Did you fix it?"

Louisa smiled. "Not something I can fix. But..."

"What?"

"Well, I was going to say that it made me think of something more I need to do here for us. We should possibly increase the oxen's water rations. But, also, I'm starting to wonder if maybe I should..."

Her mind whirred. The Martells thought she was uncommon, but she felt more pinned down by her responsibilities than ever. The Martells had thought all of the Hudsons could take care of themselves, but now Louisa wondered if her complete control was hampering that ability in her sisters.

The two women were silent for a long moment. Louisa kept her eyes down as she thought about what she wanted to say. There were so many things she had gone over and over in the week previous. She didn't even know where to start. Annie merely waited, but the longer she stayed silent, the less Louisa felt like she could articulate.

She couldn't think about this now. She had to consider her oxen and their safety.

"Nothing. It's nothing," she said, finally looking up at her sister. "It's not important. One of the Gladwells' oxen fell in its harness and that had to be taken care of."

"Taken care of? Is it okay?"

"It's dead, Annie. They had to drag it off the trail and let it—"

"I get it. Never mind. I don't..." She shook her head tiredly. "This just never ends, does it?"

"What do you mean?"

"The death. The sacrifice. I'm so overwhelmed all the time by what everyone has had to give up."

"The oxen?"

"For one. But also all the food and necessities that were taken by the Indians. People could starve because of it. Not to mention the children. Louisa, we've lost two children already—children have *died*—and that man, Mr. Buchanan, at the very beginning. All the loss and injuries and danger... How much more will we have to give up? I had no idea it would be like this."

She didn't know how to respond. "I'm sorry."

It seemed so inadequate.

Annie sighed. "You don't have to be sorry. This isn't your fault. I'm sorry; I shouldn't have said anything. I should have..." She thrust the reins at her sister. "I shouldn't have said anything. I'll go back and tell the others."

Before Louisa had quite realized what was happening, Annie had disappeared. She was shocked. Louisa had not realized that Annie was struggling so with the journey.

How could she have not seen it? Louisa had always prided herself on her vigilance, on how carefully she paid attention. Yet here was her sister hurting more than she had realized.

How could she have missed something so important?

These thoughts swirled in her mind as Louisa stood with her team of oxen. What else had she missed? It had never occurred to her that Annie would be capable of standing up to their attackers, either, and yet she had. She had even disagreed with Louisa just a few days ago. Who was this woman?

Was it possible that Louisa just didn't know her sister at all?

Soon the caravan began moving again, and it wasn't long before the Hudsons' wagons rolled by the body of the fallen oxen. It hadn't been dead long, but under the heat, Louisa fancied she could already smell the rot beginning. She didn't avert her eyes as the train passed; instead, she forced herself to look at the corpse. She forced herself to accept the possibility of losing one of their animals and at least make a tentative plan for how she would need to handle it. She forced herself to reckon with the fact that everything they had left Virginia with might not make it all the way to Oregon.

Looking up into the clear blue sky, Louisa saw that the vultures were already starting to circle. By the end of the day, there would be nothing left of that animal that the Gladwells had spent so much money, so much effort and investment on. Soon all that would be left would be the bleached bones after the wolves and scavengers had picked it clean.

CHAPTER TWENTY-EIGHT

Learning that the Gladwells had been the first family in the wagon company to lose one of their draft animals, Annie felt despondent. This journey to Oregon had been so hard for so many people in the wagon company, and it was only going to get worse. There was part of her that felt guilty that she was the reason the Hudsons were here in the middle of the plains at all, and she had to remind herself that Louisa had insisted.

Louisa always insisted, and Annie always went along with whatever she chose.

Though she knew that ultimately she would be glad to settle in Oregon with a new chance, Annie began to wonder if maybe going along with everything else that Louisa wanted from her was a problem. She was exhausted and frustrated, and every day seemed like more and more was being taken from her.

Soon the wagon train began to move again. The dead ox must have been taken care of. After Annie had handed the reins back to Louisa, she sought solitude walking beside the trail by herself. Once they got farther on, however, she realized this might have been a mistake. There, on the same side of the trail where she was walking, was the body of the dead ox.

Annie gasped when she realized what it was. She stopped. The wagons continued on the trail next to her. She couldn't deal with this; she couldn't walk right next to that carcass. Instead, she crossed between Lawrence's wagon and the Jamesons behind him to walk on the other side of the trail. A giant bird swooped overhead. When Annie looked up, she realized the vultures were already appearing for the rotting meat.

While passing the huge animal's discarded body was difficult enough, not ten yards farther they passed another abandoned item. Losing the animal had meant more than just the loss of an ox. It meant that the family now had to make hard choices, and in this case, sacrifices. Annie paused when she noticed something else in the grass ahead of her but recognized it quickly. Dragged to the side, not far off the trail, was a gorgeous, old cherrywood desk with intricately carved legs and a wide, smooth top.

Annie had slowed in her walking to take a closer look. It had been set carefully in the grass as though it merely waited for someone else to come back for it. She had no use for a desk. She knew perfectly well that their wagons couldn't hold such a substantial piece of furniture. It was clearly expensive and well-made. She wished that there was some way she could rescue it. It must have meant so much to the Gladwells if they had brought it all this way. How hard it must have been when they realized that their remaining team couldn't haul the wagon with it inside.

This was what the Oregon Trail did to people. Not only did they have to give up their homes and comforts of back east. Not only did they have to grapple with the deaths of friends, or illness, or the dangers of Indian attacks. Not only did they have to sometimes go to bed thirsty or sore. But on top of all that, even the small pleasures that the emigrants allowed themselves— books, well-loved houseplants, this hardwood desk— could not be saved.

It was enough to make anyone reconsider their choices.

But then, she thought, maybe it was also making her stronger.

Annie wondered if she would have ever been brave enough to attempt this journey on her own. She didn't get two steps farther before she realized that she almost certainly would not have been. If Louisa had not stepped in and decided for her, Annie would have likely spent the rest of her life in her small, shared bedroom in Norfolk, going through the motions of a life that no longer sparked any passion in her. She had long ago made peace with not finding love and with the idea that her life would never be more than it was.

She would have stayed there forever, not knowing what she was missing on the other side of the continent.

The trials of this journey were far more than she had any desire to put herself through. Annie would have never taken all these risks had she made her own decision.

But the Lord works in mysterious ways. Louisa had

chosen for her. Annie was learning more about what she was capable of, and now they were halfway through their trek to Oregon. Though there were still so many miles ahead of them, Annie had resolved to make the most of it.

Later that afternoon, Annie was again walking by herself, parallel to the trail. There was a slight slowing of the wagons, and Annie craned her neck to see ahead of them. A small dust-up was forming ahead and getting closer. Though it wasn't clear from this distance why, it seemed as though there were wagons heading toward her, toward the east, back the way they had just come.

"What is it?" Lawrence called to her.

Annie kept an eye on the wagons and made her way to her nephew. "Looks like folks going the other way. I think they call them turnarounds."

"They're going back?" he asked, amazed. "But they've already come so far."

"I know," Annie said. "So think about how hard it must be for them to keep going."

The boy stayed quiet, and neither of them did more than nod a greeting when the wagon of turnarounds reached them. It was an older couple, and to Annie's eyes, they looked exhausted. They didn't seem to be from the Sullivan-Mills wagon company, which means they were likely coming from even farther away.

The woman, older than Louisa, rode on the wagon seat and kept her eyes on the terrain in front of her. The man lifted his hat dejectedly when Annie nodded.

She hoped they made it back to where they were coming from, though goodness knew they were taking a mighty big risk turning around on their own.

Worrying about that family occupied her all day, and that night, Daniel Mills came by the Hudsons' wagon to check how they were faring.

"We're just checking," he said. "I know the sight of the turnarounds that we passed earlier in the afternoon could be a mite stressful for some folks. If you have any worries or concerns, we hope you can bring them to my father or Mr. Sullivan."

He or his father—the captain of the company—had periodically made rounds throughout the previous months. Sometimes they came to relay news of the following days' journey; sometimes they came to assuage worries or calm fears.

"Will they be okay?" Annie asked. "On their own?"

Daniel tried to offer her a carefree smile, but she could see the concern in his eyes. "Well, there are a few of them and a couple others left at Fort Laramie, as far as I know. That's not too far back. They'll likely stick together until they get to Independence. We just have to hope for the best."

After Daniel had gone on to the Jamesons' camp, Lawrence spoke up again.

"We wouldn't turn around, would we?" He stood up, eyes bright with excitement. "We're almost there, aren't we?"

"Maybe about halfway there," Josie said. "But halfway is halfway. I wouldn't want to turn around now."

"Me either," Margaret said.

Annie stayed quiet. The thought of heading back to Virginia after all they had been through felt impossible. But the thought that they were not even halfway to Oregon seemed even more impossible.

Lawrence took a couple steps back.

"Are you going somewhere, young man?" Margaret asked in a teasing tone.

"Oh, yes, sorry. I..." He ran a hand through his hair and looked over his shoulder into the darkness that was the center of the wagon circle. "I was wondering if I could go with Ralph tonight. I guess the boys in the Davis family are having a card game or... I don't know."

"The Davis boys?" Margaret frowned. "Well, I suppose that's not a problem. You won't be gambling, will you? And you'll stay far away from the Schmidt card game, won't you?"

"Yep!" He grinned cheerfully. "I don't got any money to gamble, and I know I'd probably lose." He laughed. "It's just a little fun."

"Be back before ten," she said.

Annie watched him dart into the darkness. After the rough year following his father's death, it was nice to see Lawrence making friends so easily. She had just been thinking how happy he seemed when Louisa spoke up.

"Are you sure that's a good idea, Margaret? We need the boy to be well-rested before tomorrow."

After all this time, all the disagreements, Annie couldn't believe that Louisa was still trying to discipline someone else's son.

Margaret didn't rise to take the bait. Instead, she stood herself, brushed the dirt off her dress, and started toward the sleeping wagon.

"Yes, rest does sound mighty good. I think I'll turn in for the night. You all will keep it down for me, won't you?"

Louisa frowned while Annie and Josie shared smirks.

After they heard Margaret settle into her cot, Louisa leaned forward to her sisters. "How is that boy ever going to learn discipline if he keeps going out at all hours? What if he turns out like those turnarounds, giving up at the slightest thing because his mother let him get away with all sorts of nonsense when he was this age?"

Annie peered at her over the campfire. "You're likening a boy spending time with his friends to the difficult choice of abandoning the Oregon Trail after who knows what hardships?"

"Well, no, of course, those are different things. But it seems to me there's a straight line from one behavior to another."

Annie could not believe what she was hearing. She stood and took a couple of steps toward the sleeping wagon. "Is there?"

She had retreated before Louisa answered. After everything they had been through, after all Annie had endured, another disagreement with her sister would be too much. She climbed into the dark wagon and got ready for bed as quietly as she could.

"I heard what you said out there," Margaret whispered.

"You're not asleep?" It was too dark in the wagon for Annie to see.

"Not yet. But I wanted to thank you. I know how Louisa can be. You didn't have to say anything."

"I know. And back in Virginia, I might not have." Annie climbed up into her cot. The dried grass in the mattress rustled as she settled herself. "I'm trying to get better at it."

"Things are different out here, aren't they?" Margaret offered.

Annie looked through the narrow gap in the canvas opening at the end of the wagon. The bright summer stars shone fiercely in the night sky.

"Things are different," she agreed, "and yet so much seems the same."

CHAPTER TWENTY-NINE

There it was. Louisa was sure of it.

After a long morning of guiding the enormous animals pulling their wagon, Louisa finally spotted the thing she had been seeking for more than a day. There was a small, dark point that they were headed to, barely noticeable on the horizon. It was impossible to tell what it was from here, but if she kept putting one foot in front of the other, she would be rewarded with her destination.

Finally.

It was only that morning, in fact, that Josie had recited facts to them from her guidebook. As she handed around cups of hot coffee to her sisters, Louisa could see that she was bubbling up with excitement.

"Independence Rock, ladies," Josie said. "Any day now, it should show up on the horizon."

"A rock?" Annie asked with a delicate frown.

"Yes! Like Courthouse Rock was back a couple weeks. I told you about this. It's just called a rock, but really it's more of a granite... mountain. Bigger than a building. It's so big, actually, that we should be able to see it for at least a couple days before we even reach it."

"Really?" Louisa said. "Why is it called Independence Rock?"

"Well," Josie said, returning to her cast iron pan. The bacon was almost done. "It's called that because we're supposed to reach it by Independence Day. It's about the halfway mark."

"Today's Independence Day," Lawrence said. "Isn't it?"

Louisa nodded. "So we're a few days behind."

"A few days behind is nothing," Josie assured them. "We'll make up the miles before September without a problem."

Louisa wasn't so sure. The wagon company had been so late in leaving their very first campsite outside of Independence, not to mention all the other unscheduled stops they'd had to make since.

Once Independence Rock was clearly ahead of them, George Mills pushed the company hard. They left camp early and settled back in late. Once, in fact, Josie had to make them all supper after dark, muttering in frustration that she couldn't find what she needed in the wagon. But the captains were intent on making it to Independence Rock as close to on time as they could manage. It was a punishing pace, and by the time they had reached Independence Rock, all were more than ready to rest in the glorious surroundings.

Louisa had never fancied herself that concerned with the natural world. Of course, she believed it was God's perfect creation and all that. But beyond that, she rarely gave it a thought. Anything outside her family and work barely warranted a thought. But now, the final morning as they drew ever closer, she understood a bit more what writers like Emerson were thinking. The enormous granite towered over the plains and filled her vision with every step she took.

By early afternoon the wagon company finally reached the foot of the behemoth and drew the wagons into a protective circle. The company would be making camp for the rest of the day and finally get a break after so many long days on the trail. All the humans and animals could use a rest, of course. But even if not, it seemed impossible to just pass by Independence Rock without stopping. It pulled them all in.

As Louisa unhitched her team for the evening, she noticed Lawrence rushing through his own chores. He was hurrying so much, in fact, that he tripped over the wagon wheel in his haste. Louisa chuckled. She had been impressed at his maturity and responsibility as they had traveled west, but then he went and fell in the dirt because he was in a rush.

She didn't like him going around with that Davis boy, which was no doubt the reason he was hurrying around. She had been awake when she heard him come back to the campsite a few nights ago—it had been well after ten, in fact. But all had seemed fine the following morning. As far as Louisa knew, there had been no shenanigans or shirking of his duties since then, so she hadn't mentioned the late night to Margaret.

"Mother," Lawrence called, as he chained the wheels of the wagons together to secure the circle.

"I think she's gone to the Van Andas' to check on the

missus," Louisa said, pointing in the direction of their campsite.

"Oh. Okay. I guess I'll go find her then."

"Is there something you need? You know I can help too."

Lawrence lit up. "Yes! Since we're here the rest of the day, I was going to go see what Ralph is doing again."

"I don't think that's a good idea."

"But, why? I took care of the animals, and I finished sharpening the ax like you wanted me to do. Aunt Josie said I could help her move the barrels in the supply wagon tomorrow morning before we leave."

Louisa racked her brain for another task to assign him. The thought of him gallivanting all over the camp galled her.

"That may be," she said, trying another tack, "but you don't want to interrupt your mother when she is helping out one of our neighbors in need, do you?"

"I think it will be fine." He started off toward that camp. "You can tell her, right? I don't want to make Ralph wait for me."

Louisa didn't have a chance to call him back before she was surprised by the arrival of a visitor to their camp. Mrs. Franklin had tentatively made her way closer and closer to the Hudson wagons, waiting to be noticed.

"I... well... Hello," Louisa said, flustered. "Can I help you?"

She cringed at how formal that sounded, how unneighborly. This woman was virtually the only person in the entire company who ever sought her out; Louisa could at least be more welcoming.

"I'm sorry," she began again. "This is such an unexpected surprise. Won't you have a seat?"

There, Louisa thought. That's somewhat better. All the same, she wished for one of her other sisters, any of them.

But Mrs. Franklin was smiling. Louisa laughed at her own awkwardness as she gestured to the only seat she had available—an upturned empty bucket.

"I didn't mean to startle you," Mrs. Franklin said as she sat gingerly.

"Oh, no, you didn't."

That earned her a skeptical look.

"Well, yes, all right, I was a little startled, but mostly because my mind was elsewhere. I was just wondering how the rest of my family was putting in their afternoon. What brings you here?"

"I wanted..." Mrs. Franklin began. She twisted her hands in her lap. "Titus told me all about your afternoon hunting the buffalo, and I got to thinking about the last time you and I talked, and I didn't... Well, I'm sorry if I was short with you that day that we met out in the grass." She looked down at her hands.

Louisa racked her brain for her memory of that day. She had been focused on gathering buffalo chips for fuel and had come across Mrs. Franklin doing the same.

"To be honest, Mrs. Franklin," she said, finally, with a small chuckle, "it is so much more often that I am short with other people that it didn't occur to me to be offended by anything you said or did."

"Please, call me Millie." She grinned. "I am so pleased to hear that. You have to understand this... Even just talking to white folks as a freed person is not easy to get used to."

"Is that why we rarely see you? It seems that you and your husband keep to yourself most of the time."

She nodded. "It's just easier. Maybe after we get to Oregon, it will be different, knowing we're in the same place, with the same neighbors for years. But it's difficult to risk after... Well, after some of the treatment that we received back in Atlanta."

"Of course, I'm not one to be gadding about and being social either. It always seems like there is so much to do, don't you find? Especially as there are so many in my family."

Millie shrugged. "Maybe it's different since it's just me and Titus, but I guess I just never feel that way. Back when we were the only ones taking care of the master's house, it sure felt like a lot. There was everything he told us to do, of course, but then a whole 'nother bunch of things that needed to get done whether he specifically said so or not. That man never once reminded me to change his sheets, but I did it week after week." She shook her head, lost in thought.

"And being wholly in charge of yourselves is different?"

Millie looked at her sharply.

"I'd say being free is quite different from being a slave, yes."

"No, that's not what I mean," Louisa said, fumbling her words. "Or, maybe that's part of what I mean. I don't understand, I'm sure."

Millie kept her lips pursed.

"I guess I'm just worrying over something myself and

dragging your life in to make it make sense," Louisa said, finally. "I don't mean any offense."

Millie seemed to thaw. "Worrying can do that."

"I'm just doing my best. I think. I don't know anymore."

"We're all doing our best. Me. You. Your family. The captains. Everyone."

Louisa nodded, thinking again about how Annie had changed over the preceding weeks.

"Will you all be coming to Pastor Montgomery's church service this evening?" Millie said as she stood to go.

"I'll have to see," Louisa said, standing as well. "But it was mighty kind of you to come by. I…"

Louisa paused, and Millie looked at her questioningly. Something had happened; Louisa felt an undeniable urge to apologize to this woman.

"Millie. Mrs. Franklin," she said. "I'm… I'm sorry for what I said. For, well, you know. I'm… I think I'm learning. At my age."

She laughed awkwardly, but Millie laughed with her.

After the other woman had left, Louisa spent a long time looking up at Independence Rock, thinking about her mistakes.

CHAPTER THIRTY

As soon as the wagon company had made camp at Independence Rock, Annie felt a burst of energy. She couldn't believe they were finally so far on the trail. She looked around at the camp, up to the top of the monumental stone. This was almost halfway to Oregon. There was still a long way ahead, but from every day moving forward, they would be closer and closer to their destination.

She had spent so long being worn down and exhausted from all they had already been through that this sudden enthusiasm felt like a gift, and she didn't want to waste it.

After checking with her sisters more than once to ensure none of them needed her help, Annie found herself with a few hours with absolutely nothing to do. Time stretched out ahead of her without structure or obligations. She couldn't remember the last time that had occurred. Usually, Louisa always had a list (and another list in reserve) of things that needed to be done.

Looking up at the monument that had guided their path for the last several days, Annie decided the best way to spend her free time would be to explore. She wanted a closer look; she wanted to see how far they had come.

Annie walked toward the granite dominating the skyline, noticing that she was not the only one who had the same idea. They followed the somewhat established path to the foot of Independence Rock, across the packed dirt that spread out around the site. A trio of young men almost knocked into her as they ran past. Further up ahead, she could spot other emigrants in pairs and groups, walking calmly up to the rock wall. It was such an exciting day, Annie wondered that everyone hadn't made the time to visit the monument.

Where the path met the stone, it was clear there were a couple different ways to climb to the very top. It soared above her, stretching dozens of feet into the sky. Annie put her hand on the cool, timeless rock and looked up. From this angle, it seemed like a nearly vertical ascent. But, when she checked either side of her, she realized there must be an easier way up.

Annie walked along the perimeter of the base, slowly grazing her fingertips on the cold rock. After several yards, she found an incline that was more accessible. Holding the hem of her dress up so she didn't trip, she took her first step, hoisting herself onto the side of the stone.

She paused, uncertain of precisely how to climb up without hurting herself.

She looked to the top to see more than a dozen people—mostly younger than her—in clusters on the crown of Independence Rock. If they had all gotten up there, she could too. All it took was a little determination and focus. And maybe a bit of that gumption that she seemed to have developed between Norfolk and here. She could do this.

With that fortifying thought, Annie leaned forward and put her hand out to spread her weight across the slant of the rock. It would be difficult still holding her dress in one hand, but she could do it. One foot in front of the other, not unlike what Louisa kept saying about getting to Oregon, she thought.

It seemed like only a few minutes before Annie had reached the top.

"Here," she heard, at the same time she saw a hand thrust in front of her face. "Let me help."

She gratefully took the proffered hand and let herself be pulled to a standing position at the top of Independence Rock. It was Arthur Davis, the older brother of one of Lawrence's friends.

"You did that all on your own? I'm impressed. Are you all right now?"

"I am. Thank you." She was breathing a little heavily from her climb but quickly caught her breath.

He waved off her thanks before returning to his circle of friends and leaving her alone.

All around her, she heard laughter and excited chatter from the young people who had also made the climb. Snippets of teasing and outbursts of wonder floated through the air around her. But Annie wanted solitude. She wanted to be able to soak in this moment on her own.

The top of the rock spread out all around her.

Though it looked almost level from the ground, once she was up here she noticed the dips and cracks that centuries of weather had wrought. It was more difficult to keep her balance than she had expected, but she found that as long as she didn't venture too far from the center, she was fine.

Annie took a deep breath, breathing in the scent of fresh grass that was carried on the light breeze. As she looked toward the west, toward Oregon, she realized she could see much farther than she would have thought possible. Far ahead, maybe a day's travel, a small wagon train cut through the landscape. Beyond that, Annie saw what looked to be a river, with low mountains even farther past.

It was beautiful.

And it was her future.

This was what she wanted. She knew that now. Annie wished she had known as much when she was back in Virginia. She wished that the idea of going to Oregon had been truly hers. She wanted to claim this. She wanted to own this choice and this path for her future. Now she owed that all to Louisa.

Clearly, Annie realized, Josie was right. Though it didn't come naturally to her, Annie knew she needed to try harder to speak up when she had an opinion. It had always been so much easier to just go along with the others. As this journey had progressed, she realized how much happier she was when she was able to speak up.

This was where she was going. And this was who she wanted to be when she arrived in Oregon. She wasn't quite sure what the next step was. She only knew that claiming her confidence like that would be a daily practice. With every choice she had, she could take the braver option instead of the apathetic one. She still had so much of her life ahead of her and could really make it something special.

Annie took a deep breath. Pulling off her bonnet, she lifted her face to the afternoon sun as she faced the west and her future in Oregon. It wouldn't be easy, but she could do this. She carefully lowered herself to the surface of the rock and sat by herself, facing the horizon as she thought over her future.

After another hour, the sun had lowered toward the horizon, and Annie was eager to get back. To get started on her life. With a wide smile, she returned the way she came, carefully climbing back down from Independence Rock. It wasn't very far at all, but in her heart, she felt as though she had just traversed miles.

When Annie returned to her own wagon, Josie was mixing a batch of biscuits.

"Goodness, your face is all pink. Where have you been?"

"I climbed to the top of the rock and took off my bonnet."

"Why on earth would you do a thing like that?"

She shrugged. "It just felt like what I needed to do," she said simply.

"All right," Josie said with a smile. "You seem happy, so I won't argue with you. I'm glad you're back, though. We'll have supper pretty soon. Could you get me some water?"

"A little early, isn't it?" Annie asked as she fetched the bucket.

"Oh, well, apparently Pastor Montgomery is having a

church service this evening. At the foot of Independence Rock, I think. Louisa told me."

"Did he come by this afternoon?"

Josie looked at Louisa, who was busy rubbing oil into Carrot's saddle. Annie followed her gaze questioningly.

"No, um... Mrs. Franklin came and told me."

"Is she a particular friend of yours now?"

"I'm not sure I would say that. But I do think that she needs some friends. To be honest, I think she's afraid of talking to many of us. She and her husband seem to keep mostly to themselves."

To Annie, this felt like the first test of her new resolve, like an opportunity to speak her mind about Louisa making friends with a former slave. She realized, however, that she didn't know what she thought about such a thing. The woman seemed perfectly nice, and if she wasn't breaking the law or hurting someone...

Maybe this new Annie would be harder to implement than she had expected.

But, she reminded herself, daily practice.

"Did you see where Lawrence has gotten off to?" Margaret asked as she came to the campfire from the east. She wiped her hands on her apron as she looked around for her son.

"I did," Louisa spoke up. "Off with that boy Ralph again."

Margaret sighed. "Oh, well. I suppose I've got to let him stretch his wings sometime. He finished all his chores, didn't he?"

"Well, yes, but I don't know that I like him just running off without telling you."

"But he told you."

Louisa blinked several times in surprise.

Annie watched the conversation with interest. The old Louisa would have fussed and fretted, pointing out all the ways the boy was not meeting her expectations, but something had changed in the previous week or so. It was small, and it was subtle, but Annie had noticed it.

CHAPTER THIRTY-ONE

Louisa took a deep breath. She sat in the grass by her campfire and leaned back to look up at the purple and orange sunset sky. She didn't mind being left alone while all of her sisters went to Pastor Montgomery's church service. In fact, she rather preferred it. The quiet was nice. Being in charge every day wore on a person. Having their home space all to herself meant at least a couple of hours of not having to worry about other people.

And there were always other people to worry about. There was her family, of course, her sisters and nephew who deserved the very best, but there was also every other member of the wagon company, the widows, the children, the men who need to stand guard each night. Everywhere she turned, Louisa found another person who maybe she could help or guide or do something for.

Even now, she could still hear the laughter and chatter carrying down from the top of Independence Rock. There must have been a couple dozen or more people that climbed to the top that afternoon, and

Louisa had worried over each and every one of them. They could fall or get stuck or get too cold to help themselves. What were they thinking putting themselves in such danger? Worrying and managing like this was how she had spent her entire life. These couple hours of reprieve were nice.

As she reveled in the relative solitude, the sound of determined footsteps approached her camp. Louisa looked up, wondering who other than her had decided not to attend Pastor Montgomery's church service. The sun had just set behind Independence Rock, so his face was mostly shaded, but Louisa would recognize that gangly youth anywhere.

"Lawrence," she said. "Goodness, what are you doing here? I didn't think we'd see you until late."

She had tried to keep the accusing tone out of her voice. Though she was still irritated that he had left in spite of her protests earlier, the fact that he was back now gave her comfort.

He sat in the dead grass on the other side of the campfire and sighed.

In this light, Lawrence looked so much older than his thirteen years. The previous months of guiding an entire team of oxen, mostly on his own, had broadened his shoulders and filled out his muscles in a way that their comfortable life back in Norfolk would never have. She imagined how ready he would be for the work ahead of him in Oregon. In a flash, images of Lawrence getting older, getting married, taking care of his spinster aunt as she aged flooded her mind.

He was becoming quite the young man.

He would be fourteen in just a few weeks, she realized. When his father had been fourteen, he had already started saving money for his first cow. He had that cow for several years and made money every week selling cream and butter to some neighbors. Tom had made a plan and stuck to it, all while Louisa hadn't even started her hope chest. Maybe Lawrence wasn't the child she had been treating him as any longer.

"Are you hungry?" she tried, after he still hadn't spoken for a couple minutes.

He sighed again and grinned. "Always."

Louisa pulled herself to her feet. As she passed her nephew, she rested her hand on the top of his head. She was rarely one for affectionate demonstrations, but he needed to know.

"You can tell me about it. If you want. Whatever happened that brought you back early. But you don't have to. I..." She cleared her throat. "I love you, either way."

Without waiting for his response, she made her way to the supply wagon to dig out some supper for the boy. Heaven knew where he had been when they were all eating supper, but Louisa realized it didn't matter. He was growing up, and she had to learn to trust him.

It took her a few minutes in the dim light, but Louisa soon found what she had been looking for and made her way back to the fire.

"It's cold." She handed Lawrence the meal. Josie had made extra of everything and then wrapped two biscuits and two thick pieces of bacon several times in a towel to keep for her nephew. "Just made tonight, though."

"Thank you," he said as he unwrapped it. "I didn't eat. We didn't— I should have come back earlier."

As he took the biggest bite he could manage, Louisa asked, "Are you sure you don't want to tell me?"

"Um..." he mumbled around a mouthful of biscuit.

"What if I promise not to get mad?" she said in a teasing tone.

He laughed, then started coughing, which in turn made Louisa laugh.

"Let me get you some water too."

In another minute, his coughs subsided, and she handed him a tin cup full of cool water.

"Are you all right?"

He nodded, cleared his throat, and drank a little more water.

"You ready to tell me what happened?"

"How come you're not with my mother?"

Louisa thought about that question, how to word her answer. "I think I just needed some alone time."

"Yeah, me too. I came back now because I kind of thought everyone would be gone. I could, I don't know, go to bed early and not have to answer any questions."

"Well," she said, keeping her voice even, "what is it you didn't want to answer questions about?"

"Aunt Louisa. You know."

"Where you went? What you did?"

"Yes, but I didn't even do it. I told Ralph I didn't want to. I came home instead."

"Then why wouldn't you want to tell us that?"

"I thought you'd be mad," he admitted. "That I had been there at all."

Louisa took a long slow breath and looked up to where the sky was turning shades of darker purple as the sun set for the night. Though the light was fading, she could still make out the silhouettes of two people on the very top of Independence Rock. Louisa would never have taken such risks herself. Now that she had seen that Annie could be brave, however, now that she had met Mrs. Franklin and seen how happy she was in this new life, Louisa was learning that maybe there were other options than simply immaculate managing. She couldn't control everything, it seemed. Maybe taking risks, and making mistakes, was just as valid as her way. Lawrence himself had proved that it couldn't be all bad.

Now that Lawrence had his supper and water, Louisa sat back down at the campfire with him.

"I know why you might think that," she said gently. "I know I tend to... have strong opinions."

She noticed him try to hide his grin, ducking his face down.

"You know it's just because I want the best for you, right?"

"I know."

"I keep thinking if I can protect you from bad decisions or other people's mistakes, then that will be all you need. But I think maybe you can protect yourself just as well."

"Okay," he said. He seemed embarrassed by the praise.

"So, does that mean you'll tell me what happened today?"

He sighed. "Yeah, I guess. I mean, I should probably tell Mother anyway. I told you a few days ago that the Davis boys were playing cards?"

She nodded, immediately suspicious but kept her thoughts to herself.

"We did. That day at least. That's what I thought we were going to do again today. But after just one hand, they started betting with real money. And I didn't— I don't have any money, but even if I did, that's not how I would spend it. Ralph's older brother Gus tried to give me credit, but, well, I know how Jefferson Carter got in trouble with that, so I said no."

"I'm proud of you for that. That must have been hard." Inside she was fuming that these young men would prey on her nephew, but she valiantly fought to keep that emotion to herself.

"It was," he said urgently. "They didn't like me saying no, and they kept pushing. And then one of Gus's friends, Clark Whitson, brought out a bottle of whiskey, and they started passing that around, and I knew what Mother would say about that. So that's when I left."

Louisa looked at the boy in amazement. No, not boy, she thought. Lawrence had displayed the integrity of a young man.

"I... I don't know what to say," she stammered, completely taken aback by the maturity he had shown.

"I knew you would be mad," he said miserably. He took another bite of his supper, chewing slowly as he avoided her eyes.

"Lawrence, look at me."

The sun had fully set now, and the two sat in the warm glow of the campfire. He raised his eyes to her.

"I'm not mad."

He seemed surprised, and really, she couldn't blame him.

"In fact, I'm impressed by your behavior. I didn't... I don't think I realized how much you've grown up over all these months. I should have seen it earlier. But I was too focused on myself. I made a mistake. And just so you know, I might make more in the future, but I will do my best. As long as you're not mad at me either."

"What's this?"

Margaret seemed to loom out of the darkness that surrounded their campfire. Louisa couldn't say how long she had been standing there or how much she had heard. She seemed to be more concerned than anything else.

"Why would you be mad at your aunt, Lawrence?"

Annie and Josie both hovered behind her, listening to the conversation.

"How was church?" Louisa asked.

"Good. Wonderful. Such a nice change, really," Margaret said with a small laugh. "But really, are you all talking about anything I should know?"

"I did something foolish today, Mother," Lawrence said. "I shouldn't have even been there."

Louisa wanted nothing more than to interrupt him, protect him from his mother, and reassure Margaret that she had everything in hand. But she was slowly learning that not only was that not always the case, but also it should not be. Though it took a bit of willpower, Louisa sat quietly for once and listened while Lawrence told his own story about his night.

CHAPTER THIRTY-TWO

Annie was still elated by her afternoon atop Independence Rock when she attended Pastor Montgomery's church service with her sisters. The unity and feelings of community that permeated the small group of worshipers delighted her even more. Annie kept the treasure of her afternoon to herself for the time being. It seemed like too big of a jewel to share with anyone yet. She was feeling more confident than she had in years—maybe ever.

When they had returned from the church service, she listened to Lawrence confessing to how he had spent his afternoon and was proud of him all over again.

But Annie didn't want to stay up and talk about it any longer. She went to bed early and lay in her cot, thinking over her next steps. They still had so far to go before they got to Oregon, but somehow this change in her made her feel like it was far easier than it had been a few days ago.

The following morning, not long after sunrise, the

Sullivan-Mills wagon train left Independence Rock to continue west. Their next target destination would be Pacific Springs. It would be the next time they could stop for longer than overnight, though they would have to push for nearly fifteen miles each day in order to reach it.

Each day they woke up early and traveled westward as fast as they could. Each night they collapsed into bed, wishing for the next time they could take a longer break.

Those were difficult days on the trail, but Annie's mind was elsewhere.

After her revelation atop the enormous monument, Annie couldn't stop thinking about all the ways that things could be different for her, how they could be better. She would need to figure out what it was that she really wanted if she was going to be sure to strive for it.

When they finally reached the new camp, the Hudsons lost no time settling in for a long afternoon. Margaret, Josie, and Louisa all found tasks to take them away from the campsite, while Annie stayed behind to brush down and take care of the oxen. The poor creatures were working so hard.

It wasn't long after they made camp at Pacific Springs that Ralph Davis came by to see if Lawrence was free. Annie didn't intentionally eavesdrop, but she couldn't help but overhear when the conversation grew heated.

"But why?" Ralph said. "This is stupid. You'll have so much more fun with me."

"Not today," Lawrence responded. "I told you. I have other things to do. Not today."

"Fine. But don't complain to me when you're stuck with a bunch of old ladies instead of having fun with us."

After the other boy had left, Annie approached her nephew.

"Is everything okay?"

He looked up in surprise. "Oh. Yeah. He just... It's okay."

"You're not going to spend the afternoon with Ralph?" Annie asked in surprise. "I thought you two were thick as thieves."

"Nope. Not now, at least. I have an arithmetic lesson with Miss Atkins in an hour, and I want to be ready for that. I still have to move Camilla and the others, too, first."

"You're giving up your free time for mathematics? I'm surprised."

"The fun can wait, I reckon," he said, sounding more like an adult than Annie thought she ever had herself. "My future is more important."

"Goodness, Lawrence, where did this all come from?"

"What do you mean?"

"Oh, nothing. Never mind. I'm just proud of you, is all."

He seemed genuinely confused. Annie didn't want to hurt his feelings by implying she didn't have high expectations of him, so she let it drop. After he went to settle the chickens under the wagon for the afternoon, Annie tried to put her thoughts into real words.

Whatever else the boy had done since they left Virginia, it was clear he was growing into a capable, responsible young man. And Annie knew it was not due to any of her own influence. Here was Lawrence, able to clearly tell his friend that he would rather learn math than play, compared to Annie, who couldn't manage to tell her own sister when she wanted to finish her coffee before she did the laundry.

When Louisa returned to camp that afternoon, Annie felt like she was bursting to tell someone.

"Louisa!" she exclaimed. "You'll never guess. Did you know that Lawrence has chosen to take another lesson with Miss Atkins rather than play with his friends?"

"Did he?" Louisa raised her eyebrows in mild surprise. As she spoke, she passed Annie to the sleeping wagon, hanging up her rifle on the hook just inside the opening. "That's interesting. Good for him."

"Did you have anything to do with this?"

Louisa laughed. "Me? Goodness no. You had better believe I would take credit for that if I had."

"True," Annie mused.

"Well, now. I see." Louisa laughed again.

"No, you understand. It's just... I'm just really impressed by him, is all. He's growing up so much."

"I've been noticing the same thing, truthfully. I never would have guessed it, but it seems as though giving him the freedom to make mistakes has nudged him into making the right decision."

Annie's eyes opened wide. "You think so? I would have guessed it was that you kept him under such strict discipline that he managed to see its value."

Louisa laughed. "I don't know about that."

"I guess we're just a good team," Annie said.

"Of course we are." Louisa turned to her sister,

offering her full attention for the first time. "Also with his mother, I suppose."

Annie laughed. "I suppose."

Louisa took a deep breath; her expression turned serious.

"We're a good team, I think," she repeated.

They were interrupted by a visitor. Annie looked up to see the company captain's wife standing patiently, waiting to be noticed.

"Why, Mrs. Mills!" Louisa exclaimed. "What a lovely surprise. Is there something we can do for you?"

"Thank you, Miss Hudson. I just came by to check again…" she said before turning to Annie. "Miss Hudson, have you given any more thought to my request?"

"Oh, Mrs. Mills, hello, yes, I mean, no. No, I haven't; I'm so sorry." Annie felt like she was rambling. She had completely forgotten the original request. "I guess I'm just not clear why you would need my help for that. It's my sister Louisa who is the seamstress after all."

Louisa nodded helpfully.

"No, thank you." She smiled at them both. "No, I think you're exactly what we need. It's more of a social, hosting role, after all. I need someone just like you. Of course, there's still time for you to decide. It's likely we won't have time for another week or so yet. You can come by my wagon any time to let me know. Now, if you ladies will excuse me, I need to go see Dr. Martell."

"Of course, yes, thank you."

"What was that about?" Louisa asked quietly as the woman walked away.

"She asked me to preside over a quilting circle weeks

ago. Though I cannot for the life of me understand why she would want *me* to do that."

"Or when she plans to hold a quilting circle while we're all doing everything just to survive this whole journey."

"I know. That's why... Well, this is the second time she's asked me. I haven't said yes yet."

Louisa looked at her carefully. "Is this what you want?"

Annie was taken aback for a brief moment. "What I want?" she repeated.

She had no idea what she wanted. But wasn't this precisely what she had promised herself she would pay attention to? Annie had vowed to be more like Louisa, to be more clear on what she wanted and do something about it.

Even if it was hard. Even if it meant saying no to someone as important as June Mills.

"What would you do?" she asked her sister.

"Me?" Louisa mused. "Well, assuming I didn't have a wagon to drive and assuming I was as charming and welcoming as you are," Annie blushed, "I still don't think I would do it. Maybe there's more to it that she hasn't told you, but I don't understand how that is an efficient or useful way for any of us to spend our time."

Annie was nodding with everything Louisa said. "Right, yes, that's what I thought too."

"So you're going to tell her no?"

Annie took a deep breath and imagined herself actually saying those words to Mrs. Mills. "Probably. I think so. Maybe."

"I can't decide for you," Louisa said, then offered

Annie a mock-shocked expression. "I can't believe I just said that."

Annie couldn't help but laugh. Who was this new sister of hers, making light of her own peculiarities and not insisting on taking care of it for Annie?

"But let me know what you eventually decide," Louisa continued.

With that, she squeezed Annie's arm lightly and went to check on the animals.

Annie had the rest of the afternoon to think over what she was going to do, but she had to do it while also completing all the chores she was responsible for. This would be the final camp with good, drinkable water for another long stretch, and preparations had to be made. The emigrants had to collect as much water as they could carry before they left Pacific Springs. They filled every bucket, pot, and canteen. Annie, Josie, and Lawrence went back and forth between the spring and the camp to bring as much water as they could. Annie made herself drink so much water she felt like she would burst.

Before turning in for the night, Annie mulled over what it would mean for her to acquiesce to Mrs. Mills's request and what it would mean for her to turn it down. She would need to make a choice soon.

CHAPTER THIRTY-THREE

The camp at Pacific Springs was where the Sullivan-Mills wagon company first started to feel the cold, and every day following felt a little chillier.

They left early that next morning and continued west, into the foothills east of the mountain range. The terrain climbed. Though subtle, the incline was still noticeable, and Louisa paid even closer attention to their teams of oxen. This would be the very last place she could handle having one of them collapse. Now that they were on the final stretch to Oregon, she felt hyper-vigilant. Each night she offered them as much water as she could, brushing them down as they cooled. Each morning she all but apologized as she hitched them up, wishing they could have more of a rest or a treat of some kind.

The animals weren't the only thing that needed a bit of extra care.

Before they had left Pacific Springs, Josie spent an hour rearranging all the family's belongings in the supply wagon. She needed Lawrence's help moving some of the heavier pieces, but this allowed her to access all of what the family needed at this stage in their journey, including a trunk that had been stuffed at the very back.

"What's in that one?" Annie asked as the other two lifted it out of the wagon.

"Blankets," Louisa answered for them. "Our extra quilts. Thank you so much for finding those."

Each of them had claimed one or two items of the warm bedding to keep them through the rest of the trip. It was still summer, but the trail was climbing, and it was unlikely to be truly warm again until they were in Oregon the following spring. The next morning, Louisa woke under the cozy blanket and almost didn't want to get up at all. She could feel the cold outside her bed, with even more waiting for her outside the wagon, and wanted to relax back into her swaddling.

And so passed every day. She had to shiver through getting ready for her day. She drove the team of oxen as gently and kindly as she could. And at the end of the day, she sat down for a warm, though occasionally meager, meal cooked by her sister before going to bed in the cold and doing it all again the next day.

Everyone in the company had the same struggling days, but some had it even worse.

As they climbed higher and higher in the hills, the trail passed more excess supplies that had been discarded by those who came before. The largest pieces of furniture now sat scattered across the plains. The only pieces that people could bear to part with now were smaller, more essential, and more heartbreaking. One afternoon, Louisa wrinkled her nose against the smell of rotting meat. Three yards later, she realized someone had tossed a side of moldy bacon off the side of the trail. Whoever that had been must have been trying to ration their meat, and in the end, didn't get to eat it anyway.

It was a difficult crossing. As the trail climbed even higher, there was too little grass for the oxen. Louisa looked over the supplies they still had and decided that they would supplement the animal's feed with oats. That was food that should have been for the family, but they couldn't get anywhere if they didn't have the oxen.

One of these cold nights, Josie took the chance of a rare egg from Camilla to bake a special dessert. She had collected black currants at their last stop and been saving them for this chance. More complicated recipes like a whirligig were a rare treat on the Oregon Trail, but it already smelled heavenly.

Louisa stood watching the rest of the wagon circle with her back to the fire. She had her shawl pulled around her and eagerly awaited the dessert that Josie was finishing up. She hadn't been looking for anything in particular, but the neighbors closest to Louisa caught her eye. The Jamesons were huddled over their fire, with no supper in sight. Louisa couldn't recall the last time she had heard Martin's fiddle. Beyond them, the Taylor family seemed to be arguing in heated whispers. All around the camp, the neighbors in the wagon company seemed tired, worn down.

"Did I tell you that little Alma Valentine has been sick for days?" Margaret said. "She's been riding inside her wagon since they left Pacific Springs. I helped Mrs. Valentine with the other little ones today, but I don't know what else to do."

"And Mrs. McKinnon came by today to see if we could spare any cornmeal," Josie added. "I had a feeling she really wanted to ask for an egg but was too proud."

"There're just too many families in need," Margaret said as she accepted her plate from Josie. "I don't feel right about eating this on my own. Why, at least two children could get a meal from what I'm about to eat tonight."

"We might be able to share some," Josie said. "When I rearranged the supplies at the springs, I consolidated a lot of the food. It shouldn't be too hard for me to check again to see what we have and measure that against how many more days we have."

"But the problem is," Annie said, "we don't know how many days we have left. We could be delayed again by Indians or weather or another death."

Her voice choked at that last. It broke Louisa's heart. So much of this journey had been so hard on her.

All of the women were looking at her, Louisa realized. She had started this journey in charge, meticulously creating their plans and details, and with this as in with the rest of it, they needed her to guide them. She looked toward the Robinsons' camp nearby, at the children sitting quietly, likely hungry with little energy. Miss Atkins, the teacher traveling with them, was by the campfire bent over a book or something Louisa couldn't see at this distance.

She thought about Pastor Montgomery holding church services and how those had so cheered her sisters.

She thought about Billy Whitson and the other boys who had stepped up to help Mrs. Buchanan when her husband was killed or the mothers who helped Mrs. McKinnon when her son died.

The words of George Mills on that street in Independence came back to her. He told her about this specifically, and at the time, she dismissed it.

"As part of my wagon company, we do expect some measure of pitching in. Everyone needs to pull their own weight, and that could mean helping out your neighbors when needed."

She smiled at her sisters. "Of course we'll help them."

Though they looked surprised at her verdict, it was plain that all of the Hudson girls were pleased with such generosity. Margaret vowed to do a little prying and discover who among the wagon train had the greatest need. Josie would ration the food as best she could and determine what they could part with. And Annie would, as ever, fill in the gaps. That was precisely what she was best at and always had been.

"I think I'd like to give up my next egg to Mrs. McKinnon," Annie said after Louisa outlined her plan.

Louisa was taken aback for a second but didn't object. "All right. Of course, that's wonderful."

Annie hadn't told her yet what she was going to say to Mrs. Mills, but maybe this one little speaking up was evidence that she could be honest with the older woman.

"Mrs. Hudson?"

Louisa looked up to see that the pastor's wife, Mrs. Montgomery, had appeared. But Margaret hadn't seemed to hear her.

"Missus... Um, Margaret?" she called again from her awkward position a full ten feet from their campfire.

Margaret had been rummaging in the back of the

family's supply wagon, looking for any little bit that she could give away. She only seemed to realize Mrs. Montgomery was calling for her when she used her first name. She stood up straight and came around the corner, a surprised expression on her face.

"Hi, yes, hello, um..." their visitor said before laughing awkwardly. "I just came to..." She finished with a shrug.

"Did you smell my sister's black currant whirligig? Don't worry, I think there's enough to share." Margaret winked at her as she moved to greet her guest. Louisa watched with interest. No wonder so many families in the camp loved her. "Come sit by the fire while it finishes baking."

"What, really?" She took a deep breath, smelling in the tart berries and pastry. "Black currant whirligig over the campfire?"

"Would you like the recipe?" Annie asked kindly.

"Oh, yes, please," Olivia responded eagerly.

"Now, Mrs. Montgomery," Margaret said, sitting next to her, "surely that's not the real reason you're here. What can I do for you?"

"I just wanted... That is, I was wondering ..." She cleared her throat. "How are you faring with Lawrence and all?"

Margaret's expression softened. "How kind of you to ask."

But before she could respond, Louisa stood from her perch at the front of their lead wagon.

"I can't stay up a minute longer," she declared.

Josie and Annie exchanged an amused look. She

decided not to notice it. Instead, Louisa said her goodnights.

"Sleep well," Margaret called to her as she climbed into their sleeping wagon.

Louisa could not keep herself from yawning as she took out her hairpins and hung up her apron. The night was cold, so she pulled out the extra quilt that had been secreted under her cot. As she lay down and pulled it over her, the rest of the family's conversation floated through the canvas covering of the wagon.

"She's been complaining all day," she heard Margaret say to their guest. "But you know Louisa. Won't take anyone's advice. Just like a toddler."

A month ago, Louisa might have stormed out there, back to the circle around the campfire, and defended herself. Now, however, she almost wanted to laugh, recognizing how true Margaret's assessment was.

It was rather a relief to be able to recognize and admit her own faults. These last couple of days, acknowledging that she didn't have to control every little detail, had been almost enjoyable. Difficult, yes, but at the same time surprisingly calm.

No wonder she was ready to sleep so easily. This might be the first night since their parents died that Louisa actually felt like she could relax. The hum of conversation carried on out by the campfire. She was still a bit cold, shivering under her blankets, but nothing could keep Louisa from falling soundly asleep.

CHAPTER THIRTY-FOUR

By this far into their journey, the routine to get everything packed up every morning had become so rote that Annie could almost do it all without thinking. Chickens back into their cages, cooking supplies back in their box, animals watered and harnessed for their day of hauling. Each member of the family had their duties, and for the first time, Annie allowed herself a moment of reflection to appreciate how Louisa's steadfastness and discipline had been so beneficial to them all. Without her strict and high expectations of them, each morning might be infinitely more chaotic and difficult.

Annie was so wrapped up in these thoughts that she hardly noticed when the Hudsons had an early visitor. Rebecca Tenney appeared at the edge of their camp. It had been too long since Annie had been able to sit down for a long conversation with her. She took a couple steps toward her friend before realizing that Rebecca seemed distraught. She was looking toward the family, waiting for someone to notice her. Rarely were visits between camps made in the mornings, and never were visits between camps made in the morning unless it was with urgent news.

Whatever it was, even just the sight of her friend sent her heart into Annie's throat.

She dropped Lawrence's bedroll that she had been on the point of packing into the wagon and rushed to Rebecca.

Annie didn't even have to ask before she revealed her reason for being there.

"It's..." Rebecca cleared her throat. "It's William Sullivan. He's passed."

Annie gasped and put her hand to her mouth. "What? No... How? Was he sick? Injured? What happened?"

Rebecca nodded, fighting back tears. "I just spoke to Mrs. Martell. Her husband was called to the Sullivans' camp late last night, and..." She shook her head. "He's gone. The doctor thought he was getting better, but the Mountain Fever just wore him down. I don't know what happens next. I'm sorry. I didn't want to get emotional. I just came to share the news."

"Of course. I understand. Thank you so much. We'll go see Mrs. Sullivan soon."

After Rebecca left to give the Jamesons the news, Annie looked around at their own campsite and felt at an absolute loss. The captain of their wagon company had died. One of the primary people who had been tasked with getting them to Oregon safely hadn't been able to do the same thing for himself. What were they supposed to make of that? What comfort could they take from such a tragedy?

"What happened?"

Annie spun around to see her oldest sister, concern all over her face.

"What's wrong?" Louisa asked.

"It's William Sullivan," she said with a deep breath. Explaining it all to her was painful, saying the words out loud, but it needed to be done. They needed to figure out what to do next. Louisa would know what they needed to do next.

"Oh, goodness," Louisa said softly when Annie finished.

Annie watched her sister expectantly. "So? Now what? What's next?"

"What do you mean?"

"I mean." She looked around, at a total loss. She laughed sadly. "You know, Louisa. You always know the answer. You always know the best thing to do. Tell me what to do now. Should we go see the Sullivans? Stay away, so we don't get sick? I'm just... I'm overwhelmed and lost."

Her sister shook her head. "That's not... I don't know. I feel..."

Annie looked at her sister carefully. Her face was pale, and she seemed to be thinking over all the news. Louisa rubbed her face with both hands.

"Are you all right?"

Louisa nodded. "It's just that this is a lot to deal with on top of everything else."

Annie knew precisely what she meant, but she hadn't thought that Louisa was affected by such concerns. Her sister had always been so strong, so steadfast, so determined in her optimism that it would all work out just according to her plan.

"I'm sorry," she said softly, pulling her sister into an embrace. Louisa felt a little warmer than usual, but Annie assumed that was because she had just climbed out of the wagon. "It's a lot, you're right." She choked up at that last.

"It's a lot."

"I didn't mean to do this. I'm so sorry. This is all my fault."

Louisa pulled away from the hug. "Annie? What do you mean? I'm worried about you."

"I'm just... I'm sorry that I made you leave Virginia at all. This is my fault. I shouldn't have even brought it up. I didn't realize it would be like this."

Louisa looked at her quizzically. "You didn't make me do anything, Annie. Remember? This was my idea."

"But—"

"But, I thought it would be good for all of us. I was so sure that this was what we all needed and that all you needed was a little push."

A moment of silence.

"Do you still think so?"

Louisa sighed. "I don't know. Yes, probably, but right now, losing Mr. Sullivan feels like a lot. To be honest, I know that we will make it to Oregon. And I think that maybe you needed this change, right? And I know that I need..."

Her voice caught in her throat.

"I don't know," Louisa said again. "But what I want to try to do is to be less... me."

Now it was Annie's turn to frown and laugh awkwardly. "Why would you be less you?"

"I want to... When I heard about everything you had done to defend Camilla—" Annie laughed "—and all of it when the camp was under attack, I couldn't stop thinking about all the ways I would have stood in your way if I could. I wouldn't have told you where the rifle was if you had asked. I wouldn't have allowed you out of the wagon if I had the choice. And, now, I think I wouldn't have let you stay in Virginia if you had expressed a desire to. But maybe I should have. I should have done all those things. Annie, I—"

A sob escaped her lips, and Louisa seemed horrified and embarrassed by her vulnerability. Annie watched her carefully as she composed herself. It was so rare that Louisa was open with her or admitted to weakness or vulnerability. She didn't want to make her sister feel any more uncomfortable, but this was what they both needed.

"Annie," she said, once she had calmed a bit, "I'm sorry. I want you to be exactly who you are, and I'm sorry for all the times that I tried to take that from you."

"You meant well."

"I meant well, but that's not enough."

"Louisa," she said softly. "Maybe it is. Maybe when people love you, intention can be good enough."

"But I want to do better."

"I know. And you will because you're you. But for now..."

Annie looked her sister up and down carefully before drawing her into a hug.

"I love you."

"I love you too."

"I'm glad we came to Oregon."

"I'm glad. I want this for you."

"I know, and that's why we work well together, right? Because we believe in each other's best intentions, even if it doesn't always work out."

Louisa pulled away from the hug but looked Annie full in the face. "But it will work out, now. Now I know that you need your space, and you know that my discipline isn't always a terrible thing." She laughed self-consciously. "And together, we can make it all work."

"Add in Margaret's generosity and Josie's planning, and we have quite the team."

"Goodness," Louisa said. "A team. I'm not sure. I rather liked being in charge."

Annie laughed and pushed her sister gently. "We'll let you pretend."

Louisa laughed too before sobering up. "We should… We need to tell the others. And see about a funeral," she said.

"Poor Mrs. Sullivan," Annie said in a whisper.

Later that morning, the Hudsons and practically every other member of the wagon company went to pay their respects to their captain and leader. Though Annie hadn't interacted with him much, it was clear how much William Sullivan's family loved him and would miss him. Watching them mourn at his graveside tore at her heart.

"William Sullivan wasn't just a friend, a husband, and a parent. He was a leader of this company." Annie looked down at her hands as the pastor continued his eulogy. "He looked after each and every one of us. He wanted every member of this party to get to Oregon, and we can't let him down."

Next to her, Josie seemed to sway on her feet momentarily.

"Are you all right?" Annie asked in a whisper.

Josie nodded, adjusted her stance, and nodded again. "Just, goodness… just a little weak is all. A bit light-headed."

Annie kept one hand on her sister's elbow through the rest of the funeral.

For yet another morning, the company did not leave camp until late morning because they had been delayed by burying one of their own. How much more of this could they take, Annie wondered.

The following day, she was not the only one who had that question. So many of the families were severely rationing the food. Without William Sullivan to help lead, the other captain, George Mills, called a meeting of all the men in the company to vote on their next move. Two different routes would get the company where they need to be, and Mills wanted their opinions. There was no question that Louisa would be the Hudson to go, but she had been failing in the last day or so. Annie kept watching for her to come back, to make sure she ate, to make sure she rested.

Josie asked for Annie's help with supper, and just as they were finishing up, their sister returned.

Louisa came back from the meeting exhausted. Annie watched her carefully, returning to the warmth of their campfire and taking a seat with her sisters. She was content to wait until Louisa was ready to talk, but

Margaret immediately started pelting her with questions.

"So? Which is it? Shorter trip?"

Louisa shook her head. "No, thank goodness. More of the men voted to take the longer route with the resources we need."

The pride was clear in her tone. Annie could imagine Louisa struggling against a crowd of men, pitting her iron will against all their power. And yet, in the end, she had prevailed.

"How close was the vote?"

"Close," Louisa answered as she accepted a bowl from Josie. "I like to think that it was my convincing Mr. Franklin and Mr. Robinson and a few of the others that made the difference, but I'm not sure. It could have just been that Mr. Harper was making enemies. That man has quite the temper when he gets going."

Annie chuckled. She had heard stories. Women talked. She could imagine how he might be in a community vote of this kind. As Annie understood it, John Harper had been the head of a big business back in New York and must be used to having his own way. And to be thwarted by a woman like Louisa must have been insufferable for him.

"So," Louisa concluded, "it will take us a week longer, but that will be a week that we can spend with fresh water, grass for the animals, and a stop at Fort Bridger so the families that need it can stock up on supplies."

"I hope they have enough," Josie said solemnly. "This late in the season, it might be hard."

Louisa nodded. "That's true. But we felt that the other benefits outweighed that risk. This way may take more days, but they will be easier days and give more of the company the chance to make it all the way to Oregon without dropping in the harness the way the Gladwells' ox did."

Focusing on finishing her supper, Louisa kept quiet for the rest of the evening. She seemed exhausted after having argued with all those men. Margaret asked questions about the route they would take now, but Louisa answered as shortly as possible. She just seemed too tired to put any effort into the conversation at all. With the way the firelight reflected off her face, Annie wondered if she was feeling quite all right. Louisa seemed to be sweating, even in the August weather.

In no time, she had eaten the little meal Josie had prepared.

"Lawrence," Louisa said, interrupting his talk of a lesson with Miss Atkins. "Tomorrow, can you be sure to double-check the latches on the hens' cages? I want to start a list of all the supplies to look for when we get to the fort."

"Yes, ma'am," he said with a firm nod.

"Good," she said, nodding back. Standing, yawning, and stretching her arms up over her head, Louisa made to leave. "I think I'll turn in. Goodness, I'm tired."

Annie looked up at the sky; the sun hadn't even set yet. "Get some rest," she called after her sister.

CHAPTER THIRTY-FIVE

What day was it?

Louisa didn't know where she was.

She couldn't remember any further back than a few moments. She tried to blink and realized her eyes were already closed, but it seemed like too much effort to open them again. She made a fist— No, she *tried* to make a fist, but the ache that coursed through her fingers and up her arm stopped her.

Where was she? What had happened to her?

The last thing she remembered was returning to her camp after the stressful meeting with Captain George Mills. She had—once again—been the only woman in attendance and felt like the only voice of reason. Louisa remembered pressing the few friends she had to vote with her and then to convince the others. She remembered sitting down, exhausted, in the middle of a conversation. She remembered feeling a bit warm and removing her shawl as she walked back to her own wagon.

She remembered going to bed... Was that where she was?

Louisa summoned all the strength she had to feel underneath her. There was a small rustling sound of dried grass. Maybe she was in bed.

But she was tired. So tired. Too tired to open her eyes. She felt hot, so hot, and realized she must have taken ill. Never before had she felt as weak as this; sickness was the only explanation. How could she have gotten sick?

Louisa Hudson had never been the kind of woman to take an obstacle without a fight. She wouldn't let whatever this was stop her. She would get better. She would rest and heal and then be on her feet again.

But, she suddenly realized, William Sullivan must have thought exactly the same thing, just a few days prior.

"Is she—"

"Shh!"

Two voices whispered in the space around her. Louisa tried to open her eyes.

"Hello?" she croaked out.

"You woke her!"

She recognized Margaret's voice.

"Go see if your aunt needs help," she said.

"Hello?" Louisa said again.

"I'm here," Margaret said. "I'm here, don't worry. Lawrence has gone to help Annie with the oxen, and I'll make sure you two both have everything you need."

"But..." Louisa mumbled.

"Shh, now. Just relax. Just sleep. You and Josie have

come down with something, and we're dealing with it. Might be Mountain Fever, but don't worry. Me and Annie and Lawrence will take care of everything while you get well. Shh, now. Just rest. That's all you need to worry about."

"Josie?"

"Yes, poor thing. You've been sleeping for almost a full day, and she came down with a fever in the last few hours. She's sleeping now; that's why I'm keeping my voice down, you know. With the two of you sick..."

But Louisa didn't hear the rest of the sentence. She had already faded out into the uncertain darkness of fevered sleep.

When she opened her eyes again, Margaret was sitting on the edge of her own cot across the wagon, but someone else was sleeping there. Louisa tried to turn her body to face her sisters, but the effort of moving all of her weight was too much. It felt as though she was burning up, that her face was flushed. Pushing back the blanket, Louisa was confused. Why had they piled on such blankets when she was clearly hot?

She hadn't realized that her teeth were chattering.

"Oh, goodness, let's get you tucked back in," Margaret murmured.

Louisa was asleep again before she felt the weight placed over her.

The next time she woke, Annie sat on the floor of the wagon, between the two cots, resting her head on her arms dejectedly.

"Annie?" Louisa said.

Her head shot up. "Oh, good. Yes. Good." She let out

a long breath. "I didn't want to have to wake you, but we need to get some fluids in you."

"Are you okay?"

Annie let out a noise that was half a sob, half a laugh. "Am I okay? Louisa Hudson, I need you to only think about yourself just now, all right? I need you to…" She swallowed hard, her eyes bright. "I need you to rest and only worry about getting better. All right? Can you do that for me?"

She nodded resolutely at Louisa, prompting her to nod back, but Louisa couldn't find the strength.

"Yes."

"Good. Now, we're going to sit you up." She folded back the blanket over Louisa. "And you're going to have some of this broth I made, and then a little bit of water, and then you're going to take another nap, okay?"

"What day is it?"

Annie paused. "I honestly have no idea. This is the second full day you've been sick, though, so you'll understand why I need you to not worry about me."

"Two days…"

"Two days. Let's get some water in you."

Louisa sipped at the tin cup that Annie held to her lips, but it all seemed like so much effort. Couldn't she just go back to sleep? Obediently, Louisa held her mouth open for her sister to spoon in a couple mouthfuls of broth. Louisa had half a thought to wonder how they were managing without her before she was asleep again. They were managing.

She didn't know how long she was in and out of sleep. Waking meant straining to recognize the voices whispering around her. Opening her eyes meant pain against the brightness. It took so much effort to move any part of her body. She couldn't be sure she had any control over it at all.

Asleep again. Awake again. Where was she? Why couldn't she move?

Louisa felt a hand on her brow.

"Mother?" she whispered.

But she didn't have the strength to open her eyes. She couldn't see her mother's loving face gazing down at her. She could only feel her presence.

A cool cloth was rested on her forehead, and Louisa sighed with relief.

Her mother disappeared, and now her sister's face floated above her.

"Annie?"

"I'm here," she whispered. "I won't leave you."

"Annie..."

"Shhh..."

"I'm sorry..."

"I know. I'm sorry, too."

"I tried."

"Shh, I know, Louisa. I know."

She heard her sister crying. But why would she be crying?

"What's wrong with me?"

"You're sick," Annie said gently. "You're just a little— You've got a fever and some aches, and we're doing everything we can to take care of you. I promise. I won't leave you."

"I'm sick," Louisa repeated, trying hard to keep her eyes open. "But you'll take care of me."

"Of course I will. Of course I will."

"Of course you will."

Louisa closed her eyes, secure, safe, loved, and cared for by one of her favorite people.

CHAPTER THIRTY-SIX

Annie sat on the edge of her sister's cot, with a pan of cool water and a rag in her lap. They didn't really have the water to spare. This wasn't how they had expected to use this water. In fact, it wasn't nearly as cool as she would have liked to help ease Louisa's fever, but it was all Annie knew to do.

"Shhhh…" Annie soothed.

Louisa struggled to open her eyes. She grimaced when just the smallest bit of light penetrated. Annie checked again to make sure the opening of the canvas at the end of the wagon was still closed. There was nothing else she could do, as far as she knew. She was helpless.

This was everything.

"Annie, you need to sleep."

She looked up to see Margaret standing at the end of the wagon, peering in.

"Come on." Margaret gestured to her. "You can't help her if you're dead on your feet."

Annie looked back at Louisa. She was the only one

still sick. Josie had gotten out of bed that morning. She was still frail and weak, but at least she was on her feet.

"What if I just sleep here?" Annie gestured to Josie's cot. "I want to be close, just in case."

Margaret's expression softened. "As long as you promise me you'll sleep."

"I promise." Annie was already taking off her shoes and pulling the blanket down to crawl in. "I'm very tired. But come check on both of us soon, will you?"

"Of course. Now, bed."

She obediently lay down and closed her eyes, but her mind was so busy with worry she could not fall asleep. It felt like she had been on her feet for days, tending to her sisters, driving the wagon in Louisa's place. But in spite of such complete physical exhaustion, she was too alert, too aware of Louisa's every breath to let herself fall asleep.

Annie didn't know how long she lay there with her eyes closed, but it wasn't long before she admitted to herself that she wasn't going to sleep. She was just waiting and listening. For what, she didn't know. But after all Louisa had done for her, now that was all she could do for Louisa.

Outside the wagon, the other Hudsons were murmuring over the campfire. In the distance, the lowing of the cattle and the laughter from other families added to the otherwise quiet evening. Annie lay in the darkness of their wagon and listened. All around them, other emigrants were making their suppers, worrying over their animals, or making plans for when they got to Oregon. The dozens of families that they had traveled with all continued on with their lives as though the most important person in Annie's life wasn't lying here struggling to survive.

A small sound emanated from Louisa's cot. Annie sat up, immediately wide awake.

"Louisa?" she asked softly, moving to her knees in the narrow aisle next to her sister.

Louisa stirred and whimpered. She must be in so much pain, and there was nothing Annie could do.

She reached for her sister's hand under the blanket. Louisa's palm was clammy, but Annie clutched it, desperate for her to know she was here, by her side.

Louisa turned on her pillow toward Annie and opened her eyes.

"You're here," she whispered.

"I'm here."

"I want..." she began before trailing off, eyes closed.

Annie waited. A sob rose in her, but she didn't want to worry her sister.

Louisa opened her eyes and seemed to steel herself for the effort.

"I want you to... be happy. I only wanted you to be happy."

"I know. I know," she said. "I will be. I am."

"Then, I've done my job," Louisa said with a soft smile.

She closed her eyes again, and Annie leaned forward, resting her forehead on her sister's arm. Louisa's breathing was labored, and Annie writhed, knowing there was no way to help her.

Moments stretched. Annie held back her sobs, listening closely. It was there, on her knees and holding her sister's hand, that Annie felt Louisa take her last breath. Her chest rose and fell and then did not rise again.

Annie prayed quickly, desperately, hoping she was mistaken, but there was nothing. Louisa Hudson had passed.

She sat quietly by herself for at least thirty minutes, thinking over her sister's life and what she had meant. It was only when she heard Josie putting away the dishes from supper that Annie roused herself to share the news with the rest.

It must have been written all over her face. The moment Annie climbed out of their sleeping wagon and turned toward her family, Josie gasped.

"Is she...? Oh, no, Annie."

Annie nodded, unable to stop her tears. "She's gone. She's..." She swallowed hard. "She's gone."

The remaining Hudsons came together in a hug. After all they had been through, after all Louisa had guided them through, toward their new life in Oregon, the worst had happened. Annie didn't know how exactly they would manage to go on. All she knew is they would have to for Louisa.

"I'll send Lawrence to let the captain know," Margaret said through her tears.

"No, I want to do it," Annie said determinedly. "I'll go."

"But, really—"

"I want to go."

Annie set off through the wagon circle before anyone could stop her.

Deaf to anyone calling after, she found herself at the Mills campfire soon after. Mrs. Mills looked up from the dishes she was cleaning and stood when she recognized her visitor.

"Why, Miss Hudson," she said with a bright smile. "How lovely. I hope you've come to tell me that you'll help me host that sewing circle?"

It took all of Annie's patience to not interrupt her. As it was, she didn't even try to return her smile. "No, I'm sorry. I've come to tell the captain that my—" She cleared her throat. "My sister Louisa has died. And ask if we... If we can..."

Her throat closed up as thick tears began to fall again. Saying it out loud proved impossible. She shook her head in frustration at herself, unable to do this one thing for her sister.

"Oh, my dear," Mrs. Mills said gently, reaching out to take Annie's hand.

"What's this then?" Mr. Mills said as he approached the pair.

Annie was grateful that his wife relayed the details so she didn't have to say it again. It would be hard enough for her to get used to the fact that her strong, independent sister was no longer there for her, let alone to have to tell people that.

"I'll have word sent to the pastor," he said gently. "We can bury her in the morning if that's acceptable."

She nodded.

"We can't stay here, Miss Hudson," he had said kindly. "Since the sickness is most common in high elevation, we need to keep moving till we're out of the area. In order to keep as many people safe as we can. Many have recovered, but we can't risk any more."

"I understand," she said.

"I'm so sorry for your loss."

With that, he left Annie to be comforted by his wife and tended to the number of pressing items on his attention.

"What can I do for you, dear?" Mrs. Mills said. "Would you like me to walk you back? Have you eaten?"

"No. Yes. I don't... Thank you." Annie shook her head to clear the cobwebs and looked at Mrs. Mills again. "I'm fine. Thank you."

She had already walked away when she heard a gentle, "I'm so sorry," floating behind her, but she didn't stop.

The next morning, a small group of mourners gathered at dawn to say good-bye to Louisa Hudson. As Annie looked around, she was initially affronted that the group was so small. But she spotted the Franklins. And the Martells. These people cared about her sister. Louisa had not been very social while traveling west, but the friends she had made were dear.

Rebecca Tenney stood just behind Annie. She put a hand on her arm briefly, just to let her know she had a friend.

Annie stood between Josie and Margaret, holding each of their hands. Pastor Montgomery offered a prayer of thanks and grief over their sister. Annie suppressed a smile, thinking about how Louisa would have liked this funeral. She would have been itching to get back to work, insisting people could mourn her while they got other things done.

In Annie's memory, Louisa loomed large as an example of discipline and generosity. She would always be Annie's best example of doing what she believed to be best, no matter the obstacles. Annie would have to live in honor of that.

The pastor finished his prayers, and the murmur of "amen" rippled around the small gathering. Tears poured down Annie's face; she blinked them away but made no other effort to dry her eyes. Losing Louisa would be a pain she felt for the rest of her life.

Several of the young men stepped forward, shovels in hand, to complete the burial. Annie felt rooted to the spot watching them. Watching these strangers, these boys, perform this final act of service for her older sister all but overwhelmed her.

Louisa had sacrificed so much for Annie, for all of the Hudsons. She had called off her own betrothal. She had worked ceaselessly to provide for both of her younger sisters, and in the end, she had let go of everything she had built in order to give Annie a better life. Through all of the haranguing and attempts to control, Louisa had still only ever been doing what she believed was best for her family.

It wasn't until they were actually on this journey across the continent that Annie realized how much she had depended on Louisa.

And now, in this final moment, Louisa needed Annie.

But it required Annie to speak up.

She could do this for her sister.

"No," Annie said softly.

But no one heard her. No one paid her any mind. And she was sick of it. Louisa had always pushed her to stand up for herself and to take what she wanted. This was the final thing that Annie could do for her oldest sister, who had given up so much of her own life to take care of her.

"No," Annie said more loudly.

She startled Jefferson Carter into pausing, and he looked at her questioningly.

Annie stepped forward and gestured for him to hand over the shovel. He frowned in confusion.

"Miss Hudson, I'm happy to—"

"No," she said again. "Please."

Jefferson didn't make her plead anymore. He handed over the tool and stepped back.

Annie choked back a sob as she looked down at the shallow grave. She could do this. This last gesture. This last sight of her sister.

She swallowed hard as she slid the shovel into the pile of dirt and lifted it up and over Louisa's body.

CHAPTER THIRTY-SEVEN

The next several days were a blur to Annie and all the Hudsons. If it hadn't been for the fact that they only had to follow the Robinsons' wagon, they might not have gotten anywhere at all. The fewer decisions they had to make, the better. Even supper every night was a strain for Josie.

Annie found her sobbing over the coffee in the supply wagon just the day after Louisa's funeral.

"Shhhh, shhh," she said, wrapping an arm around her sister.

"I'm sorry," Josie said, wiping her face on her apron. "I don't know what got into me. I just came across a whole bag of coffee that hadn't been touched—I didn't even know it was in here—and thought all over again about how much Louisa did to care for us."

"She got us this far," Annie said. "I think she probably did a lot for us that we may never know about."

Josie started crying all over again, and Annie held her. Her own tears seemed constant now; she didn't even notice until Josie teased about her leaving a wet spot on her shoulder.

"Well," Josie said with a deep breath. "She certainly wouldn't want us standing around crying over her. Can you imagine?" She laughed. "Wasting time with feelings when there was work to be done?"

Annie laughed at the thought. Was this what the rest of her life would be like? Imagining how Louisa would react to this or that? She wiped her tears and got to work.

To make up the extra days it took them to follow the longer route, the captain sent the word that they would be leaving camp at first light every single morning. It was a punishing pace; more than once, Josie tried to sleep in the wagon as it traveled during the day. She was still so weak from her illness that the constant work and short nights of sleep threatened to bring her down again.

Annie's own workload had gotten significantly larger. She had taken Louisa's spot driving the lead team of oxen every day. There had been some discussion of combining the wagons and making do with just one, but Annie had been adamant.

"We need do everything we can to honor what Louisa wanted for us. She chose two wagons for a reason. She bought all these supplies and gave us all this space because she believed it would be best."

"But, Annie, honey," Margaret said. "It's so much. It's too much for you. We'll be all right with just the one wagon."

"No," she said stubbornly. "We have to do this. This is all we have left."

"She's right," Lawrence said, speaking up for the first time. "We'll be okay, Mother. Please."

Margaret shook her head but didn't argue any further. Annie hadn't articulated this thought, but the idea of working herself so hard felt cathartic, as though it was her punishment for surviving when Louisa had not. Her oldest sister had worked herself so hard that her body had not been able to fight off the illness, so now Annie could do this for her.

And so, every morning, Annie roused herself before dawn. As often as she could, she let Josie continue to sleep and scraped together a breakfast by herself. Sometimes it would be a cold biscuit. Sometimes, Margaret would be up as well, cobbling together a few mouthfuls of beans and rice. Coffee helped, but not enough to combat that lack of sleep they always seemed to be operating under. But always, always, Annie proudly suffered through any hunger or exhaustion to carry on the work that Louisa had begun.

Louisa had been adamant in the wagon company taking this longer route because it offered plenty of grass and water for the animals. But as they trudged westward, seemingly without rest for days, Annie was all but blind to the riches of the landscape around her. She just focused on getting them all to Oregon.

A few days after Louisa's burial, Annie was in the family's sleeping wagon with a lantern, looking for her pen and paper. She had an idea that maybe if she could find the words to write to Isaac about her sister's death, it would be easier for her to deal with the reality of it herself. It had been so long, however, since she had even thought about writing to him, let alone had the time for it, that she couldn't quite remember where she left her supplies. There wasn't much of them. They would be tucked somewhere out of the way. She was on her knees digging through one of the trunks that had been wedged in the back of the wagon behind the cots.

The trunk contents were a mix of linens, extra pots and dishes they didn't need on the trail, and a handful of well-loved books. Annie smiled to herself as she pulled out the copy of *The Legend of Sleepy Hollow*. Louisa had been so strict about limiting what they brought west, but she couldn't deny herself the luxury of carting this two thousand miles. It seemed so incongruous for practical, reliable Louisa Hudson to love a ghost story so much, but she did. It was such a strange, unpredictable quirk in spite of her rigidity.

Annie set the book aside, vowing to read it herself once she had a chance, and caught her breath. In the back of her mind had been the thought that they would need to find Louisa's purse before they got to Oregon. She would have wanted them to be taken care of and so would have tucked away her funds for starting their new life. And here it was. Stored with her favorite book.

Feeling a bit as though she was invading her sister's privacy, Annie picked up the small purse and opened it. And then dropped it immediately in surprise.

Inside the purse was a combination of banknotes and heavy gold pieces. Annie couldn't even guess how much was here, but it was more money than she had ever seen in her life. It could be well into the hundreds of dollars. It was likely enough money to set all of the Hudsons up for a good long while in Oregon.

Regardless of the exact amount, it was more than

enough to purchase whatever supplies the family might need between here and there.

Annie made a quick decision and replaced the purse where she had found it, under the book, under a quilt and a serving platter, and closed the trunk up again.

"When we get to Fort Bridger," Annie said to her sisters, "we should stock up on as much as we can."

They had been talking when she climbed out of the wagon but fell silent when they heard her words.

"Do we have enough money, though?" Josie asked. "I think we can still make what we have stretch if we need to, supplemented with game or whatever we can catch."

"We have enough," Annie said. "I found Louisa's purse and..." She laughed at the sheer joy of it. "You will not believe it. We have more than enough. Plenty. And if we somehow managed to spend all that we have, then we can also use any additional supplies to help others who might not have as much as we do."

"Like Louisa said we could do," Josie added softly.

"Exactly. Yes!" Annie said. "She gave up so much to get us this far. We can help stretch her effort and her influence. If we buy enough flour, we can make sure that there's plenty to share around when others' stores get low."

Margaret was grinning too, pleased at this proposal. "Oh, I just love this. How long till we get there?"

"I think maybe tomorrow," Annie said. "Should be soon, at least."

"Where did you find that?" Josie asked. "I had forgotten all about it."

"The chest in the back of the wagon. Where some of the personal items are. I found one of Louisa's books, too…" She trailed off, thinking about going through her sister's belongings without her sister being there.

"Louisa would love this plan of yours," Josie said softly. "I'm so glad you said something."

Annie just smiled. She didn't trust herself to say anything without breaking down in tears again. But as long as she was making Louisa proud, she was happy.

CHAPTER THIRTY-EIGHT

Reaching Fort Bridger was the reward they received for the punishing pace Captain Mills set the wagon company to make up for not taking the cut-off. Annie had only been leading their team of oxen for a few days, but already she didn't know how Louisa had managed for so long. It was exhausting and difficult, made more so by the fact that she was missing her sister.

The wagon company arrived at the fort in the middle of the August afternoon and would stay the rest of the day. Annie left the animals in Lawrence's care and prepared to make her way to Fort Bridger.

"All right," Annie said. "I'm off to the fort. Is there anything specific I need to look for?"

"Whatever you find, but we should get more oats if possible," Josie said, looking through their stores. "The oxen have eaten quite a bit, and I imagine we'll need to give them more before the end."

"Oats," Annie repeated. "Got it. What else?"

"Bacon if they have it. Really, any meat or jerky. I

only have a few more meals' worth of meat to feed us and after that…"

"Meat. All right. I can do that." Annie nodded confidently, committing this all to memory. "Is there anything we don't need any more of?"

"Well…" Josie said doubtfully as she picked up a half-full bag and checked what was underneath. "To be honest, if we can afford it… we could use anything. Like we talked about, even if we don't eat it, there are plenty of folks less fortunate that we could help out. And you never know if—"

"If any of it will be stolen," Annie finished for her. "You're right."

Josie nodded somberly.

"All right. I'll see what I can do."

Annie was looking forward to this. It would be a test of her gumption, a good chance for her to show herself how much she had learned from Louisa. Maybe she would have to haggle for a lower price or insist on someone to help her back with all her purchases. The thought of being so forward and assertive scared Annie, but she wanted to do better about that.

For Louisa.

Annie didn't take the full purse of money with her. There was far too much, and she would be anxious the whole time with that much on her. Instead, she pulled out what seemed a reasonable amount and clutched it in her tight fist. Walking to Fort Bridger, Annie saw that it looked similar to the previous fort, surrounded on four sides by tall, sturdy walls to protect the buildings against attack, though with lower walls, hunkered close to the ground.

Many other emigrants from her wagon company had the same idea. Annie found herself walking toward the fort amidst a half-dozen others. She looked around at their worried, expectant faces and only felt calm. Louisa had done such a remarkable job at planning for them that Annie didn't have to worry about her own family. They would be just fine.

No sooner had that thought flitted through her brain than it was dashed out by the sight of a frenzied woman. Annie was dismayed to see Mrs. McKinnon striding toward the group walking into the fort, shaking her head and appearing distraught.

"There's nothing," she called as Annie's group approached.

"Say that again," Mr. Findley insisted.

"Nothing here. The shelves are stripped bare. They don't even have any ammunition so we can find our own food. How am I going to...?"

Her voice trailed off as she continued her rapid pace back toward the wagons. Annie stood still, at a loss for what to do. There seemed no point in continuing on to the fort if there were no supplies, but then maybe she should still check for herself.

But when she looked around and noticed the desperation on the faces around her, Annie thought better of it. If there was anything left, her family was the least in need of any of them. She could easily step back and give other people a chance.

Instead, she turned around and made her way to their campsite. There were still plenty of hours of sunlight left in the day, and Annie had laundry to do.

Leaving Fort Bridger the next morning, Annie was

determined to stay positive. This was the route that Louisa had chosen, after all. She couldn't have known that the fort wouldn't have any supplies. And, besides, the Hudsons did actually have enough food to get them to Oregon. Not a lot, but enough.

She felt bad for the other families, though. Walking to the stream that ran next to the fort, Annie noticed how many of the others in the wagon company had hollow cheeks and seemed even more exhausted than she did. They were reaching the final stretch of the trail, and whatever food they all had left needed to last as long as possible.

That first day, the trail turned toward the north. They headed to the mountains for a couple of days to more safely pass through the range and travel around the Great Salt Lake. Though it felt a bit out of the way, Annie chose instead to be grateful to not be walking into the sunset every afternoon. There was not much else to be grateful for. The trail in this stretch was rough and dry, and everyone's nerves were shot.

One early morning, as Lawrence went off to collect their teams of oxen, Annie heard Margaret gasp as though in panic.

"Oh, goodness!"

"What is it?" Annie asked, hurrying over.

"Oh." She put a hand over her face and laughed. "I just plumb forgot my boy's birthday. He'll be fourteen tomorrow."

"Is it really tomorrow?" Josie asked as she handed each of them mugs of coffee. "I knew it was coming up. I've been thinking about it."

"So have I," Annie admitted, "but I don't know what

to do. Maybe one of you could drive his wagon? Give him a day off? If Louisa was here…"

"If Louisa was here," Margaret said, interrupting, "we would have started planning this a week ago. But, you're right. I can drive the wagon for a day at least. If he helps me hitch up the team. That's a wonderful idea."

"And I've been saving some black currants and eggs to make the whirligig again."

"Oh, good," Margaret said. "He loved that."

"I'll keep thinking. There's bound to be something else extra we can do. He's had such a rough year already."

"And if you don't come up with anything, it's just fine. He's a good boy. He doesn't expect anything."

Annie sighed, but she knew Margaret was right. Even so, she put her mind to it and spent the following twenty-four hours thinking about what she could do.

By supper on Lawrence's fourteenth birthday, she had come up with just the thing.

"One last gift," she said, after supper. The three women had spent the whole day trying to cater to Lawrence as much as possible, and now that supper was over, Annie found her chance. From beneath the folds of her skirt, she pulled out Louisa's copy of *The Legend of Sleepy Hollow* that she discovered in the trunk.

"This was your aunt's. I remember you told me—"

"I love these stories!" Lawrence said excitedly, accepting the proffered gift.

"And you've been working so hard to improve your reading. I know Aunt Louisa was proud of all you were doing. I bet you didn't know that she loved ghost stories too."

"Really?" His eyes were wide.

"I know." Annie chuckled. "It's hard to believe. It's only right that you should have this book. Happy birthday."

His eyes shone, and he paged through the slim novel. "Thank you."

"Well, my boy, the last serving is for you, of course. Happy birthday!" Margaret said,

Lawrence set down the book and accepted the plate gratefully but didn't immediately take a bite.

"Is everything okay?" Josie asked.

"I just was thinking if maybe someone else might like this last piece instead."

Annie laughed in surprise. She couldn't help herself.

"Lawrence Hudson. You may be fourteen, but goodness if you don't have the heart and generosity of a man who has seen a lot in his long life."

"Aunt Annie," he said, seemingly embarrassed. "It's just... You know."

"Who were you thinking?" his mother asked.

"I'm not sure. Miss Atkins, maybe. Or Mrs. Montgomery. Or anyone really. No one else has had whirligig like this in ever-so-long."

"Mrs. Montgomery did enjoy the taste she had a couple weeks ago," Margaret reminded him. "And I think they're having quite a difficult time of it. The pastor has to rely so much on the generosity of his congregation."

"Then that's where I'll take this," he said, standing up. "I'll be right back."

"Hold on one minute, Lawrence." Josie darted to the supply wagon and returned shortly with two eggs in her hand. "She might be embarrassed to accept so much from us, so maybe just leave these where she'll find them."

After he disappeared into the dusk toward the Montgomery wagon, Margaret said in a low voice, "Did you happen to hear what else the Montgomerys are dealing with?"

"Yes!" Josie exclaimed. "How exciting for them, but what a time to be on the Oregon Trail. The poor dear. Hopefully, the eggs will give that new mother-to-be a little bit of her strength back."

"Heaven help any woman who tries to cross this continent pregnant. We'll have to look after her as much as we can," Margaret said.

After a handful of days pushing west over the high desert, the wagon company finally reached a haven of green. Annie led the team up, up, up the trail behind the Robinsons, until finally, they crested the hill, and the trail wound down into the lush Bear River Valley. This late in the summer, they were surprised to find so much high grass remaining. Even with all the other wagon companies that had come through here, their animals had barely made a dent in the foliage. There was still plenty. For a couple days, they followed the wide, flowing river through the valley, luxuriating in the bounty all around them. The mountains surrounding the valley were not yet snow-capped, but there was plenty of water and green everywhere they looked.

If only the entire journey could have been like this.

Margaret again took a turn driving the second wagon, so Lawrence could spend an afternoon hunting with the Davis boys. He came home with an armful of game that Josie and Annie skinned, dried, and salted as quickly as they could. Josie made the Hudsons a veritable feast that night, rabbit stew with wild onions and rice. It was no matter if the forts didn't carry supplies when they could supplement their meals like this.

The trail climbed out of the Bear River Valley into the high desert, where they again had to ration their water. Annie was well used to this by now. She had gotten quite good at noticing when she was just thirsty versus when her body was absolutely crying out for water. For several days, they struggled in the August sun and high elevation until they reached the gates of Fort Hall.

When they stopped to camp at the fort, Annie again made her way to the stores with cash clutched hand. The fort was two stories tall and built from roughly hewn logs. No windows provided a glimpse inside, and the whole thing felt more or less thrown together. Annie picked her way across the barren land and black lava plains that stretched all around the structure. She reminded herself that they would be okay. If this fort also proved a disappointment, they would still have enough food to survive to Oregon, especially after the Bear River Valley.

When she walked inside, however, she let out a long sigh of relief. Though the shelves and barrels were not overwhelmingly full, there was enough.

And enough was all Annie had asked for.

With the cash her older sister had left behind, Annie purchased a side of bacon, jerky, a bushel of dried apples, and more. This would be plenty to feed them for the remaining few weeks, and she could leave what supplies remained for other families.

And she hoped it would only be a few more weeks. Most wagon companies crossed the mountains into Oregon sometime in September. At the rate they were going, it seemed it might be closer to late September or maybe October, but that was still just a few weeks from now.

They would make it. They had to make it.

CHAPTER THIRTY-NINE

When they reached the part of the trail that ran parallel to the Snake River, Annie sucked in a breath. It was stark and intimidating, yet beautiful in its own way. The trail approached a canyon at an angle before turning slightly and running along the top of it. From where she remained at the top, leading the wagon, it was easy to hear the rush of water even though she couldn't see it. The canyon was too deep, the river far below.

They spent several days this way, following the curve of the river, but with the water too far away to do them any good. The trail itself was not wide in this section, and Annie found herself tense at the end of every day, as though her body was just waiting for something terrible to happen.

One afternoon, Annie walked alongside her team and busied her mind thinking over all the things they would need to take care of once they reached Oregon. Meeting her intended in person for the first time, finding a home or homes for all of them, learning about her neighbors and her new town. She suddenly remembered that Isaac had said he was buying her a piano, and Annie felt herself grinning at that new delight to turn over in her mind.

Thus distracted, Annie didn't notice that the wagon in front of her was slowing until she had almost run into it. As the wagon train slowed to a stop, Annie felt a pulse of frustration. They were far from where they needed to be before making camp. But she took a deep breath and waited. There was nothing she could do; no point in getting angry about it.

Still, she wondered what the holdup was. This narrow trail was dangerous enough to travel along, but staying put meant it would be even longer until they found someplace safe.

The lead ox nuzzled her ear, tickling her.

"I know," she murmured absently.

Surely someone would come back to let them know what was happening and why they had stopped.

"What's this about?" Josie asked as she approached from behind.

"Don't know. I can't even see around the Robinsons."

"Maybe I'll go check it out?"

"If you want. I figure they'll tell us eventually, and what else are we going to do in the meantime?"

Josie laughed. "Can you imagine Louisa saying something like that? Just waiting? The very idea!"

Annie smiled, but the thought of her sister was still so painful. She had been trying to step into Louisa's shoes, helping make decisions and leading the family, but she would never truly be like her sister. Louisa had such command of herself and of others. Annie could only pretend to.

"Well, since there's nothing else to do…" Josie said as she made her way up to the front of the caravan.

As Annie stood waiting, she looked up and around at the canyon where they had stopped. She hoped it wasn't anything serious. The longer they stayed here, the more anxious she got. It was ridiculous, of course, but Annie felt like they were being watched. She shivered at her own thought and admonished herself to stop being silly.

Josie appeared around the side of the Robinsons' wagon.

"Did you find out?"

Josie nodded, eyes wide. "It's bad… or, well, good, actually. Both." She sighed deeply. "Mrs. Van Anda is having her baby, so that's exciting. I don't know any more details, but Mrs. Stephens said there didn't seem to be any reason to worry."

"So, then, the bad news?"

"There's been another death."

"No," Annie whispered. "Not again."

"John Harper. He… he fell. Down into the canyon."

"What on earth was he doing so near the edge?"

"I don't know. Mrs. Stephens hadn't heard the details. But as far as she knows, we're going to make camp just a little ways ahead so men can collect the body and he can have a proper burial. And so Mrs. Van Anda can have a rest. And I think the pastor will hold a service tonight, too."

"Goodness. That's so much all at once." Annie felt a wave of exhaustion. She wanted to curl up in bed and sleep this all away. "But I suppose…"

"I know," Josie said, smiling sympathetically. "Just when it feels like we've hit our limit, something else comes along and pushes us further. I know. It's a lot."

Annie sighed and looked back out into the canyon, past a bend, into the deep recesses, and got that feeling again. She just wanted to get out of here.

The rest of the afternoon, Annie went through the motions, driving her wagon, making camp, eating supper. Filling each of the many roles that she had to fill in order to get her family to Oregon. Each task she completed by rote. If she let herself think too much about it, she wasn't sure she'd have the energy to continue.

When supper was over, Margaret led the way to the clearing outside of the camp circle where the worship service would be. Again, Annie simply followed along, letting her sisters decide for her. She felt like she only had so much energy for such things and wanted to conserve what she could.

Many emigrants had the same idea that night, and Annie stood with her sisters in the crowd. Pastor Montgomery had found a spot just outside the circle of wagons, near the canyon with tall rock walls rising behind them. It was the perfect venue to hold a church service, especially on that night when so much love and pain was present in the company.

As he and his wife led everyone in singing, Annie closed her eyes and listened. Not all the voices were in key, but every person there worshiped with their whole heart. It made Annie miss her church choir back in Norfolk more than ever. Maybe, she thought, if they settled near the Montgomerys when they got to Oregon, she would be able to sing in a choir again. Music had been part of her life since she was so small, and these months without it had been more trying than she expected.

The pastor closed out the service with a prayer, particularly calling on the Lord for mercy on those who were in mourning. It was likely he was thinking about Miss Harper above all, but Annie thought she could use some of that mercy too. Every hour that passed without Louisa was painful, and she didn't see any sign that would be letting up any time soon.

The congregation broke up, and the Hudsons walked slowly back to their campsite. They crossed the secure perimeter of the wagon circle and began the long way across the open center.

"Miss Hudson?" a deep voice called to them from behind.

All three women turned to see that both of the Franklins had followed them from the service. Here in the center of the circle of wagons, cattle and other animals milled about. One of the Mills family's cows crossed the open space between the two families as the Franklins walked closer.

"Mr. Franklin?" Annie asked. "Can we help you? Is something wrong?"

She tried to remember what Louisa had told them about this couple; if only she had more time with her sister. As the dark-skinned pair drew closer, Annie realized that this was the woman she had been in line behind at the post office in Independence all those months ago. This woman who had seemed so unencumbered was, in fact, a freed slave.

It seemed amazing that Louisa had been friends with her, but at the same time not surprising at all. If anyone she knew would do the unexpected and buck society's expectations, it was Louisa.

"Nothing is wrong," Mrs. Franklin said. "I'm so sorry to alarm you. But we wanted to pay our respects. Your sister was one of the only people in this entire company that was kind to us, that treated us like people."

"Oh, surely not," Margaret said, aghast. "Why, there are so many kind families here. How could none of them be neighborly?"

Annie glanced at her sister-in-law.

The expression on Mrs. Franklin's face was unreadable in this light, but she paused before responding. "Yes, ma'am. That's so. But your sister, Miss Hudson, was one of the best. She will be greatly missed, I'm sure."

"Greatly missed," her husband echoed.

"Thank you so much for saying so," Annie said. "She didn't... Well, she told us a little bit about your story and seemed to greatly admire you all as well. We really appreciate..." Her voice cracked, but she soldiered on. "We really appreciate your kindness toward our sister."

Left unsaid was the knowledge that Louisa could be prickly and hard-headed and the fact that she always had put work ahead of making friends. But whatever her faults, it was clear that she had made an impression on these two. Annie's gratitude was all that mattered. Louisa would be remembered fondly by people outside of the Hudson family. She couldn't ask for anything else.

John Harper's funeral was held the next morning, but Annie could not bring herself to attend. There were plenty of ways she could justify the choice to herself—she had never even spoken to the man, so it didn't seem as though his sister would expect it of her. But in the end, Annie knew that regardless of the reason, the fact that she had decided on what she wanted was a big change for her. Louisa used to bow out of social obligations all the time; Annie had always admired that bravery, and now that she was doing it herself, understood how freeing it could be.

"Goodness, that poor lamb," Margaret said as she brushed out her hair that morning in preparation to attend the funeral. "So young and now all alone. I can't think of how hard it must be for her. You know, when Tom died, I was just about lost, but at least I had my boy, and I had you all, and I had my home. But Miss Harper only has a wagon and virtual strangers. I'd love to go see if she needs help."

The two women were in the sleeping wagon after breakfast. Annie didn't quite agree with Margaret but wasn't sure precisely how to articulate her disagreement. She had no practice doing so. Speaking her mind at the actual moment she felt it was something Louisa did, not her.

But this was precisely what Louisa had taught her over the last five months.

"Well, yes, but," Annie tried to say gently to Margaret. "We also need your help here. We've lost someone, and Josie was so sick. I hope, if you feel like you have extra energy later, maybe, you can go check on Miss Harper? But... here..."

"Yes. Yes, of course, you're right," Margaret said. "Of course. I'm being silly. Thank you for saying something."

She reached out and took Annie's hand, squeezing tightly.

After Margaret left for the funeral, Annie thought about how much easier that had been than she had expected. She had braced herself for a fight or at least sullen anger, but Margaret had taken it all in stride. Maybe this wouldn't be too difficult.

CHAPTER FORTY

The delay for Mrs. Van Anda's baby meant that the company did not reach the camp at Shoshone Falls until after sunset. As Annie settled the wagon and the animals for the night, she could hear the distant roar of the enormous waterfall not far past the circle of wagons. Josie's guidebook had promised beautiful views and fresh water, but that would have to wait for the next morning when they had some light.

Over breakfast the following day, Margaret and Lawrence were arguing over whether or not he needed a bath while they were here with all the water.

"Son," she said, "I know you are fourteen already, and I'm sure quite capable of many things, but please. Have mercy on the rest of us."

"Hey!" Lawrence objected over his aunts' laughter.

Josie stopped laughing abruptly and looked up at their visitor. Buck Robinson stood waiting to be noticed.

"Ladies," he said, removing his hat politely. "Captain Mills has called a quick meeting of the men in the company. I'm happy to go as your representative if you like. I know your sister usually was the one—"

"I'll go," Annie said, standing up. She didn't give herself time to second guess the decision. If it was the thing Louisa would have done, then Annie would do it, too.

There was a brief pause in the conversation, but no one objected.

"All right, Miss Hudson." He waited.

"Oh. Now?"

Mr. Robinson chuckled. "Yes. Would you like to walk with me?"

"Here's your shawl," Josie said, handing it to her.

"Whatever you decide is fine with us," Margaret added.

Annie nodded resolutely and followed Mr. Robinson toward the Mills wagon.

"Do you know what this is about?"

"No, ma'am. Some of the other men have been whispering about how we haven't seen hide nor hair of any Indians in a few weeks, so it might be something to do with that."

"Indians," Annie repeated in awe. But she didn't slow her steps. Whatever decision needed to be made, she would do her part.

"Or maybe something else. He's got all kinds of folks under his care, you know. Maybe it's good news."

Neither said anything further. They had reached the outer edge of the crowd of men forming a half-circle around the Mills' camp. Annie couldn't see anything over the heads and shoulders of all the others. She thought she'd just listen from where she was, but soon

Mr. Robinson was nudging her ahead of him. Then Mr. Cole, Mr. Gilroy, and so many others noticed that she was there and politely ushered her along to the front of the group.

Annie smiled to herself, thinking about how Louisa would have just elbowed her way forward. Maybe she didn't need to be like her sister in *every* way.

"Gentlemen," Mr. Mills began.

Annie stood just behind Mr. Jameson's shoulder, listening and trying not to draw attention to herself.

"I'm afraid I have bad news. As you may know, we have been crossing the territory controlled by the Shoshone Indian tribe for the last few days."

Annie's stomach dropped.

"Considering what they are likely capable of, they have been very kind and generous in allowing us to pass through unmolested."

There was a confused murmur rippling around the crowd.

"But we cannot deny that it has been a hardship for them. After all, the longer that we are here, the less they have access to the fish and game that sustain them the rest of the year. Every animal we hunt is one less for them. They believe that our wagon company owes them for allowing us passage."

"Do they want war?" an angry voice called.

"No, they don't. I don't think we want that either. The chief and his men came to speak to me last night, and I believe we've come to an agreement."

Annie's hands felt clammy with worry, but she was more than grateful that Mr. Mills had been able to put off any further confrontation. She had been able to stand up to one of those warriors once, but she wasn't certain she could do it a second time.

"I have agreed that we will pay a toll."

Annie sighed in relief.

"A toll?" Pastor Montgomery spoke up from somewhere behind her. "We don't— Some of us don't have much to spare, Captain."

"I ain't got no cash!" another voice called.

"How much do they want? What do they think they're going to do with banknotes?" came from the other side of her.

"Please, gentlemen," Mr. Mills said, lifting his hand for quiet. "They originally demanded twenty dollars per wagon—" a murmur of dismay surrounded Annie "—but I convinced the chief that we simply don't have that. Instead, you all need to go back to your wagons, speak to your wives, and return here with every single bit of supplies that you can spare."

"Like what, for example?" Mr. Jameson asked.

"Shirts. Tools. Sugar. Trinkets. Anything that they can't readily get or make themselves will be worth quite a lot to the Shoshone. They will be here in an hour, so please come back here with your toll items as quickly as you can."

The group started to break up. Mr. Jameson almost ran into Annie when he turned to go.

"Oh! Miss Hudson. I didn't see you. Are you...?" He frowned, confused, then seemed to answer his own question and his face cleared. "Can I walk you back?"

"I would appreciate it, yes, thank you."

They walked in silence for a minute before he ventured another question. "Are you girls— you ladies doing all right, then? I mean, with your sister gone, I imagine it must be an additional burden on the rest of you. I can send over one of my boys if you need…”

“Thank you, but no. We’re doing as well as can be expected. As you might guess, Louisa was rather thorough in her preparations.” Annie laughed lightly. “She made sure that more than one of us could drive the team and that we always had plenty of knowledge about what everyone else was doing. It’s been difficult to get used to, but we’re managing.”

“She was a fine lady,” he said fondly. “I didn’t talk much to her, but any woman who can do what she did must be a marvel.”

“Thank you.”

They had reached the Hudsons’ camp.

“I’ll let you get to your family,” he said, tipping his hat.

“What was that all about?” Margaret asked, looking at Mr. Jameson’s back as he headed to his own camp. “Is everything all right?”

Annie explained what Captain Mills had told them, explained why, and finished with the news that this all had to be done as soon as possible.

“The tribe will be back in less than an hour,” she concluded, “and I don’t want to be there when they return.”

“Yes,” Josie said adamantly. “Of course you don’t. Let’s get to work.”

Lawrence had already gone to the Davis camp to learn how to repair a wagon seat, so Annie ended up moving most of the heaviest things in the supply wagon.

“I’m sure there must be food we can spare, but I hate

to offer that if there are other things we can find instead," Annie said, as she stepped over a sack of flour into the space farther back in the wagon.

This area of their supplies, all the way at the rear, had barely been touched since they left Independence. Small pieces of furniture, multiple trunks full of belongings, and a handful of valuable, sentimental objects were carefully stored back here out of the way. Nearly everything in this section of the wagon was something that Louisa had planned on the family needing once they set up house in Oregon. Things that would be expensive to replace on this side of the continent but held enough value that she couldn't leave them behind.

"Do you know what is in these?" Annie asked her sister.

Josie shook her head. "I could guess. At least one of them is probably what Louisa would have needed to start up her business again, don't you think?"

"Oh... I had forgotten."

Annie stepped back to look at what Louisa had deemed valuable enough to take with them and think. Louisa wouldn't need many of these things now—the many needles and thread, the bedside table that had belonged to their parents, her dresses that wouldn't fit any of the other Hudsons.

When she moved, Annie bumped into a long wooden box that had been lined up against the wall of the wagon. Her skirt got stuck on the rough corner, and when she disentangled them, she stepped back to look. It was almost as long as she was tall, but very shallow, and she couldn't think what was in it.

"Help me with this one," she told Josie.

Between the two of them, they managed to lift it out of its corner, and Annie held it in place while Josie used a crowbar to pry up one of the planks.

She gasped.

"What?"

"It's Louisa's mirror. That tall, ornate one from her shop. Oh…" Tears filled her eyes. "She loved this mirror."

Annie remembered. "She spent so long saving for it."

"And now she'll never need it again."

"Let's take the Shoshone this," Annie said after a pause.

"This? A mirror? But—"

"Mr. Mills said anything they can't readily get would be valuable to them, and this big mirror certainly fits the bill. It's possible they've never seen one before, or they have but nothing nearly this big."

"But Louisa saved so long to get it."

"Louisa gave up so much to get us this far. And she's not going to be starting any business in Oregon now. You know she would rather we give this big, heavy, luxury item that none of us will use, rather than give them any of our clothes or food or other essentials, right?"

"Well, I suppose." Josie sniffed and wiped her tears. "It's just so sad."

"I know. I know, and… it's hard, but I really think this is the best thing we can do. The best way we can honor all the sacrifices that she made to get us here."

Josie nodded. "You're probably right."

"But I can't carry it alone. So let's take it now and be back before the chief returns."

CHAPTER FORTY-ONE

The wagon company's camp had been at the top of the canyon, looking out over the Shoshone Falls. They left just after midday, following the trail that took them away from Snake River and down into another canyon. Annie marveled at whoever had been the first man to dare take a wagon through this terrain. The trail was so narrow she had to stay close to her animals, constantly worried about getting caught underfoot. She certainly never would have chanced it if she wasn't certain that hundreds of other emigrants had already come this way.

The descent was manageable, though slightly nerve-racking, but the ascent back up the other side of the canyon seemed nearly impossible. Everyone in the caravan was delayed as the wagons in front figured out the best way to climb up out of the gorge. Annie waited in the throng with the rest of the wagons, thinking over her choice that morning.

Decision-making had never come easy to her. That was a good portion of the reason why it had been Louisa who'd decided the Hudsons would all move to Oregon. Annie always shied away from disagreement of any kind, and whenever she expressed an opinion or tried to impose her will, there was the risk of conflict.

But that morning, she decided they would give away Louisa's prized mirror.

A day or two before that, Annie had also decided that they would not yet give away Louisa's dresses and aprons. The Hudsons might still be able to use them, and Annie was loath to let them go just yet.

Both times, she knew, she had been taking a risk. She had been making a choice that Josie or Margaret might not agree with. It could have started a more heated discussion or even an outright argument.

"Miss Hudson?"

Annie turned to see Mrs. Mills walking toward her. She looked back to the foot of the trail and realized that some of the families had started their ascent. The Mills wagon would be at the front, but apparently, Mrs. Mills would walk up separately.

"I thought you'd like to know that my husband said the Shoshone were quite pleased with your mirror. It was one of the more valuable things we had to offer them, and it went a long way to make up for some of the more meager offerings the other families could contribute."

"Oh, I'm so glad. I hoped it would do some good since I'm not sure when we would use it. It was my sister's, you see."

"An excellent choice. And now that that is behind us, I wanted to ask one last time if you would be able to help me with a quilting circle. As we've discussed several times." She wasn't smiling this time.

Annie wilted inwardly. She could hear the pointed tone behind the woman's words. This was the third time she had asked, after all, and in Mrs. Mills's mind, what she wanted should have been simple to provide.

But Annie didn't want to.

She didn't want to sew at all, and now that Louisa was gone, she certainly didn't have time for any extra chores. She didn't want to host anything or be in charge of other people. Simply put, there was no reason she would do this thing if she weren't guilted into it.

And Annie realized that if she didn't start standing up for herself, that's exactly what would happen.

She stood up straighter and squared her shoulders.

"No."

The woman blinked in confusion. "I'm sorry?"

"I'm sorry. No, I don't think I can spare the time, you see. There's always so much to do, and with my sister gone now..." She trailed off, allowing the other woman to fill in the blanks herself.

"Well." She smiled sadly. "I confess myself to be disappointed, but... I suppose I understand." She looked behind Annie, at where their wagons waited. "I should let you get on with your day. I believe my son will be around shortly to explain the best solution to get everyone to the top."

With that, she turned and walked off. Annie imagined she must be quite upset; she wasn't sure if the woman was used to being turned down.

It had not been much of a confrontation, but even so, Annie found her heart beating fast.

But she had done it. She had said no when she meant no, and she was none the worse for it. Perhaps if Mrs. Mills had been a bigger influence in her life, it would have been more difficult, but as it was, Annie was grateful enough to just get through it.

Now she had to get through the relatively simpler ordeal of getting her wagons to the top of the canyon.

As Daniel explained when he got to their family, some families would again have to part with their furniture or their prized pieces. The incline out of the gorge was so steep that the worn-down animals couldn't hope to lug the wagons to the top. To aid them a bit, the men chained every two wagons together and rearranged the draft teams so that eight would be pulling up the linked wagons.

The oldest Jameson boy, Lewis, came to help Lawrence chain the Hudsons' wagons together. Lawrence and Annie walked together at the front of their teams, encouraging the animals to make the hard climb to the top of the canyon again.

The poor creatures were winded and slow-moving when they finally reached the top.

"Are they okay?" Lawrence asked as they unhitched the double team.

"I hope so," Annie said. "We've still got to get over the mountains, and I don't know how we'll do it without all of them working together."

Even with such a treacherous ascent behind them, the wagon company kept pushing westward, higher in elevation, desperate to make it to Oregon before winter, before some of the more unfortunate families ran out of supplies. Without the fourth of the Hudson girls, the food they carried could stretch longer. Every other day or so, Josie would make an extra portion of food to quietly, surreptitiously gift to those who needed it. Margaret kept an eye on families like the McKinnons or the Buchanans, the families that had lost a member or been utterly ransacked by the Indians. There was always someone else in need, and they tried to share their good fortune as much as possible.

The Oregon Trail curved away from the Snake River and the canyon around it, before returning back to the water. At Three Islands Crossing the water would be shallow and fordable, as long as they took their time, and the trail would then continue northwest to Fort Boise. It would take the company two full days to get all the wagons across. Each one had to be done slowly, so as not to get caught in the sandy muck at the bottom, and across a narrow stretch of river that was the shallowest.

Though the Hudsons were generally near the back of the caravan, Captain Mills wanted to allow the more vulnerable of the families to cross first this time. This meant that with the Hudsons missing both a member of their party and not having any men save a fourteen-year-old-boy, they were sent to cross in one of the first groups.

When the time came, Annie remembered how Louisa had so bullied her in the crossing of the Platte and promised herself she would do no such thing now. She trusted Josie and Margaret to know what to do. If she needed help, she would ask for it.

She led her team to the water's edge and wrapped the reins around her hand. With a deep breath and a confident command of her animals, Annie took the first step into the river.

It was cold and surprisingly faster than she anticipated, but Annie knew she could do this. She knew all of them could do this. Louisa had gotten them so far, yes, but more so, she had prepared them for crossings and obstacles just like this.

Annie put one foot in front of the other, slowly, carefully, watching where she stepped while still keeping the animals moving, so the wheels didn't get stuck. It seemed to take forever, and yet, soon she felt more solid ground under her feet and looked up to see she had reached the other shore.

CHAPTER FORTY-TWO

As they had been one of the first families to cross Three Islands Crossing, the Hudsons got to spend the rest of their time resting around their own campfire. The wagon company would stay in this spot for the night, so once they were out of the water, the Hudsons made camp. Annie quickly got out of her wet clothes and into dry ones and allowed herself a short moment of rest. Josie had started a pot of coffee brewing, and Annie inhaled the bitter smell fondly. That would warm her up.

Margaret headed off to help one of the families that had come to rely on her, and Josie bustled about mixing up a batch of biscuits. Annie knew she should probably be helping Lawrence reinforce the hooks on the supply wagon that held their tubs and buckets. But first, she wanted a few moments to herself.

Nothing even remotely close would provide the same views that Independence Rock had, but Annie wanted to get up high. She set her mug of coffee on the wagon seat ahead of her, grabbed her skirt to keep it from getting caught on the wheel, and climbed up.

Once there, she settled in, marveling at how much of the camp she could see from even this height. Throughout all the nearly six months since they had left, Annie had almost never climbed up on the actual wagon seat. None of them ever rode up there, and there was never another reason to when they were in camp. But today, as the rest of the wagons slowly made their way across the wide river, Annie made this moment of solitude for herself.

Wrapping her fingers around the warm mug, Annie looked in one direction out over the dozens of wagons and the campsites being set up. There was a relaxed quiet to the gathered families, a lull after the danger of the river. In spite of all the hardships they had thus far been through, Annie began to truly believe that they would make it to Oregon. In spite of all they had risked and lost, she could actually see herself getting to the other side safely and making a home. She had come such a long way and learned so much about herself and what she needed to do for the relationships in her life. As long as she lived, Annie would never be grateful enough to Louisa for what she had given her.

Looking the other direction, Annie's gaze fell across the broad expanse of high desert plateau and scrub. Ahead of them, they still had to cross a handful of small tributaries and begin the climb into the mountains. She had never had such pressures put on her body as she had over the last few months.

To the west was her new life, with her future

husband. To the west would be the full embodiment of the person she was becoming.

Annie remained on her perch, procrastinating on the chores she needed to do long into the afternoon. One by one, the other wagons forded the river and found their places in the camp.

"You'll never guess," Margaret said.

She had been away from the Hudsons most of the day, helping the mothers with their cold and wet children and making her rounds to keep everyone in a good mood. Annie hadn't seen her for hours, but when she appeared just before supper, she was full of news and gossip.

"After everything that has happened, now this too. Poor Caroline—Miss Harper—had an axle break in the water. Her wagon is simply stranded six feet from the bank."

"No!" Josie exclaimed. "Oh, that poor dear. And after she was so determined to drive the wagon after her brother's death. What is she going to do now?"

"Well, I was wondering if maybe we should ask her to join us," Margaret said simply.

"What, really?" Annie asked.

"Yes. Why not?"

Annie stared at Margaret. Margaret, who had never hesitated to stand up to Louisa when she disagreed. Margaret, who always went out of her way to help anyone who needed it. Margaret, who was now suggesting that they bring a complete stranger into their home, into their intimate lives on a level that they never had before.

Annie's hands started shaking, and she had to remind

herself that these were her sisters. These women loved her. If she couldn't outright disagree with these two, who could she?

"Lawrence can go back to sleeping under the wagon like he did when Louisa was alive," Margaret was saying. "She will have some food she can contribute, and I'm sure we can find room for whatever personal belongings she'll have. It won't be many, I'm sure. Yes, as far as I'm concerned, it's an excellent idea. She gets a bit more support, and we get another pair of hands."

"Josie?" Annie said hesitatingly. "What do you think?"

Annie couldn't bear to give her own objections yet. Maybe she wouldn't have to.

Josie shrugged. "I don't see why not."

"Exactly," Margaret said. "I'll go ask her."

She had already taken a couple steps when Annie found her voice.

"Wait!"

Margaret turned back.

"I don't want... uh." She cleared her throat. "I'm not sure that's a good idea?"

Her heart pounded in her ears in that brief moment before Margaret responded. How mad would she be?

"Why not?" Margaret frowned.

"I..." Annie made tight fists and used the tension to propel her words. "I don't want to."

"You don't want to what?"

This was not going how Annie had thought.

"I don't want another person here. I... She's a stranger, and I really would prefer that we not take on any other burdens if we can help it."

Margaret stood up straighter. Annie was still, technically, taller than her, but her sister-in-law, with all her definite opinions and confident chin, seemed to loom over her.

"Well. All right. I suppose I can understand that. But, Annie, it's not up to you alone," she finished softly.

Annie felt her face flush.

"I'm really glad you spoke up," Josie said. "It's important that we know what you think about it."

"You don't have to humor me," Annie said.

She was a maelstrom of emotions—embarrassed to be so ungenerous, frustrated that they weren't listening to her, but also amazed that she had so openly disagreed with her sisters and they had been so kind to her. What had she been afraid of?

"We're not humoring you," Margaret said. "I think maybe," she glanced at Josie, "taking a vote is the most fair, isn't it? There's no safety or danger reason to not invite Miss Harper, so with everything under consideration, I think we should do it."

"So do I," Josie said. "All right, Annie?" She peered into Annie's face.

"Okay," she said. "I understand. Yeah. That's... I'll be just fine. I just wanted to... Thank you for listening."

Josie pulled her into a hug. "See? Wasn't that hard, was it?" she whispered.

"I'll go ask her now," Margaret said, setting off again.

After she left, Annie took a deep breath and thought over the whole conversation. That wasn't even really a fight, was it? She thought over some of the arguments she had witnessed between Louisa and Tom or Louisa and a store clerk, even. All Annie had done was speak up about something she wanted. Her sisters had listened. And they had a discussion about it. None of it was nearly as bad as she had prepared herself for.

Annie grinned to herself as she calmed her beating heart. She could do this. She could be more brave and be the person Louisa had hoped she would be.

"What did she say?" Lawrence asked when his mother returned. It was one of the only sentences he had said in between bites of supper. Annie would have to see about buying more food when they visited the next fort.

"She was resting. Daniel Mills is helping her take care of things and told me he'd pass along the offer. He's too polite to say so directly, but he did suggest that several other families, including that of her best friend, had offered, so we probably shouldn't expect much."

Josie peered at Annie and said teasingly, "What do you think, Annie? Relieved?"

"Yes," she burst out without thinking. "Goodness. I don't know what I would do with a stranger around here."

"You'd have to learn to speak up for yourself all over again, I guess."

"What are you going to do when you finally meet Isaac?" Margaret teased.

"Oh." Annie buried her face in her hands. "I hadn't thought of that."

The other women both laughed.

"Annie," Josie said seriously, "really, are you all right with all of this? Is there anything we can do?"

Annie looked back up at her sisters, grateful for

them, grateful for the safety she felt in their presence. Grateful for everything she was learning.

"You know... A few months ago, or even a few weeks ago, I would have been something of a mess, especially in thinking about what it would be like to meet Isaac for the first time. But now... I think I might be okay."

"I'm sure you will be okay."

The three Hudson girls hugged again, wishing all the time for the fourth one that would forever be missing.

After leaving the shores of the Snake River for the final time, the wagon company headed farther west to Fort Boise, where they camped overnight. The fort was mostly out of supplies, but it was situated on the Boise River, which was full of salmon this time of year. Margaret roped Martin Jameson into helping the Hudsons all learn how to fish. It was a skill that had almost never been useful in their hometown of Norfolk, with as many professional fishermen as lived around there, but they would need to know in Oregon.

That first night, the salmon made a delicious soup that warmed them, with the rest of the catch dried and salted for the coming days.

After Fort Boise, the trail stretched across another long, hard terrain. Captain Mills pushed them to make as many miles each day as they could. They suffered through torrential rain and bone-chilling cold, but they kept going. The rain gave way to mud and then deep ruts and dips in the dirt. And after that stretch of high desert, they would start their final climb into the Blue Mountains. As Annie led her wagon westward, she looked up to the snow-capped mountains, where the weather would only get worse, and tried to steel herself for the final push.

CHAPTER FORTY-THREE

This late into September, Annie woke every morning and pulled on as much of her warm-weather clothing as she could. Wrapping a scarf around her neck three or four times, she hurried in her morning preparations to get a campfire going as quickly as possible. She drank more coffee just to stay warm during these final weeks than she had the rest of the trip leading up to this point.

The trail had begun its climb into the mountains. From the level surface of the plains, these mountains had seemed so high, so insurmountable, but now that they were in the middle of them, it felt as though they went nowhere. Each day was higher and higher, without seeming to reach the top. And as the trail grew higher, the air grew thinner, the weather colder.

As Annie and Lawrence led the teams, Josie checked on them every hour or so, making sure they were warm enough and that they had gotten enough to eat. She had heard about the dangers that previous emigrants had suffered—starvation, being snowed in before reaching the other side—and was anxious about the same thing not happening to them.

But Louisa had more than prepared them for the journey. Even Josie was surprised that they didn't have to do more rationing. As Annie watched the other members of the wagon company wasting away, she conferred with her sisters to share as much of the food they had remaining as possible. Leaving Independence weighed down with so many hundreds of pounds of food had seemed extravagant at the time, but now Annie was grateful.

Where some mothers had to send their children into the woods on either side of the trail to scavenge for the barest edibles, like acorns and roots, Margaret surreptitiously visited these same mothers, leaving them small gifts of a cup of rice or parched corn. Josie warned her to be careful, that they couldn't afford to feed everyone in the camp. But still, Margaret persisted.

One morning, when they had been in the mountains for nearly two weeks, Annie climbed out of the wagon, expecting to find a layer of ice across the top of the oxen's water buckets. When she reached the campfire, she found Josie forming half a dozen biscuits.

"No more meat," she said without looking up. "We finished the bacon yesterday, and I didn't realize it. All that's left is a bit of flour and this last helping of beans." She shook her head. "Maybe Lawrence can try hunting later tonight, but since everyone else in camp has the same idea, I don't know that it will do any good."

"Do you hear that, Margaret?" Annie said. "Please leave the food that's left for us. For your own son."

"It's only a little bit longer," Margaret insisted. "And

some of these children… Goodness, if you could see them, you would understand. They're just wasting away. It breaks my heart."

"Leave oats for the oxen, though, please," Annie pointed out. "This high up, there's nothing else for them."

"And can you imagine getting this far and losing an animal?" Josie said with a shudder. "Eighteen hundred miles pulling a wagon, and we have to leave everything here because you thought someone looked hungry."

"They *are* hungry," Margaret insisted, smiling at the teasing. "But, thank goodness, it won't be too much longer. I think we should have some relief soon."

"Really?" Annie asked. "That's news. What do you mean? Don't we still have another several days before the other side?"

"Oh, I thought for certain I had told you. I didn't tell you? I can't keep track of who I tell what to anymore. Well, listen to this." Margaret leaned forward, with hands clasped. "George Mills sent his son Daniel and that Findley boy up on ahead. They can move faster just on horseback, and they're to find the closest settlement and return here with supplies."

"No!" Annie exclaimed. "When did he do this?"

"Well, let me see, it must have been a week or so ago now. I would think we should expect them nearly any day. That's what Julia Davis told me at least, and you know she's close friends with Mrs. Mills."

"I didn't realize we were so close to the end," Annie murmured.

"Any day," Margaret repeated.

But as close as they may have been to the other side

of the mountains, there were still miles to go. Annie finished the rest of her coffee and the final bites of beans that Josie had fixed and stood.

"Come on, Lawrence. One more day."

In the sharp, dry air, she and Lawrence harnessed their teams with numb fingers—knots and buckles were too difficult to manage with their gloves. He had been growing so fast, his boots nearly didn't fit any longer. Annie saw the grimace cross his face as he stepped in the too-tight shoes. Just a few more days, she told herself. They would be in Oregon in no time.

The wagon company set off at a slow pace that morning. The trail itself was difficult enough; no smooth dirt providing a clear path, it had been all but cut directly into the mountainside, and each driver had to go as slowly as possible to avoid the stones, pits, and uneven ruts that covered the trail. Beyond that, however, it was a mix between a steep incline and sharp turns, weaving around the rockface, immovable trees, and lethal drops.

If she had to guess, Annie would say they had only made maybe two or three miles of distance before noon. She looked up at the snow-capped mountain towering above her and wondered when this would all end.

At midday, the wagon train stopped. The animals needed to rest after having hauled the wagons up through the thin air in the mountains. Though many of the families didn't have enough food to cobble together a meal, they too were grateful to stop for an hour or so. Annie wondered if today would be the day that one of them gave up, that they would have to leave behind an emigrant who just had no more left to give. The months of labor and stress had worn most every member of the company down. It was a wonder some could put one foot in front of the other.

But they were so close. From Josie's guidebook descriptions, Annie knew that they could reach the tallest point on the trail and head down the other side into the Willamette Valley any day now. On the other side would be plenty of food and water, as well as help and space to make a home for the winter. It would be warmer once they got out of the mountains. Annie—all of the Hudsons, really—were lucky to have someone waiting for them on the other side.

Where the Mills or the McKinnons would have to build a home themselves as fast as possible, Annie had Isaac. Isaac, her betrothed, was waiting for her, just a few dozen miles away. He would have a home and plenty of food, and the comfort that she had left behind in Virginia was just about within reach. He would already have a home waiting for her.

Where the company had stopped at noon was a small spring, so at least everyone could get a drink. Josie gave them each half a biscuit, cold since she had baked them hours earlier. As they each chewed quietly, the Hudsons sat huddled around the campfire, trying to warm as best they could. Annie was exhausted.

Too tired to speak. Too tired to think.

So tired that when she began to hear energetic voices, she wondered if she imagined it. Annie looked around for the unfamiliar, strong voices calling throughout their camp. She looked up to see at least half a dozen men coming up over the ridge toward them.

CHAPTER FORTY-FOUR

Looking up to the source of the strange voices, Annie felt her heart leap in her chest as hope and adrenaline coursed through her. This was what they needed. This is what they had been looking toward for days. This was hope. This was the help that Daniel Mills had gone after.

As she stood, the relief party from Willamette Valley appeared over the ridge of the hill.

They were still too far away for Annie to speak to them or even for them to notice her, but it was clear from the start that the group of men, young and old, were here to help. The group spread out, some carrying heavy bags, some leading horses laden with their own burdens. As each man or pair approached a member of the wagon train, they withdrew sacks and packages and all manner of supplies. The emigrants received the gifts with heartfelt gratitude. For some of these families, this would be the first full meal they had had in weeks.

One, in particular, drew her eye: a broad, barrel-chested man with an enormous blond beard. Annie's breath caught in her chest. Could it be? Those kind eyes looked familiar, but she didn't dare waste time digging her old letters out from the trunk.

Though her natural instincts told Annie to wait, to hang back until the group approached her, she knew that's not what Louisa would have done. Waiting and deferring was not how her sister had managed to get the family all the way to Oregon. It took some courage, but Annie reminded herself she had resolved to do better.

This was the perfect chance.

Taking those first steps away from her campfire, Annie approached the group of men making their way through the Sullivan-Mills wagon company. A tall, thin young man pulled a couple apples out of the bag he carried and handed it to Mrs. Van Anda with a kind smile. Annie was too far away to hear what he said to her, but the joy in her face was unmistakable.

The blond-bearded man broke away from the group and seemed to spot Annie approaching. It was him. She was sure this was the man she had left Virginia for.

"Mr. Wheeler?" Annie asked tentatively.

She watched as his expression went from confused, to surprised, to absolutely joyful.

"Miss Hudson?" he asked breathlessly, crossing the space between them in only three long strides. "Annie?"

She nodded.

"Oh, thank goodness," he said, his body sagging in relief. "I haven't heard from you in months, and I know how rough that stretch of trail is, and it's already so late in the year, and..." He trailed off and allowed himself a good look at her. "Well, that's neither here nor there.

You're here. And we're here to help y'all get the rest of the way."

"Who is we?" Annie asked. "What are you doing here? Did Daniel Mills find you?"

"Yes, ma'am, he did. Many of us down in the valley know to keep a lookout for wagon trains this time of year. Those folks that had such a hard time crossing down near Truckee Lake a couple years ago have got us scared. But this year... well, I tell you, knowing that you and your sisters were on your way here has made me nervous as a long-tailed cat in a room of rocking chairs." He shook his head at the memory.

"I guess we're a little later than we had hoped," Annie allowed. "I'm sorry to worry you."

"No matter. You're here now. We'll get you folks fed and stay with you the next few days until we're all down and safe in the valley together. And then... Well, I hope that you haven't changed your mind, is all I will say for now. I'm mighty happy to be able to get to know you in person, Miss Hudson."

"Please call me Annie."

He looked her in the eyes and smiled, waiting a beat before repeating. "Annie. And you must call me Isaac."

She nodded in return, though she couldn't yet say the name out loud. There was too much happening, too many things to think about for her to fully accept that she was now standing in front of the man she had promised to marry. This was her future, but she couldn't think beyond her present.

"Now, don't you worry," he said, taking her hand in one of his and patting it gently.

Annie felt tears welling up. Louisa had always been

the one to assure her she didn't have to worry. What a relief that her intended husband was so kind, so generous. How fortunate she was to have come all this way and managed to find herself a safe home.

Isaac seemed to sense that she was at a loss for words. He looked around. "Is that your family?"

"Yes, they—" Her voice broke. "Before I introduce you, I need to tell you…"

In a few broad strokes, Annie relayed their experience coming west, culminating in the tragedy they had suffered in losing Louisa. Isaac listened, concerned and heartbroken along with her.

"Oh, no," he murmured. "Can I… Would it be all right if I hugged you?"

Annie blushed and looked around at who might spot them. But she didn't care if anything looked improper. Louisa had taught her that—if she knew what she was doing was right, who cares if someone thought her odd. This man was her betrothed, after all. She nodded, and he wasted no time in catching her up in a bear hug, holding her tight as she let go of her stress and pain of the previous months.

"I'll take care of you," he promised, murmuring into her hair.

For the first time since Louisa had died, Annie Hudson felt like everything would be okay. She had food, shelter, family, and love. What else did she need to start her life in Oregon?

She pulled away from the hug, suddenly remembering. "Did you really buy me a piano?"

Isaac laughed heartily at the abrupt shift in conversation. "Yes, I really did."

Annie's mouth hung open. "But— but—" she stammered. "The expense? And... how..."

"I told you in my letter, didn't I? I just wanted you to feel at home as soon as possible. I wanted to show you that... well, now, you're just as a valued member of my household as I am. It wouldn't feel right to be getting myself a new horse or some such and not something for you. Once I resolved to do it, it wasn't as hard as I thought. In fact, it was just unloaded off a ship in San Francisco a week or two back. Should be up here before Christmas, I'm thinking."

"Thank you," she said softly. "Thank you so much. I can't..." She shook her head before beaming up again.

"Don't thank me yet, now. Wait till you see your new home before you go deciding you love it."

Annie laughed—her first true happiness since Virginia, since before Louisa had died.

"Now," Isaac continued. "Let's go see your family and get some of this bacon cooking up for y'all."

Annie took his hand and led the way.

THE END

Download your free book — *HANNAH'S HOPE* — at ATButler.com/Hannah

When Hannah Sullivan's family decides to head west to the Oregon Territory, she's exhilarated. The small town where she grew up was fine when that's all she had to choose from, but as soon as the horizons and opportunities open up, Hannah finds a whole new world, just built for someone as competent, kind and warm as she is.

Sign up for A.T. Butler's mailing list today and receive Hannah's Hope for free! Dive into a story where romance blossoms against all odds, and be the first to hear about new releases, exclusive content, and special offers. Don't miss this chance to fall in love with Hannah and Benjamin's story.

ATButler.com/Hannah

Thank you so much for reading *Frontier Sisters*, book 3 in Courage on the Oregon Trail.

This was the first book of the series that isn't a romance at its core, and as such it's rather special to me. I only have one sibling of my own—a brother two years younger—but both of my parents are one of six children, so I grew up with lots of extended family, and all those sibling dynamics on display each holiday season. There are stories about shifting allegiances and loyalties and knowing the very specific way one can needle their sibling.

When my dad read this book, he asked me if Louisa was based on anyone in particular, very clearly implying she was like an older sister he knew well (not me). She wasn't. Not specifically. But ... oldest sisters are a cliche for a reason, aren't they?

Part of why I wanted to write this book was to give sympathy to those oldest sisters who are just trying their best to hold everything together and if other people would just *listen* better it could all go so much more smoothly.

Life doesn't work that way, of course, but fiction does. We can at least see inside the mind and motivations of a woman like that. I'm a little bit sad that she won't be around for the Oregon At Last book series.

Both Annie and Margaret have books though—two and seven, respectively.

Thank you so much for being on this journey with me. The excitement and the hardship and the heart that our pioneers go through every day. We'll be with the Sullivan-Mills wagon company for a long time still.

A.T. Butler
October 2024

FREE PRINTABLE OREGON TRAIL MAP

Sign-up to download a FREE custom printable map of the Sullivan-Mills wagon company's journey on the Oregon Trail.

You'll also get news of future releases, updates for promotions and discounts, as well as occasional other exclusive goodies, created just for my subscribers.

https://atbutler.com/ot-free

The next book in COURAGE ON THE OREGON TRAIL series is available now.

Grab UNYIELDING HEART here!
(on Kindle and Kindle Unlimited)

Is it too late to go back home?

Beth McKinnon and her family have already lost so much. Forced from their home, pared down belongings, they seek a new chance out west for their five children.

But when her son Alexander dies early in the journey to Oregon, Beth disappears into herself and struggles to find a reason to continue the trek westward.

Without every member of her family, will this harrowing struggle for survival even be worth it?

All the books in the Courage on the Oregon Trail series take place within the same wagon company's trip west and run concurrently. They can be read in any order.

Can Caroline find her new path or will this journey be the end of everything she thought she had achieved?

For all the stories of how these brave pioneers got to Oregon, look for the book series Courage on the Oregon Trail by A.T. Butler.

Oregon At Last Series:

Journey's End (Caroline's story)

Christmas in Oregon (Annie's story)

Snowbound Promises (Nora's story)

The Pastor's Baby (Olivia's story)

Frontier Fortune (Rebecca's story)

Reluctant Spring (Sadie's story)

Summer of Promise (Margaret's story)

ALSO BY A.T. BUTLER

Courage On The Oregon Trail Series:

Westward Courage

Faithful Trail

Frontier Sisters

Unyielding Heart

Wild Promise

Fierce Dreams

Seeking Home

Trouble and Grace

Oregon At Last Series:

Journey's End

Christmas in Oregon

Snowbound Promises

The Pastor's Baby

Frontier Fortune

Reluctant Spring

Summer of Promise

Juniper Falls Series:

The Juniper Hotel

Building the Dream

Snowflakes and Sugar Cookies

Jacob Payne, Bounty Hunter Series:

Trouble By Any Name

Danger in the Canyon

Justice for Jasper

Blood on the Mountain

Outlaw Country

Death By Grit

Desert Rage

Arizona Legend

Fool's Demise

Silent Night

Bountiful Justice Series:

Loyalty's Price

Riding for Justice

Trail of Redemption

Other Western Novels by A.T. Butler:

Hawke's Revenge

Short Stories from Juniper Falls

ABOUT THE AUTHOR

I grew up in the southwest—California Missions, snakes and constant threat of drought weaving the backdrop of my childhood.

But it wasn't until I moved to Texas a few years ago that the magic and mythology of the American West began to seep into my soul.

I'd love to write about western adventures, strong women and noble men for a long time.

If you enjoyed this book, a review on your favorite retailer would be greatly appreciated.

- A

www.ingramcontent.com/pod-product-compliance
Lightning Source LLC
Chambersburg PA
CBHW021233190726
48289CB00005B/1302